DETECTIVE LOG

Stone Richardson

WEDNESDAY, JUNE 11

Jessica Hanson came into the precinct today and confessed to having witnessed the <u>murder</u> of Olivia Stuart.

Problem: Jessica says she saw this in a vision after she bumped her head during the blackout.

Possible? Maybe. . . or maybe not. But stranger things have happened. It's worth checking out. Eric says I'm just looking for an excuse to see her again, but that's crazy. Jessica and I were over a long time ago. And nothing's changed. . . or has it?

Dear Reader,

Sometimes your life can change in a heartbeat. For the residents of Grand Springs, Colorado, a blackout has set off a string of events that will alter people's lives forever....

Welcome to Silhouette's exciting new series, 36 HOURS, where each month heroic characters face personal challenges—and find love against all odds. This month a tough-hearted cop and a tender lady must join forces to solve the murder of Grand Springs' most beloved citizen. Stone Richardson is the kind of man who believes only in what he sees, but Jessica Hanson has a way of showing him things in a whole new light....

In coming months you'll meet a sexy tycoon who is searching desperately for a woman he has met only once; an industrious reporter who has one chance to save his high school sweetheart—and his unexpected daughter; and a bride on the run who must depend on a sexy stranger for protection. Join us each month as we bring you 36 hours that will change *your* life!

Sincerely,

The editors at Silhouette

FOR HER
EYES ONLY
SHARON
SALA

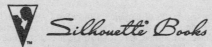

Published by Silhouette Books

America's Publisher of Contemporary Romance

Special thanks and acknowledgment are given to Sharon Sala for her contribution to the 36 HOURS series.

 SILHOUETTE BOOKS

FOR HER EYES ONLY

Copyright © 1997 by Harlequin Books S.A.

ISBN 0-373-65009-4

Printed in U.S.A.

Sharon Sala

has captured the hearts of countless readers with her award-winning novels, published under her name, as well as the pseudonym Dinah McCall. An Oklahoma native with the pioneering spirit of her forefathers, she believes in following her heart and her dreams.

* * * * * *

Dedication

I believe these things to be true:

A kiss will last but a moment in time, but the sound of laughter will echo for years.

You can make love to a man with all of your heart, but if you can make him laugh, his heart will be yours.

Sorrow will come in and out of your life, but if you can look toward tomorrow with a smile on your face, you will somehow endure.

I dedicate this book to the people who know the healing power of laughter.

Share it and it will be with you always.

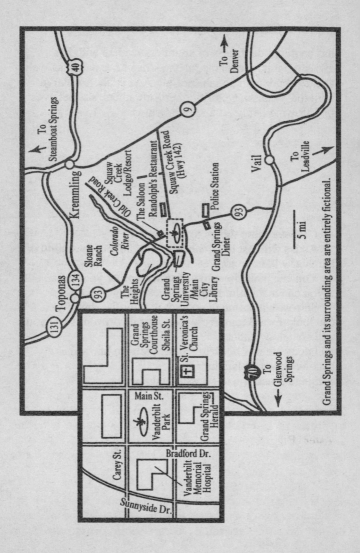

One

Thunder rolled outside the walls of Squaw Creek Lodge, ripping through the gray, overhanging clouds. Rain splattered against the shake-shingle roof before running onto the ground. It had been raining for so many days it seemed as if heaven was weeping. And while it was fashionable to cry at weddings, Jessica Hanson thought this was ridiculous.

She sat hunched over her computer, determined to concentrate on getting out the payroll for the lodge employees, and not on the wedding about to take place in the nearby ballroom. As she flipped through the time cards, her lower lip slid out of position just enough to pass for a pout. A sign to those who knew her best that she was more than slightly annoyed. She knew the couple who were about to get married, yet she hadn't been invited to the wedding. But she was honest enough to admit that part of the reason could lie in the fact that she hadn't been back in Grand Springs long enough to reestablish her place within her old circle of friends. Jessica's reason for leaving Grand Springs two years ago had been traumatic enough for her to break all ties with her past except for those with her sister, Brenda. And although she'd been back a little over two months, she had yet to see the man who'd been her reason for leaving.

Stone Richardson.

Just thinking his name made her heart hurt, and she blinked back a quick spurt of tears as she let the memory of him back into her mind. *Stone*—as in...*with a heart of.*

Then she sighed. Damn his ex-wife, Naomi, and damn his hard heart, anyway. It wasn't Jessica's fault Naomi had done everything within her power to prove that it was Stone's job as a cop that had ruined their marriage and not Naomi's own lack of understanding or willingness to accept him for who and what he was.

Jessica glanced at the clock. Almost six-thirty. Long past quitting time. She hammered on the keyboard with renewed intensity, determined to get through with the payroll before she left.

Her brief affair with Stone had ended without anyone, and that included Brenda, ever knowing it had happened. Stone had refused to trust another woman enough to give their future a chance, and Jessica hadn't been willing to settle for being a cop's sexual outlet.

She'd told herself then and she still thought it now—the best and worst thing that ever happened to her was loving Stone Richardson. Coming back to Grand Springs had been Jessica's way of proving to herself that she was over him. And although she'd been back for two months now, she had yet to see him face-to-face. When that happened, then she would know if her two-year, self-imposed exile had worked.

Her fingers flew as she entered data into the computer, while her mind was stuck in the past. Laughter from the gathering guests was faint, but she heard it all the same. She rolled her eyes and frowned. If she could have seen herself, it would have lightened her mood. She looked more like a pouting child who'd been put in a corner for something she hadn't done, than the consummate professional she considered herself to be.

A sudden clap of thunder made her jump, and when the lights flickered, she paused, her fingers poised above the keys as the battery backup to her uninterrupted power supply beeped a quick, nervous warning. The everlasting rain that had been falling in Grand Springs for days was getting on everyone's nerves. It only followed that something besides tempers would finally give way.

"No, no, no," she begged, staring at the flickering screen. When the power held, she sighed in relief and returned to her task. Just a few more cards and she would be finished.

Cool air circulated within her small, self-contained office as, moments later, she hit the save key. It was done! A smile of satisfaction crossed her face.

Jessica leaned back in the chair, stretching as she listened to the contented purr of her computer's hard drive. Her shoulders ached and her neck was tired, and out of habit, she reached up and pulled out the pins holding her hairdo in place. It rolled from the topknot and onto her shoulders without so much as a tangle. Since it wouldn't hold a curl, it only stood to reason it wouldn't hold a knot, either.

Her hair was thick and straight and a color her sister, Brenda, called dishwater blond. She'd been told all of her life that she looked a bit like the actress Goldie Hawn, minus the giggles, of course. It hadn't helped Jessica's opinion of herself at all. She didn't want to be minus anything. She wanted...

Before she could finish the thought, the room went dark, lit only by the pale green screen of the computer still in operation. The backup battery on her uninterrupted power supply began beeping a frantic warning for her to shut the system down before all was lost.

Frantically, Jessica exited the program, breathing a quiet sigh of relief when she switched off the computer. She hadn't had time to print out the checks, but payroll had been saved. However, now that the screen was dark, she couldn't see a thing. Outside her office, she heard the sound of a folding chair tumbling to the floor, and then an unnatural silence.

"Perfect. Just perfect," she muttered, and wearily laid her head down on the desk to wait for the power to resume.

A man's muffled voice sounded as he ran past the outer door to her office, and Jessica thought he said something about fuses and flashlights. Flashlights! There was one in the file cabinets by the door. Although good sense told her to stay put until the power returned, she pushed her chair back from the desk and then stood. It was her first mistake.

The absence of light was disconcerting. It made the air seem thicker, her balance less sure. Circling her desk with hands outstretched, she was forced to orient herself by touch alone. When she bumped the edge of the desk with her knee, she winced. Even though she was wearing slacks, the fabric wasn't heavy enough to prevent the bruise that was bound to appear.

"Fish guts," she muttered, rubbing at the ache in her knee.

When she could bend it without further pain, she moved again, still aiming for the file cabinets by the door. Once more, the absence of light threw her off balance and she staggered, this time stumbling backward. Her sleeve caught on something sharp, and when she heard fabric rip, she groaned. That had been her favorite blouse.

Another ripple of thunder sounded overhead as something thumped against the outside of her door. A muffled curse and then a slight moan drifted beneath the crack. It gave her a modicum of satisfaction to know she wasn't the only one fumbling around in the dark. Still fuming over the tear she'd put in her blouse, she started forward. It was to be her second mistake.

The office that had been her refuge now seemed close and confining, and in a panic, she hastened her steps. Seconds later, something hard and round rolled beneath her shoe, and in dismay, Jessica remembered the umbrella she'd tossed on top of a cabinet hours earlier. Even as she'd been walking toward her desk, she'd heard it roll off and onto the floor. She'd meant to go back and pick it up, but the phone had rung. And then she'd sat down and started to work and thought nothing more of it...until now.

The sensation of moving through space without seeing where she was going was frightening. All she knew was that her feet were no longer on the floor and she was on the way down. And then pain shattered her consciousness. She'd found the file cabinets...the hard way.

Lamplight flickered in a corner of the room.

Jessica groaned and clutched at her head as she rolled toward the glow, but the act of moving had not been wise. Her stomach lurched and she gritted her teeth. With a moan, she closed her eyes as she grabbed at the floor, waiting for the world to quit bucking.

She took a deep breath and, choosing one of her more colorful epithets to express her dismay, dug her fingers into the carpet's pile and muttered.

"Rat feet. Rat feet. Dirty little rat feet."

Quick bursts of bright colored lights went off behind her eyelids as she rolled into a sitting position and covered her face with her hands. When her fingers came away damp and sticky and she discovered part of her hair was stuck to her forehead, she began to shake.

Testing the place where her head hurt the worst, she was horrified to feel a large gash and a steady stream of blood flowing out and down. Her head was throbbing. The room wouldn't stop spinning. And she needed help. She closed her eyelids, gritted her teeth and took a slow, deep breath.

When agony had subsided to a dull, pounding ache, she opened her eyes again, this time focusing on the lamp and the soft, yellow glow across the room, and she wondered if she would be able to move. When someone suddenly walked between Jessica and the light, her first thought was that help had arrived. But the woman by the desk didn't look up.

"Help me," Jessica said, but the woman didn't move. In fact, Jessica could have been invisible for all the reaction her plea evoked.

She blinked slowly, trying to coordinate the action between a fresh surge of pain. The woman's image kept wavering in and out of her consciousness, and she knew she was going to pass out again. Frantic for help, Jessica lifted her arm, waving in the woman's direction as she tried once more to gain her attention.

"Help me. Please, help me."

And then the woman turned and walked to the end of the desk, revealing her identity. Jessica went weak with relief.

"Olivia! Thank God it's you."

It didn't seem odd to Jessica that Olivia Stuart, the mayor of Grand Springs, would be here at the lodge. After all, she was the mother of the groom who was about to be married. Where else might she have been? But Jessica didn't think to wonder what Olivia would be doing in her office, smiling when she had so obviously been injured. All she knew was she was no longer alone.

Once again, Jessica tried to stand and got no further than her knees before the room began to spin. She paused on all fours with her head down and her arms trembling from the effort of trying to hold herself up, then slumped back to the floor with a moan.

"Olivia, I can't do it alone. You're going to have to help me."

To Jessica's disbelief, Olivia kept smiling. Then, out of the shadows, a second figure suddenly emerged. Jessica instinctively shrank back against the wall as someone grabbed Olivia from behind. A hand was clamped roughly over Olivia's mouth, and then Olivia was shoved forward by the momentum of the attack, pinned against the end of the desk and the attacker's body. Jessica gasped. Some stranger...a tall, powerful woman...was trying to hurt the mayor!

The struggle between the two women was horrifying. Olivia's arms flailed helplessly as the assailant's grip seemed to tighten. Jessica watched as Olivia struggled, trying to pull free of the woman's clutches.

And then it seemed as if everything began to happen in slow motion. Something glittered in the assailant's upraised hand. Jessica moaned and covered her mouth, suddenly aware that she could very likely be the woman's next victim.

Dear God, she thought. *It's a needle! A hypodermic needle!* A vein throbbed horribly at the back of Jessica's neck, blinding her to everything but the motion of the needle as it was plunged into the back of Olivia Stuart's leg.

Moments later, when Olivia crumpled to the floor, Jessica began to scream. Led by the sounds of her distress, Jessica's co-workers soon found her—alone and unconscious—and bleeding profusely from a wound to the head.

Vanderbilt Memorial Hospital was a beacon in the darkness that had fallen upon Grand Springs. Operating on backup generators, faint light spilled out of the windows and doorways and into the streets beyond. Ambulance sirens screamed a warning as the first of the victims to fall prey to the blackout began to arrive.

Stone Richardson had been thrust into the ongoing scene at the hospital, almost from the onset of the blackout. After transporting an accident victim to the hospital in his own car, he found himself caught up in the turmoil going on inside. Although he was a detective on the Grand Springs police force, every able-bodied officer was working where they were most needed. And judging from the chaos in the emergency room, this seemed to be a good place to start. Caught between people in need of assistance and those who'd accompanied the injured to the hospital, he found himself in the role of referee. Twice in the last few minutes, he'd been forced to get between a doctor working on a patient and the person who'd brought in the injured person. Panic was rampant.

"Hey! Back off and let the doctor do her job!" Stone

ordered, yelling to make himself heard above an angry biker's shout. When the biker, who called himself Red, took a swing at him, Stone shoved him up against a wall.

Nearby, Amanda Jennings, one of the doctors on duty, did what she could to staunch the flow of blood spilling down the other biker's face. Red grabbed at Stone's arm in frustration.

"But that's my buddy she's—"

Stone glanced at the hand locked around his wrist, and then looked back up at the biker as his voice lowered to a menacing growl.

"I don't care if he's your fairy godfather. Either you sit down and shut up, or you're going to spend the night in jail for assault."

At that point, Red might have recognized more than the voice of authority. The gleam in Stone's eyes was warning enough for him.

"Fine with me," Red muttered, and glared at the lady doctor before slinking off to the waiting room.

Without taking her eyes from her patient and the stitches she was putting in the side of his face, Amanda Jennings muttered a quick, fervent thanks.

"Glad you were here," she said shortly.

Stone nodded. Dr. Amanda Jennings was all business, even though her size belied her strength. She was only a couple of inches over five feet tall, but her skill more than compensated for her lack of height.

"Glad I could help," he answered, and headed back into the hallway where humanity streamed by at a steady, frantic pace.

An ambulance slid to a halt just outside the door, and Stone stepped aside as paramedics came running into the building with a patient strapped fast to a blood-splattered gurney. From where he was standing, he got a quick glimpse of the woman beneath the sheets. She was young and slender, her long blond hair steadily staining with a blood flow the paramedics had been unable to staunch. He winced. Another person had fallen victim to the Grand Springs blackout.

As the gurney moved past him, Stone's heart, quite literally, stopped. It was only for a moment, but the skipped beat was evidence of the shock of his recognition. He knew that upturned nose. He'd seen that mouth many times before. He'd kissed it more times than he could count. And he still remembered the shock he'd felt upon learning that Jessica Hanson had left Grand Springs without so much as a goodbye.

He hadn't known until she was gone how much he'd cared for her, but even then it hadn't been enough to make him go after her. Stone wasn't stupid. He'd learned the hard way that being a cop and being married weren't always synonymous, at least not for him. He'd cared for Jessie. He'd loved making love with her. But he wasn't going to ruin another woman's life and dig his own hole in the world any deeper by repeating his mistakes.

By the time he got the impetus to follow the paramedics down the hall, they had disappeared into a trauma room. While he was struggling with the fact that Jessie was back in Grand Springs and he hadn't known it, never mind how she had come to be covered in blood, another altercation began to take place between two sets of desperate parents who were vying for a doctor's attention. He moved toward them with fixed intent.

Jessica didn't remember the ride to the hospital, or of being wheeled into ER amid a flurry of shouts and activity. When she did begin to come around, she opened her eyes and screamed, reacting instinctively to the sight of a portable X-ray machine being lowered into place above her. Someone grabbed at her hands, then spoke. The woman's voice was calm, the tone reassuring.

"Take it easy, dear. You're in a hospital."

Jessica shuddered and moaned, then tried to relax, unaware that she was already crying. From the other side of the curtain, a child began to shriek, and in the opposite corner of the room Jessica could hear someone groaning. Pain shattered her cognizance.

Hospital? Why am I in a hospital?

Minutes passed, but to Jessica, they could have been hours. Perspective and time had no meaning. There was only the pain and confusion holding her fast to the bed.

Sometime later, she woke up again to find herself on a gurney in a hallway. Disoriented by painkillers and a headache of mammoth proportions, she knew little about what was going on around her until someone touched her arm.

"Take it easy, Jessie. You're going to be all right."

Jessica blinked and then groaned. That voice and those wide, imposing shoulders were all too familiar. She looked up into stormy gray eyes and let her gaze wander to that stubborn square jaw before she looked away.

Stone knew she had no idea he had followed her as she'd been moved from the trauma room, or that she'd been parked in the hallway, waiting to be taken upstairs. She also had no way of knowing, nor did Stone think she would have believed, that he'd refused to budge from her side until someone came to get her.

"Bat barf," she muttered, and missed seeing his grin.

If it hadn't hurt so bad, Jessica would have glared.

"I'm bleeding," she muttered inanely, and reached toward her head.

Stone's expression gentled as he caught her hand. "Not anymore, Jessie. You're going to be all right."

"Not in this lifetime," she muttered.

Stone frowned but didn't have time to answer, as the long-awaited orderly finally appeared, moving Stone aside as he grabbed at the foot of Jessica's bed.

"Sorry, sir, but they're admitting her. You can see her tomorrow during visiting hours."

Stone turned Jessie's hand loose and felt a sense of panic as the orderly wheeled her away. The need to say something more was choking him, but all he could manage was, "Hey, honey, take care of yourself, okay?"

Jessica felt him patting her knee as she was wheeled away.

"I am not your 'honey,'" she mumbled, before falling back asleep.

Someone yanked at the sheet beneath Jessica's right leg and then rolled her onto her side. With an audible groan, she opened her eyes and grabbed for the bed rail. A pair of nurses-in-training were changing the linens on her bed.

"We're sorry, Miss Hanson, but this won't take long, and you'll feel so much better with clean sheets on your bed."

Jessica looked at the name tags on their uniforms, then gritted her teeth and hung on. She could have used a painkiller, and she was fairly certain that the clean sheets A. Wren and S. Dexter were determined to give her wouldn't do a thing for the throb in her temples.

Wren rattled the ice in Jessica's pitcher and then set it down, satisfied that there was an ample supply.

"Isn't that a shame about Mrs. Stuart," she said.

Jessica's heart kicked out of rhythm as Dexter tucked the corners of her sheet tightly into place. Memory was coming back in swift and sudden flashes. Olivia had been attacked right in front of her eyes! Guilt flooded her conscience. How could she have been so crass as to forget such a thing?

Dexter nodded. "It's so sad for her son, Hal, too. Imagine having your own mother suffer a heart attack on the day of your wedding!"

Jessica frowned. They had it all wrong. It wasn't a heart attack. Someone had stabbed Olivia. She'd seen it happen. She touched Wren's arm and started to argue.

"But, I saw…"

Wren, not to be outdone, patted Jessica's arm and continued with the story as if Jessica hadn't uttered a word.

"They said someone found her on the floor by her kitchen table. When they brought her in last night, she was all dressed for the wedding."

Jessica closed her eyes. Teal. The dress was a teal-colored silk. Her head was swimming. None of this was making a bit of sense.

"It wasn't by *her* table, it was by *my*..."

For all the good it did to say it, the two women were still ignoring the fact that Jessica was trying to speak.

Dexter thrust her arm beneath Jessica's neck, then slid a fresh pillow beneath her head.

"Here you go, dear. Easy does it."

Wren poked a thermometer in Jessica's mouth and began to take her pulse. Once again, Jessica found herself unable to say what was on her mind.

Dexter picked the bloodstained sheets from the floor where they'd been tossed and waited while Wren yanked the thermometer out of Jessica's mouth and made the necessary notations on the patient's chart.

"Have you seen where the Stuarts live?" Dexter asked. "I swear, some people have all the luck. That house is fantastic. I always wanted one like that."

Wren stuck her pen back in her pocket and patted Jessica's arm. "Yes, well, that house won't do Olivia Stuart any good anymore. You can't take it with you, you know."

Jessica was too shocked by what she was hearing to respond. *How could they have found Olivia in her house? She was in my office, I saw her!*

Dexter's voice lowered to a theatrical whisper. "They said Dr. Jennings and Dr. Howell worked on her forever and it was just no use."

Jessica gasped, and this time when she grabbed at Wren's arm, she got their attention.

"She's dead? Olivia Stuart is dead?"

Wren and Dexter glanced nervously at each other, suddenly realizing they'd been gossiping about hospital business in front of a patient.

"Are you a member of the family?" Wren asked.

"No, but—"

Relief spread over both of their faces. "Just rest, dear. It's the best medicine for what ails you."

Having dispensed their opinions, Dexter and Wren quickly disappeared, leaving Jessica in a state of confusion. *Olivia wasn't in her kitchen. She was in my office, and she didn't have a heart attack. Someone tried to kill her.* Then she gasped. Someone hadn't *tried* to kill her. If Olivia was dead, then the attack had been successful.

But the more Jessica thought about it, the more confused she became. The nurses would have no reason to lie, and it didn't make sense that someone could attack Olivia in one place and then move her body clear across town and dump it in another place without being seen. Granted, there was a blackout, but the lodge had been crawling with guests.

A fresh wave of pain moved from Jessica's head to her neck and shoulders. She bit her lip to keep from crying out and closed her eyes. And the longer she lay there alone, the more convinced she became that the blow to her head must have caused her to suffer hallucinations. It was the only explanation that made sense.

She refused to let herself examine the fact that about the same time she was having the hallucination, Olivia Stuart was suffering a heart attack on the other side of town. The coincidence of it all was mind-boggling, but she hurt too much to sort it all out.

Settling back against the pillow, she took a slow, deep breath, trying to convince herself it was going to be all right. In the midst of her thoughts, the door to her room flew open, banging against a nearby chair. She opened her eyes and stifled a groan.

In all her tall, blond beauty, Brenda Hanson burst into

the room carrying an armful of wilting flowers. "Jessie, darling! Are you all right?"

Jessica had no time to answer before her sister leaned across the bed and gave her a kiss, unintentionally squishing the IV fastened to the back of her hand and poking the stem of a gladiola up her nose.

"Ouch," Jessica muttered.

"Ooh, sorry," Brenda said, frowning as she straightened, then staring at the apparatus they'd stuck in her baby sister's body. The frown deepened as her gaze moved from Jessica's hand to her head.

"Ooh, yuck, they shaved off part of your hair, didn't they."

Jessica's hand flew upward in a fit of panic. Slipping her fingers beneath the edge of the bandage, she felt bare skin, then groaned and let her hand fall to the bed with a thump.

"Dog fleas. As if I'm not invisible enough already."

Brenda sighed. She loved her younger sister dearly, but was of the same opinion their parents had been before their untimely death some years earlier. With regards to looks, fashion sense and her worth on the open market with men, Jessica was clueless. Brenda was all for subtlety herself, but not at the expense of style and looks.

Brenda poked her finger near the edge of the bandage with a sympathetic tap. "I'm sure it will grow back in no time."

Jessica's chin quivered. "With my luck, that's not necessarily a given."

Brenda ignored her remark and moved on to a different topic, waving the drooping flowers under her sister's nose. "They're a little wilted, but you must remember it's the thought that counts. The power is still off, and Marcel's Bouquet was letting everything go at half price."

In spite of her misery, Jessica had to grin. Leave it up to Brenda to find a bargain in a blackout. She brushed her fingertips across limp lavender petals.

"They're very pretty, but I don't have anything to put them in."

"It doesn't matter," Brenda said. "Grand Springs is on water rationing until the blackout is over."

Jessica snorted softly. "It's been raining for days and we're now short of drinking water?"

Brenda laughed and waved her hand above her head with a flirty flip. "You know the old saying, 'Water, water everywhere, but not a drop to drink.'"

Jessica closed her eyes as a fresh wave of pain rolled up her back to the top of her head.

Brenda's lighthearted expression faded as she stared at the stark white bandage on her little sister's head. She set the wilting flowers aside and brushed a hand lightly across Jessica's forehead.

"What happened, sweetie? About an hour ago I got a call from someone telling me you'd had an accident. When I found out you've been here since last night, I started to pitch a fit. But I suppose with all that's been going on, we're lucky they called at all."

Brenda's sympathy was too much to handle. Tears trickled from the corner of Jessica's eyes as Brenda patted at her arm.

"I fell in my office. Against the file cabinet, I think."

Brenda glanced at Jessica's head again and winced. "Poor dear."

Jessica had the distinct impression that Brenda's concern was more for her missing hair than the wound she'd suffered.

"Oh, did you hear the news about Olivia Stuart?" Brenda said, suddenly changing the subject.

The room started to turn, and Jessica was thrust into the past with a swiftness she wouldn't have believed. She was only vaguely aware of her sister's voice droning on somewhere in the background, as her attention had become focused on an entirely different scene.

Rationally, she knew she was in the hospital, but her

mind seemed removed from her body. The room went dark, and, unable to fight the overwhelming sense of being out of control, once again she found herself witnessing Olivia Stuart's attack. And then the image disappeared as quickly as it came, leaving Jessica weak and shaking and gasping for air.

Concerned for Jessica's sudden pallor, Brenda grabbed her sister's hand. "Are you all right? Should I call a doctor?"

Jessica closed her eyes and tried to calm her racing heart. "No, whatever it was is gone."

"Still," Brenda muttered, "I think I should let them know that you're not quite up to par."

Jessica tried not to glare and wondered what it would be like to be beautiful and dense, then decided it wouldn't be a good trade-off. She liked being able to balance a checkbook, as well as a job and a life. She rolled her eyes at Brenda's inane remark.

"Of course I'm not up to par. I have stitches where my hair used to be."

Brenda's laugh tinkled like crystal chimes in a gentle breeze. Jessica snorted softly in response and both sisters smiled at each other. There *was* some truth in the old saying that blood was thicker than water.

Stone Richardson walked into the precinct, his steps dragging, his expression lined with fatigue. He'd slept in his car in fits and snatches, and dried blood stained the toes of his boots, remnants of the time he'd spent in ER last night.

Erik Chang, an officer on the force and one of Stone's friends, looked up as Stone walked in.

"Your ex-wife called, and the chief's waiting to see you," he said.

Stone's eyebrows rose, and he thrust a hand through his hair, spiking the short, thick strands. He hadn't heard from Naomi in years. Why now? he wondered.

"Well, they're both going to have to wait," he muttered, and reached across his desk for the coffee cup on the other side of a stack of files.

"There's no coffee," Chang said.

On his way to the break room, Stone stopped, then pivoted. The frown between his eyebrows deepened as Chang added, "Because there's no power, remember?"

Stone's expletive was brief and to the point. He glanced down at the half inch of yesterday's coffee coating the bottom of his cup, considered his jangled nerves and tossed it back like a dose of bad medicine.

Chang shuddered and looked away so that no one would see him gag. For a cop, he had a remarkably weak stomach.

Stone dropped his jacket on the back of his chair as he headed for Frank Sanderson's office. He knocked once, then went in without waiting for an invitation.

The chief looked up, took one look at the drawn expression on his detective's face, as well as his blood-splattered clothing, and frowned.

"Were you hurt?"

Stone looked down, only now realizing how he must look. "No, it's someone else's blood."

"Then, go home and get some sleep. Come back when you can think straight."

Stone's right eyebrow arched. "Why, mother, I didn't know you cared."

"Shut the hell up and do what I said," Sanderson ordered. "This blackout isn't over yet."

Stone's attitude shifted. "Sorry," he said quietly. "But it was one hellacious night."

Aware that his men had worked without routines or orders, filling in where they were needed most, Sanderson asked, "Where were you?"

"Vanderbilt Memorial."

Sanderson thought of Olivia Stuart. She'd died there last night. God knows how many others had followed her exit.

Glancing at the blood splatters on Stone's shirt, he repeated himself. "Do what I said."

Stone's shoulders slumped under the weight of exhaustion. "Yes, sir."

He shut the door quietly behind him and picked up his jacket on the way out of the precinct. His stomach growled—more from hunger than the cold, stale coffee he'd tossed down moments earlier. And he kept remembering the blood in Jessica Hanson's hair and then, later, the lost, frightened expression on her face as they'd wheeled her away. He wanted—no—needed to know if she was all right. And as soon as he got a couple of hours' sleep he would go back to the hospital and see for himself.

Two

Jessica watched with a wary eye as the nurse who was accompanying Dr. Noah Howell on his rounds removed the IV from her hand.

"Just take it easy when you get home," Noah said as he signed off on Jessica's chart.

Jessica glanced at the dim, flickering light in the hallway. Since she'd been admitted, she'd spent most of her time sleeping and was still confused about the time that had actually passed.

"Is the power still off?"

He nodded. The last few hours had been chaotic, and it would seem there was no end in sight.

"Yes, we're still operating on generators, although I'm told that the crews are out in full force. I'm sure it won't be long before power is restored. For now, all you need is a bed."

Briefly fingering the small white patch of gauze above her right eyebrow, she winced. "That and a new head of hair."

"We didn't cut away all that much," Noah said.

Jessica tried to smile. "That's easy for you to say."

He smiled and patted her on the knee. "It's not so bad. And it will grow back. You'll see."

She sighed. "Sorry. I don't usually whine. After all, what's a little missing hair compared to everything else that's been happening."

The smile disappeared from Noah Howell's face as he thought back. Of everything that had happened in the past hours, the thing he regretted most was losing Olivia Stuart. No matter how hard they'd tried, it hadn't been enough to save her, and somehow, that still surprised him. Just before she died, she'd whispered the word "coal." Soon afterward, they'd lost her. Masking his weariness, he tried to focus his concerns on the patient before him.

"You have the instructions the nurse gave you. I'll see you back in my office in a few days to remove the stitches, okay?"

A few days. What else, Jessica wondered, could happen between now and then? She nodded. "Okay." Then she added, "These phones aren't working, and I need to call my sister so she can come get me and take me home."

Dr. Howell paused at the door, glancing back at the phone near her bed.

"The switchboard operator was one of last night's victims, and her replacement is out of town on vacation. It's been so chaotic, we decided to channel everything through the nurses' stations on each floor. I'll have someone call her for you at the desk."

Moments later, she was alone. She glanced at the clock. It was close to five p.m. She thought of going home to a house without power, without refrigeration—possibly without a means of communication. She looked down at the wad she'd made of the covers and tugged at the neck of the hospital gown she was wearing. While the aspect of those discomforts was disheartening, the idea of crawling into her own nightgown—and into her own bed—was enough to make it all worthwhile.

She sat up and looked out the window. On the surface, everything about Grand Springs seemed the same. The lush green of the majestic mountains marking the skyline of the city were capped by low, overhanging clouds, but for now, the rain had stopped. The sky was dark and overcast. Night would come early.

Dusk was near. Normally, streetlights would be coming on and people would be closing down businesses and hurrying home for the evening meal. But not tonight. The streets were eerily empty, and the lack of vehicles on the roadways seemed an ominous sign of impending doom.

Suddenly, she wanted to be home. To find the familiar within her own house before dark. Throwing back the covers, she got out of bed and went to the closet. Brenda had brought her clean clothes as well as the discount flowers. At least she wouldn't have to go home in torn and bloody clothing.

But getting dressed wasn't as simple as she'd expected it to be. Every time she leaned down, the room started to spin and she was forced to grab onto the bed to keep from falling. It took all she had just to put on her underwear and jeans, and by then she was in a cold sweat. Barefoot and clutching a T-shirt to her chest, she staggered to a nearby chair, where she sat staring at the tennis shoes still in her closet. They were less than a yard away and it might as well have been a mile. Hating this feeling of helplessness, she closed her eyes and leaned her head against the wall.

"Bug breath."

It was a fair comment on her condition, as well as her state of mind.

This time when Stone entered Vanderbilt Memorial, he went in the front door and took the stairs on the right to the third floor. He came out of the stairwell, his long stride carrying him down the hall with single-minded intent. Under the weak glow of the generator-powered lighting, the shadows beneath his eyes seemed darker, the strain lines at the corners of his mouth deeper, and the sun-bleached highlights in his hair gleamed like wheat in a noonday sun. His expression was grim. It was what his friends called his "cop face." But all he needed was some more rest. And that would come, after he'd seen for himself that Jessie was really all right. He'd tried to talk himself out of this trip all the way to the hospital, yet when he'd parked and gotten out of his car, he knew he would never have been able to rest without seeing her face...hearing her voice...even suffering the guilt he would feel when he saw her. He had to know she was all right. Then he could rest.

"Richardson, haven't you gone home yet?"

Stone paused and turned. Noah Howell was coming out of a room he'd just passed.

"Hi, Doc. I thought I would look in on Jessie Hanson. Last night, they said she'd been put in 339. Do you know if she's still there?"

Noah nodded. "But not for long. I just released her to go home. In fact, I'm on my way to the nurse's desk to call her sister to come and get her."

Stone didn't stop to think why he was offering, he just blurted it out before he changed his own mind.

"Don't bother. I'll see that she gets home okay."

Noah grinned. Stone's defenses went up.

"Get that look off your face," Stone warned. "Just because I'm concerned about an old friend, it doesn't mean anything. Hell. I dated her sister once. Besides, she's just a kid."

"If my memory serves, she's twenty-six, old buddy. That's hardly robbing the cradle," Noah said.

Stone ignored the comment and knocked, waiting for an invitation to enter. When it came, he went in, unprepared for the woman inside.

Jessica jerked as the knock sounded on her door. Still sprawled in the chair with the T-shirt clutched to her chest and expecting one of the hospital staff, she spoke without thinking.

"Come in."

When Stone walked into the room, she gasped and grabbed her shirt with both hands, holding it up beneath her chin.

"How dare you!" she muttered, and tried hard to glare, but frowning made her head hurt worse.

Stone was transfixed. He'd expected her to be safe in bed and covered up with a sheet, not half dressed and sprawled out in a chair with a shirt clutched to her front like a shield. All he could think to say was "You told me to come in."

Jessica's lower lip slid forward. "But I didn't know it was you."

She looked so lost and hurt sitting there. Stone fought the urge to hold her.

"Sorry, do you want me to leave?"

She nodded, then groaned. If only she could remember to speak instead, it would be a lot less painful.

"Are you all right?" he asked.

She grimaced, closing her eyes to steady the sudden sway of the room.

"Of course I'm not all right!" She sighed, trying to relax the tension knotting at the back of her neck.

Stone frowned. The past two years had certainly changed one thing about Jessie. She never used to be so angry.

"I told Doc Howell I'd take you home."

Jessica's eyes flew open, and the shirt began to slip. When it revealed two mounds of creamy flesh held fast beneath a white lace bra, Stone reacted by pointing at the T-shirt.

"You gonna wear that home or just carry it?"

Jessica's eyes teared in frustration as she stopped its escape. "I got dizzy."

His expression softened. "Need some help?"

She hesitated.

"Come on, honey. I've seen it before."

The look on her face was priceless, and Stone knew he'd reminded them both of something better left forgotten.

Jessica's ire rose. "Just turn around, you mealymouthed snake."

He grinned slightly as he turned. "Dare I turn my back on a woman who's just called me a snake?"

Jessica glared at his backside, reminding herself to ignore the wide shoulders, narrow hips and long legs as she thrust both arms in the shirt, yanking it down over her head in haste. But she'd forgotten the bandage at the edge of her hairline and yelped in pain when the neck pulled too tight for comfort.

Stone spun, took one look at the predicament she'd put herself in and stalked across the room without waiting for an invitation.

"Easy," he warned, and pulled the shirt back up enough to give himself room to maneuver. She started to sputter. He frowned. "Calm down, damn it. I'm trying to help."

When she muttered something he didn't understand, he figured it was better to let lost curses die. This time when he eased the shirt down, he started the opening at the back of her head first, then pulled it toward the front, stretching the fabric as it slid past the bandage. When it cleared her nose, he looked down. Two orbs of pure blue were gleaming up at him with malevolence.

"You're welcome," he drawled.

She resented his arrogance. Why did devastating men always smirk?

"What are you doing here?" she asked.

The question took him off guard. What *was* he doing here? Last night had resulted in a multitude of disasters that had sent literally dozens of Grand Springs residents to the hospital. And Jessica wasn't the only one he knew who'd been admitted. Why had he felt the urge to make sure she, above all others, was going to be okay? Uneasy as to how to answer her, he blurted out the first thing that came to mind.

"I was on my way home. Thought I'd stop by."

"You live on the other side of town."

His eyes narrowed. He wasn't prepared to pursue the issue. Not with her. Not even with himself.

"I know where I live. Do you want to go home or not?"

Jessica's shoulders slumped. "Yes, please."

Satisfied to be back on firm ground, Stone nodded. "That's fine, then." He looked down at her feet. "Where are your shoes?"

Jessica pointed toward the closet and started to cry. Not loudly, just huge, silent tears spilling out of her eyes and down her face.

At that moment, something tore loose inside of Stone that had nothing to do with compassion. If he hadn't been so rattled by a particular tear hanging on the edge of her lip, he might have realized the emotion for what it was. But he was, and he didn't, and by the time he got the shoes on her feet, the notion of pursuing the thought had long since passed.

Their drive home was silent. A half hour later, he pulled into Jessica's driveway and parked. Every house on the block was little more than a dark shape against the shadows of the coming night. Now and then a weak glow of some lantern or candle could be seen shining through curtains, but it was the depth of darkness out on the streets that made Jessica jumpy.

After offering to carry her inside, and getting a quick glare for his efforts, Stone settled for walking her to the house. Lit only by the glow of a three-quarter moon, he guided her to the porch steps. They were at the door before Jessica drew back in dismay and slapped her hand against the side of her leg.

"Wormy, wormy fudge," she muttered.

He chuckled beneath his breath. One thing he'd loved about her was the uniqueness of her colorful language, but even that sounded gross to him.

"What's wrong?"

"My keys are in my purse, and it must be back in my office at the lodge."

"Not to worry," Stone said, and slipped a small lock pick from his jacket pocket. Moments later, the lock clicked and the door swung open. He stepped aside.

"Don't mention it."

She glanced up at him in silent appreciation. "Thank goodness you're on our side."

Stone followed her in, shutting the door behind him. "Got a flashlight or candles?"

"Both in the kitchen. Top drawer on the right."

He traded the lock pick for his own small flashlight. "Wait here. I'll be right back."

When he started toward the back of the house, Jessica frowned.

"How do you know where the kitchen is?"

"I'm following my nose."

She sniffed. He was right. The scent of burned bacon was still evident.

Smart aleck.

But she didn't voice her thoughts. She didn't have it in her to complain anymore. An old Elvis Presley song came to mind as she leaned against the wall to keep from falling. Yes, her legs *were* shaky, and her knees were *more* than weak. She *was* definitely all shook up, but from the accident, of course. *Not* from the fact that she'd just spent the better part of an hour with a man who'd haunted more than one of her dreams.

Jessica closed her eyes and took a slow, deep breath. When she looked up, he was coming toward her, carrying a lit candle. His face was cast in shadow, but the cut of his cheekbones, a broad slash of jaw and his lower lip were highlighted by the soft yellow glow.

Exhaling slowly, she watched as he set the candle on a nearby table and then led her toward the chair beside it. She sat.

"Here," Stone said, and dropped her flashlight into her lap.

Suddenly the intimacy of being alone in the darkness with this man was too much. She'd spent two years trying to forget how it felt to go to sleep and wake up in his arms.

"Goodbye, and thank you for bringing me home."

His easy laugh did things to her nerves she didn't need to feel.

As Stone chuckled, it crossed his mind that his ex-wife would have cried and clung with every ounce of her being. She'd hated his job as a cop, but she'd hated her lonely life as a cop's wife more.

"Damn, honey. I've had the brush-off before, but never so sweetly."

Muttering beneath her breath, she looked away. "That wasn't a brush-off, and stop calling me 'honey.'"

He cupped her chin, tilting her face until she was forced to look at him.

"Hey, you."

Now her nerves were really on edge. There was a low, breathless quality to his voice that she'd never thought she'd hear. At least, not when speaking to her.

"What?"

"It's been a long time, hasn't it?"

Jessica's heart started to thump erratically. "Long time since what?"

His voice deepened. "Since we've been together."

"I've spent two years trying to forget," she muttered.

"So that's why you left without so much as a goodbye."

She swallowed, trying to get past the pain. "You'd made yourself painfully clear," she said, and then looked deeply into his eyes. "There wasn't anything left to say…was there?"

He looked away, and then back. "Will you be afraid?"

She gripped the arms of the chair as her heart skipped a beat. *Afraid? The only thing that ever scared me was losing you and I survived that. This is a piece of cake.* But she didn't answer.

"If you are, I can have a patrol car swing by here every so often to make sure you're okay."

She gritted her teeth. "I'm not afraid of the dark, and I want you to go."

He sighed, then stood up, hesitating. Sitting there in the

dark with nothing but candlelight by which to see, she seemed awfully small and so alone. He couldn't bear to leave her...at least not like this. He thrust his hand in his pocket and pulled out his card.

"If you need me, the number is on the card."

Jessica fought an urge to cry. Her fingers curled around the card as he shut the door behind him. Even after the sound of his car engine had faded away, she sat unmoving, clutching the card as if it was her lifeline to normalcy in a world lost in darkness.

She fell asleep in the chair, and when she awoke, the candle was out, yet the room was not dark. Disoriented, it took her a moment to focus on the fact that the light she was seeing was coming through the windows, and that it was growing brighter and brighter with each passing second.

Tension pulled the muscles at the back of her neck, and her breath began to shorten. Her fingers dug into the arms of the chair as the familiarity of her home began to change before her eyes. Unable to look away from the light, she stared into a nightmare that wouldn't let her go.

Olivia Stuart smiled as she walked around the kitchen, adding the finishing touches to the ensemble she'd chosen for Hal's wedding. Teal was her favorite color. Somewhere between true blue and green, it accentuated her coloring to perfection. She paused in front of the sink and picked up a picture that stood on the windowsill, smiling to herself as she remembered the day it had been taken. Eve had been fussing with her hair, and Hal had been laughing at her futile attempts to make it glamorous. Even as adults, they were good children.

Just as she started to move toward the table, to pick up her purse and the umbrella lying there, the scent of flowers drifted into the room. A slight frown drew between her brows as she tried to identify the scent. Gardenias! She was smelling gardenias!

A hand came around her mouth without warning, and Olivia dropped the picture and shrieked, swallowing her own cry as the fingers upon her face clamped too tightly for the sound to escape. Fear shattered her control as she reached behind her, trying to tear free. The struggle was brief. Shock turned to pain as a sharp, burning sensation pierced the back of her leg.

She remembered thinking that this didn't make sense. Her leg had been stabbed, but there was pain in her chest. She reached out, gasping desperately for air. She wasn't going to make Hal's wedding, after all.

My son...my son.

Pain blossomed and burst, splintering throughout her body in a white-hot heat.

Jessica jerked. The bright orb of light was still present, but there was a constant, repetitive thump that hadn't been there before. She blinked, then blinked again as she realized this wasn't part of the dream. Someone was knocking on her door.

It took her a moment to switch gears, and when she did, her first thought was that Stone had come back. And then she heard her sister's voice.

"Jessica! Are you in there? Jessie, it's me, Brenda! Let me in!"

Jessica blinked again, her perception of what she'd just seen suddenly clear. The light was nothing more than the headlights of Brenda's car shining through the sheer curtains at her front window.

I must have been dreaming again.

"Be right there," she called, and headed for the door. As soon as she turned the knob, Brenda came rushing in and threw her arms around Jessica's neck.

"I went to the hospital and they said you'd been dismissed! Why didn't you call?"

"The phones in the rooms were out of order."

Brenda threw up her arms in disgust and pointed to Jessica's phone on a nearby table. "Is yours?"

"I don't know. Stone brought me home. I didn't think to check."

Even in the shadows, Jessica was aware of her sister's shock.

"Stone? As in Richardson?"

Jessica shrugged. "Do we know another? For Pete's sake, Brenda, come inside. I need to sit down."

Brenda's mouth pursed. "Obviously you've been keeping secrets from me. However, we'll discuss that later. You need to be in bed. Here, take my flashlight."

"I have one somewhere," Jessica muttered, looking back toward the chair in which she'd been sitting.

"No. Take mine and don't move," Brenda said. "I'll be right back."

Jessica waited while her sister killed the car engine, turned off the lights, then returned, carrying an overnight bag in her hand.

Jessica pointed the beam of the flashlight at the small blue bag. "What do you think you're doing?"

"Spending the night. And don't argue. You have a concussion. You shouldn't be alone."

Jessica groaned. The last thing she needed was a babysitter, but from the look on Brenda's face, it would seem she was getting one, just the same.

"You're a mess," Brenda said, fingering Jessica's matted hair and drawn expression. "Come with me. I'll get you cleaned up and tucked in a bed."

"I don't need to be tucked in. Besides, someone told me water is being rationed."

"Up to now, you haven't used any, so I'd say you're allowed a quick bath. And you know what Mother used to say. Everything will look better in the morning."

Jessica sighed. She knew better than to argue with Brenda when she got on a roll.

"Then, will you help me wash my hair? It feels awful."

Brenda hugged her. "We'll have to be careful not to get your stitches wet, but I suppose something can be arranged."

"Then, okay. But you have to stick to your side of the bed."

In the glow of the flashlight, Jessica saw her sister grin.

Jessica awoke in a panic and sat straight up in bed. Her heart was pounding, and the scent of gardenias was thick in her nostrils. She covered her face with her hands, fighting the urge to cry. Why was this happening? Why did she keep having this same awful dream, over and over and over?

Brenda sighed and rolled onto her back, one arm outflung on Jessica's pillow, the other trailing off the side of the bed. Jessica glanced down and frowned. As if the dreams weren't bad enough, Brenda had a tendency to take her half of the bed from the middle. She patted Brenda on the shoulder.

"Brenda!"

Brenda snorted softly, muttering something in her sleep. The pat turned into a shove. "Brenda!"

Brenda groaned and cracked an eye. "What?" Then she remembered where she was and why she'd come. When she saw Jessica sitting up in the bed, she came awake in an instant.

"What's wrong? Are you in pain?"

"No, but you're going to be if you don't move over," Jessica muttered.

Brenda blinked like a baby owl. "Sorry," she said, and scooted back to her side of the bed.

With a defeated sigh, Jessica tried to go back to sleep. But she kept seeing the needle glittering in the lamplight as the assailant plunged it into the back of Olivia Stuart's leg. Something kept telling her there was more to what she was seeing than just a dream. Long minutes later, she rolled over.

"Brenda. Are you asleep?"

Brenda shoved a lock of hair from her face. "I'm not now," she mumbled.

"Have you ever had a vision?"

Brenda rolled over. "Jessie, honey, does your head still hurt?"

"Of course it does. But one thing has nothing to do with the other."

Brenda eyed the clock and groaned. "It's three in the morning. Don't you think we could save this conversation for daylight? You need your rest. I need my rest. Go back to sleep."

"I'm afraid to," Jessica said in a quiet, resigned tone.

Brenda sat up, her attention caught. "What do you mean?"

Jessica picked at a loose thread on the edge of the blanket without answering until Brenda yanked the blanket away.

"Jessica Leigh Hanson, I asked you a question."

Jessica's smile was slight as she looked up. "You sounded just like Mother."

Dismayed, Brenda sighed and slid her arm around her sister's neck. "Jessie, if you don't talk, I can't help."

Jessica frowned. "I could talk from now to daylight and I still don't think you can help. In fact, I don't think anyone can help."

"You'll never know until you try."

Jessica sighed. "I keep having this dream about Olivia Stuart dying."

Brenda's voice softened. "Oh, honey. That's understandable. You must have been in the ER when they brought her in."

Jessica shook her head. "I don't think so. If I was, I don't remember. I don't remember much of anything after I hit my head." *Except Stone Richardson...but that doesn't count.*

"Maybe talking about it will help. What were you dreaming?"

"She was by a table."

"Who was by a table?" Brenda asked.

Jessica rolled her eyes, trying not to let her frustration show. "Olivia Stuart," she repeated. "At first I thought she was at my desk, but she wouldn't come help me."

Brenda brushed the hair away from Jessica's bandage and patted her arm. "Honey, head injuries do weird things to people. Maybe you just—"

Jessica drew back in frustration. "I knew you would say that, but it's not so! I know what I saw. I mean... I know what I saw in my dream, and in my dream, Olivia Stuart did not die from a heart attack. She was stabbed."

Brenda gasped, for the moment caught up in the telling. And then she remembered. "But don't you see? Now you know for certain it was just a dream. I heard that the doctors and nurses at Vanderbilt worked on her for some time. They would have seen a stab wound. There would have been blood. Lots of blood." She patted Jessica's arm. "It's just a bad dream caused by the blow to your head."

Fighting exhaustion and tears, Jessica laid back down and pulled the covers up to her chin as her sister rolled over to her side of the bed. Wrapped in quiet and lulled by a false sense of security, Jessica began to settle. But at the edge of sleep, her voice broke the silence.

"She wasn't stabbed with a knife. It was a needle. A hypodermic needle...in the back of the leg."

Brenda thrust her foot into the leg of her jeans and yanked them up while Jessica watched from the bed.

"Thank you for spending the night with me," she said.

Brenda smiled. "That's what sisters are for." And then the smile quirked. "That is, when there are no good-looking cops around."

Jessica refused to look at Brenda. Her heart was so full of memories that she feared if Brenda saw her face, she would know. "I already told you. I have nothing in common with the man. You're the one he dated, not me."

"And there's your answer. Dated. As in...past tense. Also, that was ages ago. I haven't given him a thought in forever."

Yeah, well, I wish I could say the same.

Brenda stuffed her nightgown into her bag. "There. I think I have everything. I need to go home and feed the cat and check my messages." She glanced toward the clock and realized it was running. "Oh, look! The power is back on."

Jessica followed her sister's gaze and sighed. At least one part of this nightmare was over.

Brenda continued, unaware of Jessica's disinterest. "The boss is out of town and probably frantic because no one's there. However, I doubt there's a soul in town who's interested in redecorating their home right now."

Jessica nodded. "I know. I was in the middle of payroll at the lodge when the power went off. Everyone's probably having a fit because their checks will be late."

Brenda picked up her bag and then fixed her baby sister with a long, assessing stare.

"Jessie."

Jessica looked up.

"About last night and what you said..."

"What about it?" Jessica asked. Her voice was defensive and she knew it.

"If I were you, I wouldn't be telling just anyone that you're having hallucinations. They might get the wrong idea."

Jessica's lower lip slid slightly forward. "What if it's not a hallucination?"

Brenda shrugged. "I still wouldn't be talking about them." Then she glanced down at her watch. "I've got to run. You've got juice in the fridge and cereal in the cabinet. However, your milk is sour."

"Oh, yummy."

Jessica's sarcasm was not lost on Brenda. She grinned. "I'll call you later. Stay in bed. Rest. I love you."

Jessica rolled her eyes. "In spite of your incessant need to boss me around, I love you, too."

Brenda left, and then moments later, came back on the run.

"Jessie, have you seen my car keys? I can't find them anywhere. I thought they were in my bag, but they're not."

Without waiting for Jessica to answer, she began turning the bedroom upside down, looking under cushions and then dashing into the adjoining bathroom to see if they might be there.

Just as Brenda slammed a cabinet door, Jessica began to lose track of where she was. The air in front of her seemed to shift, and suddenly she had a clear and perfect vision of a set of keys sticking out of the lock on a trunk. She got out of bed just as Brenda came out of the bathroom.

"Shoot," Brenda muttered. "I can't seem to find them—"

"You left them in the trunk lock last night."

In the act of looking under the bed, Brenda froze. Slowly, she looked up, meeting her sister's gaze over the edge of the mattress.

"What did you say?"

"I said, they're in the lock on the trunk."

Realization dawned. Brenda remembered opening the trunk to get her bag. Yes! That *was* the last time she'd had them! She got to her feet with a look of relief on her face and was almost out of the room before it hit her.

Jessica hadn't been outside. In fact, she hadn't been out of her bed since Brenda had put her there last night. She stopped and turned.

"Jessie?"

"What?"

"Why did you just say that?"

Jessica shrugged. "I don't know. I just suddenly saw them dangling out of the lock."

The hairs stood up at the nape of Brenda's neck. She shivered, refusing to give way to what she was thinking. "Nothing more than a lucky guess. That's all it could be."

Jessica's expression didn't change. "Go see if I'm right."

She listened, and when she heard the sound of a car engine firing, she shuddered and crawled back into bed.

Toad tracks. Now I am scaring myself.

She lay back on her pillow and flung her arms above her head in a dramatic gesture of disgust. The longer she lay there, the more convinced she became that something out of the ordinary was happening to her. The question remained—what was she going to do about it?

Three

That night, Jessica ate her evening meal by the light of the moon. Although the power had been restored all over town, she still felt the need to escape, and the dark of her backyard was as far as she could go. She sat on her porch with a can of pop in one hand and a peanut butter and jelly sandwich in the other, unwilling to move indoors.

Grape jelly squished out of the edge of the bread as she took a big bite. Before it could drip, she caught it with the tip of her tongue and swallowed it whole. It wasn't exactly fine dining, but for Jessica, who at her best was just a fair cook, it sufficed.

Thanks to a co-worker at the lodge, her car was back in her driveway and her purse was safely on a chair in her bedroom. But her stitches kept pulling beneath the bandage and her long hair was driving her crazy. The longer she sat, the more she thought about cutting part of it off. At least, the part that was making her nuts.

It shouldn't be all that hard. She had scissors, and thanks to the power company, a good light by which to see. Since she could work any computer program on the market, she could surely cut her own hair without making a mess. Besides, Dr. Howell had given her a jump start by shaving the part around her stitches. All she had to do was tidy it up a bit.

An hour and a half later, she stood before her bathroom mirror, staring at herself in disbelief. Yes, she was a whiz with figures, but she should have remembered that she couldn't sew on a button without bringing blood.

The length was gone, just like she'd wanted. But so was the shape and the style. And for hair that was remarkably straight and limp, she'd somehow given it a life of its own. It no longer lay on her head. Instead, it sort of sprang from it, like new sprouts on a severely pruned tree. Oddly enough, the new cut gave her gamine features an engaging quality that her old style had not. The flyaway do was, in its own way, quite charming. But Jessica couldn't see the charm for the harm. She dropped the scissors in the sink and sighed.

"Mouse poop."

That pretty much said it all.

The next day dawned with an inevitability she couldn't ignore. She needed to go to Squaw Creek Lodge and finish the payroll. When she got in her car, her nerves began to draw. A short while later, she turned into the parking lot and sat with the engine running, staring up at the grand log-and-stone edifice with dread. And as she stared, the same thought kept running through her mind. *This is where it happened.*

But she wasn't referring to the accident. It was what happened afterward that was making her nuts. While she sat, lost in thought, someone knocked on her window. She turned with a jerk, expecting to see Olivia Stuart's ghost.

But it wasn't a ghost. It was Sheila Biggers, secretary to the manager of the lodge. Jessica glanced at herself in the rearview mirror as she killed the engine. No use putting this off any longer. At least she wouldn't have to go inside alone.

Sheila squealed. "Jessica, ooh, your poor little head." She pushed aside a swag of Jessica's gypsy-cut hair to peek at the bandage beneath and made a face.

But Jessica didn't bother to answer, because Sheila Biggers could shift conversational gears faster than a drag racer on a hot track. They started toward the lodge, and Sheila continued without taking a breath in between.

"Did you hear! That bride-to-be, Randi Howell, disappeared the night of the blackout! The Stuart wedding never did take place!" She took a deep breath and moved on to another subject. "I love, love, love your hair! Who did it?"

Jessica's mouth dropped. "Really? You don't think it's too drastic a change?"

Sheila reached out to touch the ends of Jessica's hair. "I always said you looked like Goldie Hawn. Didn't I say you looked like Goldie Hawn?"

"Yes, you did, although I must say I never saw why."

"Never mind, because I was wrong. I see it all now. It's the hair that does it. It's not Goldie Hawn. It's Meg Ryan, although you have a much cuter chin." She fluffed the back of Jessica's hair with her fingers and shrieked in delight when it fell back in disarray. "Cute, cute, cute!" She glanced up, realizing that she was already at her office. "Gotta run. Talk to you later."

Jessica continued down the hallway, wondering how far a cute chin would take her in life. She opened the door to her office and turned on the lights, then hesitated, almost afraid to shut herself in the place where she'd first had the dream. When nothing out of the ordinary happened, she stepped inside and closed the door.

A dark stain shadowed the carpet near the bank of file cabinets. Blood. Her blood. She shuddered. A couple of steps farther, she saw her umbrella sticking out from beneath the desk where it had rolled after she'd tripped. She picked it up and put it safely on top of the cabinets where it belonged.

When she sat down behind her desk and turned on the computer, a feeling of well-being settled upon her. The familiarity of her desk, her computer, her things, eased the tension she'd been feeling. Now maybe everything would return to normal.

Before the program came up on the screen, she caught a glimpse of herself in the reflection and grimaced. Everything else might be normal, but her hair was not. Although it still made her look like a waif, there was an unplanned benefit to the shaggy style. The wild fall of bangs across her forehead hid the lump of white bandage quite nicely. Then the program came up and her reflection disappeared and she forgot about everything except payroll checks.

Less than an hour later, she picked up the house phone. Her part of the job was finished. Now all she needed was Jeff Dolby's signature on the checks and she, along with the other employees of Squaw Creek Lodge, would get paid.

It should have been a simple call. Punch in the three numbers that dialed the manager's office, then tell Sheila that the checks were ready to be signed.

She punched the numbers, and as she'd expected, Sheila answered the phone. But Jessica didn't tell her the checks were ready. Between dialing and waiting for her call to be answered, something else started to happen. When she heard Sheila's voice, she started to shake. And when Sheila raised her voice to repeat her hello, Jessica heard herself shouting.

"Your house is on fire!"

Sheila's gasp was audible. "Who is this? If this is a joke, it's not funny."

Sweat beaded on Jessica's upper lip as she stared down at her desk. The checks were right before her, but she didn't see them. All she could see were tiny orange-red tongues of flame eating their way up a kitchen wall. Her voice deepened, and she spoke in a vocal shorthand, trying to impart the urgency of what she was seeing.

"In the kitchen! Up the wall. Fire! Smoke! Hurry! Hurry!"

The line disconnected, and Jessica dropped the phone and laid her head on the desk, fighting an overwhelming urge to cry.

Some time later, she made herself get up. Her hands were still shaking as she walked down the hall toward the manager's office. When she went inside, she made herself look. Just as she'd expected, Sheila's desk was empty.

What have I done?

But there were no answers, only questions. Taking a deep breath, she knocked on Dolby's door. When he called out for her to enter, she did.

Trying to focus on something besides the vision she'd just had, she laid the checks on the manager's desk.

"I thought you might want to sign these now, since we're a couple of days late getting them out."

He looked pleased. "Good job! I wasn't sure you'd show up. I take it you're not suffering any ugly aftereffects of your fall?"

"Hardly any at all." *Except for losing my mind.*

"Wonderful! Wonderful!" He picked up a pen. "Have a seat, will you? Give me a couple of minutes and they'll be ready to go out."

As she sat down, she realized that Jeff Dolby was sporting a new hairpiece. For once, she was thankful she had something besides her own problems on which to concentrate. It was all she could do not to stare. This month's hairpiece was dark and wavy, which was a unique contrast to the one he'd worn before. This one rode his bald dome like a loose saddle on the back of a swayback horse. It was there, but it just didn't fit.

Jessica sighed and closed her eyes. She knew about not fitting in. It had been the story of her life. Now, with this *thing* that kept happening to her, she felt like more of an outcast than ever. Tears burned at the back of her throat as she struggled with her composure.

Dolby's pen scratched across the surface of the checks as he wrote his name in small and contained flourishes. When he got to the last one, he looked up.

"If you don't mind, Miss Hanson, I would appreciate it if you would distribute these. Normally that's Sheila's job, but she got an emergency phone call and had to leave, and since these are already late—"

He shoved them toward her, expecting her instant acquiescence.

Jessica stared at the checks, but couldn't bring herself to move. She tensed, then cleared her throat.

"She did?"

He nodded, unaware that his hairpiece went one way as his head went another. In spite of the oddity of Jeff Dolby's hair, it was what he'd said that gave her pause. She licked her lips, wanting to ask, but afraid of what he might say. Moments passed, and finally, she could stand the suspense no longer.

"I hope it wasn't serious."

"Well, yes, I believe that it was," Dolby said. "She called me just before you came in." He paused, and then continued. "You know, it was the strangest thing. She got an anonymous phone call here at the office. Someone said her house was on fire."

"Oh, my," Jessica said, and felt the skin on her neck starting to crawl.

"As it turns out, the call was on the up and up. If it hadn't come, her house would have burned down. She said most of the damage was confined to the kitchen."

And then Dolby gasped and suddenly bolted from his chair. His hairpiece slid forward over his left eye as he made a grab for Jessica. But he was a couple of seconds too late.

She slid out of her chair in a faint.

Smelling salts stunk. Enough so that wherever Jessica had gone when she fainted, she came back in a rush.

"Easy now," someone said.

She looked up, noting that Mr. Dolby had more natural hair up his nose than he had on his head.

"Don't move just yet. Take a couple of deep breaths and relax. When you feel able, we'll help you up."

One of the maids was cradling Jessica's head in her lap

while another mopped at her face with a very wet cloth that smelled of disinfectant.

At least I will be clean when I die. "What happened?"

"You fainted."

She covered her face with her hands.

"Bat barf."

Dolby patted her arm. "Now, now, you're going to be fine. I appreciate the fact that you came in this morning to finish payroll, but I think you came back too soon. We've called for an ambulance. They're going to take you—"

She pushed them aside and sat up with a jerk, then clutched her head with both hands, reeling as the room began to spin. Someone pushed her head between her knees and she found herself looking at a dried raisin that was stuck in the carpet. It was a fitting analogy to the way she felt.

"I'm not going back to the hospital," she said. "I don't need a hospital." *All I need is a new brain. Mine broke.*

The sound of sirens could be heard coming up the road leading to the lodge.

Jessica groaned. "Send them back."

Her request was too late. Paramedics came in on the run, followed by a couple of curious cops who'd been on their way to the lodge to interrogate the hired help about the missing bride and had decided to follow the ambulance instead.

When Stone Richardson followed the medics inside, it had been in the line of duty. A "just in case he was needed" decision that soon brought him up short. At first, he didn't recognize the woman on the floor. But then she looked up, and he saw past the new haircut to the face beneath and found himself on the floor at her side.

His gruff voice and gentle touch were nearly her undoing.

"Damn it, Jessie, what have you done to yourself now?"

Jessica's hand went to her hair, then she paused, uncertain as to which disaster he was referring—her hairdo, or the fact that she was about to go for another ambulance ride.

"She fainted," Dolby said.

Jessica eyed the paramedic, who was fastening a pressure cuff on her arm. She refused to lie down. "I'm fine. They shouldn't have called you, and I am not going back to the hospital."

Stone heard what she said, but he had his own opinion of what she needed. She was pale and near tears, and the thought of Jessie unconscious and helpless did things to his heart he didn't want to consider.

"You will if they say so," he said, angry with himself and the emotions he kept feeling whenever Jessie was around.

Stone's bossy attitude was more than Jessica was ready to accept. She gave him a sidelong glance. "Don't you have someplace else to be?"

"No."

Disgusted at being the center of so much unwanted attention, she closed her eyes and slumped forward, laying her head on her knees in a gesture of defeat.

Jeff Dolby patted his hair, making certain it was still in place, then touched Jessica's shoulder in a comforting gesture.

"We can muddle along without you, dear. I suggest you take off as much time as you need to recover from your injury. If need be, I'll call in a temp."

She groaned. Just after she'd started working at the lodge, she'd come down with a virulent flu bug that had taken its toll on the whole staff. Then the temp agency had sent a man who'd reorganized her entire filing system and crashed the computer. Fixing Dolby with a crushing stare, she gave him fair warning.

"If they send Lester Cushing, I quit."

Dolby looked taken aback and then nodded nervously.

"Don't worry. I'll see to it personally. You just get well. That's all that matters."

The paramedic began gathering up his things. "Miss Hanson, your vitals are normal, but I think you should see a doctor just the same. You can't be too careful about head injuries."

"I'll call Dr. Howell when I get home," she said. "I just need to go get my purse and keys."

Restraining her intent, Stone pointed at one of the maids who was standing nearby.

"Would you please go to Miss Hanson's office and get her purse?"

Jessica started to argue, when he silenced her with a look.

"Look, Jessie. I suggest you use what's left of that hard-headed brain of yours. You just passed out. You are not going to be driving anywhere. I'll take you home."

Jessica slumped again, this time muttering the most disgusting slur she could summon on short notice.

"Tick teeth."

Stone grinned. "Yeah, well, the same to you, lady."

Startled, she looked up in time to see him wink. She felt herself blushing and looked away in disgust. *I am immune to his charms. I am immune to his charms.* The mantra did not work.

While Jessie was stewing quietly, Stone stood up. His partner, Jack Stryker, made no attempt to hide a grin.

"Stuff it," Stone said as they walked to the other side of the room.

Jack whistled softly between his teeth and shrugged. "I didn't say a thing."

"You didn't have to," Stone said. "I saw that smirk."

"I take it we're going to delay the investigation of Randi Howell's disappearance."

A faint flush spread across Stone's cheeks. "Look, Jessie is a good friend, okay?"

Jack's grin widened. "From the way you hit the floor

when you saw her down there, I'd say she's more than your friend. However...I could be wrong."

Ignoring his partner's comments because they were too damned close to the truth to comment upon, Stone turned and then suddenly bolted across the room. Jessie was struggling to her feet. He should have known she wouldn't do a damned thing he said.

A few minutes later, Jack leaned in the car window, sympathetically eyeing Jessica's pale face as Stone fastened her seat belt. He knew Stone had been right in wanting to help her. This blackout had messed up a lot of lives. He supposed it was fortunate they'd happened along.

"Miss Hanson, I'll bring your car to your home when I pick up Stone, but I need to talk to a couple of people here at the lodge first," he said.

Jessica's lips trembled as she handed him the keys to her car. "Thank you. I appreciate your help."

Stryker walked back toward the lodge as Stone pulled out of the parking lot. He gave Jessie a sideways glance.

"How come you appreciate Jack's help and mine annoys you?"

Jessica stared out the window. *Maybe because I don't dream about going to bed with your partner.* She took a deep breath and fought back new tears.

"Detective Richardson, I appreciate your help."

He tried to laugh off the hurt he kept feeling as she continued to shut him out. "Dang, you sweet-talking woman. You're just liable to sweep me off my feet."

She refused to comment.

Stone tried another subject. "I see you cut your hair."

She burst into tears.

Startled by her reaction, Stone swerved the car to the side of the road and jammed it into Park. Worried, he slid his hand up the back of her neck.

"Are you sick? Do you want me to—"

His touch, his consideration and those damned gray bedroom eyes were going to be her downfall. Desperate to put some distance between herself and the man who could be her Waterloo, she turned on him without warning.

"Stone Richardson, if you don't put this car into gear and take me home, I will never forgive you."

Torn between anger and dismay, he moved back to his side of the car.

"Lord love a duck, Jessie Leigh, you'd make a preacher lose his religion."

Then he grabbed the steering wheel with both hands. The car took off from a parked position like a turpentined cat, leaving black rubber and smoke to mark its passing. A short while later, he turned the corner leading down her street and slid to a stop at the side of her driveway, leaving just enough room for Jack to park.

Jessica breathed a quiet sigh of relief and reached for her seat belt, anxious to make a getaway before she embarrassed herself even more than she already had.

"Thank you for bringing me home."

This time his laugh was little more than a gruff bark. "You don't get rid of me this easy."

Before she could argue, he was out of the car and helping her up the walk. When they reached the door, he stopped and turned.

Pinned beneath his watchful gaze, she realized he was waiting for her to open the door.

"Just a minute," she said, fumbling through her purse for the keys. "I know they're in here." And then she remembered she'd given them to Stryker. She looked at Stone. "Oh, no, I gave them to your partner."

"Allow me," he drawled, and before she could think to argue, he had pulled the lock pick from his pocket and, once more, picked the lock to her front door.

She started to comment, but changed her mind when he stepped aside and pointed forcefully.

"You! Inside!"

"But I—"

He took her by the hand and pulled her after him, shutting the door behind them.

"Damn it, honey, you are trying my patience to—"

It was once too many times to ignore. Without thinking, she drew back and let fly, thumping his arm with the bulk of her purse.

"Stop calling me 'honey'! You gave up that right when you walked out of my life!"

Stunned by the fact that not only had she hit him with her purse, but she was yelling at him, Stone yelled back.

"I'm not the one who walked out, you are."

In spite of the ominous swing to the purse she still clutched in her hand, Stone held his ground and wished he hadn't given up the right to hold her. Right now he would give a whole lot to have her in his bed and his arms. The blue in her eyes had turned dark and angry. Staccato bursts of her breath brushed his face. Stone remembered thinking that she was close—but not nearly close enough to suit him.

The next thing he knew, he'd yanked her into his arms and was kissing those sweet, pouting lips. Tasting her shock and the echoes of her words, and knowing it was never going to be enough.

Jessica went from stunned to surrender in just under three seconds, unprepared for the jolt of emotion that tore through her. The only thing she remembered thinking was that she'd wasted the last two years. She hadn't gotten over a thing.

Stone took a deep breath and turned her loose, and in those moments before he moved away, something precious passed between them that they couldn't take back. Unspoken, but obvious, just the same.

"Stone, I—"

His voice was gruff, but his hands were shaking. "Get in bed."

She took a sudden step backward. Where had all the tenderness gone?

He groaned. "I didn't mean it like that," he said softly, and took a deep breath while trying to calm his racing pulse. He reached out, lifting the fringe of her bangs to look at the white bandage beneath. "You have to be careful. I still think you should call the doctor. Head injuries are tricky."

Her fingers brushed the surface of her mouth. "Not nearly as tricky as you."

He flushed but held his ground. "I will not apologize for what just happened."

She lifted her chin and walked back to the door, then opened it and stood aside, waiting for him to leave. As he stepped out, she slammed the door behind him. When she was certain there was at least three inches of solid wood between him and her, she shouted, "I don't recall asking for an apology."

Stone froze in midstep and then pivoted. His hand was on the doorknob just as a familiar click sounded. His eyebrows arched in disbelief. The little witch! She'd locked him out.

"What about your car keys?"

"Drop them through the mail slot, and thank you for the ride."

"You call the doctor or I'll do it for you!" he shouted.

She didn't answer, and he could hear the sounds of her footsteps as she walked away. Torn between elation and frustration, he kicked at a rolled-up newspaper lying on her porch and sent it flying. It landed on top of a nearby bush.

"Damned woman." He dropped down on the top step, waiting for Stryker to come with her car.

It didn't dawn on him until later that he'd actually thought of her as a strong, capable woman, not one who cried and begged and blamed as Naomi had. But by the time he'd come to that conclusion, Stryker was pulling into the driveway in Jessie's car.

Jack got out with a mile-wide grin on his face. "What are you doing out here?"

"None of your damned business," Stone muttered.

Jack held up her keys. "What about these?"

Stone stuffed them through the mail slot in the door. They rattled as they hit the floor, and the moment they were out of his hand, he realized he should have kept them. Now there was nothing to keep her from getting back in the car and driving. And she was just stubborn enough to try it.

He sighed in frustration and headed for his car. Maybe he could find peace of mind in his work.

Jessica sat huddled on the floor in the hallway, listening for the sounds of Stone's departure. She was afraid to sleep—afraid she would dream. But the real truth was, she was even afraid to think. She hadn't been asleep when she'd seen Sheila's house on fire. She'd been at her desk and minding her own business.

Her lips still tingled, and she thought of Stone and shivered with sudden longing, wishing that things were different. Wishing that she wasn't so certain she was about to come apart at the seams.

He was an officer of the law, trained to help, trained to serve. She'd been injured. It only stood to reason he would consider it his duty to offer assistance. However, she reminded herself, he'd had no earthly reason to kiss her just now as he had. Except, she reminded herself further, she *had* been irritating him unnecessarily. Maybe he'd done it just to shut her up. She inhaled on a soft, helpless sob. Well, it had worked. She felt lost and rudderless, uncertain of what would come next.

She leaned her head against the wall and closed her eyes. Tears trickled out from beneath the lids, and she bit her lip to defend herself from the threatening flood. The truth be told, Jessica Hanson was afraid—afraid of herself, and afraid of what she might see next. She got to her feet and went to bed. Right now it was the only place she felt safe.

Horror shattered the joy in *Olivia Stuart's eyes as a hand clamped across her mouth and she was shoved forward, pinned between the table and the unyielding body of her attacker. The overpowering scent of gardenias mingled with a sudden pain in the back of her leg. Moments later, another pain, different and more threatening, mushroomed in the center of her chest. Her arms flailed outward and upward. She would never see her son again.*

Jessica woke with tears streaming down her cheeks and the scent of gardenias swirling around her. She sat up with a jerk and took a long, deep breath.

"Why," she whispered, and buried her face in her hands. "Why is this happening?"

She crawled out of bed and walked through her house toward the kitchen, comfortable in the darkness and with the familiarity of her own things. She poured herself a cold drink of water and drank it from start to finish without pause. When it was empty, she set the glass in the sink and then looked out the window to the night beyond.

Moonlight bounced off the nearby hedge, coloring the neatly clipped branches in a cold, silver glow. She shuddered as echoes of the last three days crept back in her mind.

Olivia Stuart's attack.
Her sister's lost keys.
Olivia Stuart's attack.
The fire at Sheila Biggers's house.
Olivia Stuart's attack.

Something she hadn't considered suddenly occurred. She hadn't been wrong about where Brenda's keys had been. She hadn't been wrong about the fire at Sheila's house. She started to shake.

Then, what if I'm right and they're wrong about the reason for Olivia Stuart's death?

The longer she stood, the more certain she became of what she must do. Like it or not, she had to talk to the authorities. If she didn't, someone would be getting away with murder!

Four

Stone Richardson's day was already screwed when he walked into the precinct on Wednesday morning. Thanks to the blackout, there was a backlog of cases they might never get through. And when a handcuffed hooker called out his name and then winked, he muttered beneath his breath in disgust. There was a real good chance that the day might never get better.

Ready to get down to work, he draped his sport coat on the back of a chair and reached across the permanent stack of files on his desk for his coffee cup.

Stryker, who sat across the aisle, was on the phone. When he looked up and saw Stone, he put his hand over the receiver long enough to give Stone a message.

"There's a man waiting to see you. He said Dr. Howell sent him."

Stone nodded. "Tell him to have a seat. I'll be right back."

He headed for the break room, moments later, pouring what was left in the pot in his cup, dregs and all. When some of it splattered on the toe of his boot and the edge of his jeans, he frowned, then took a quick sip on the way out the door, thankful it had missed his white shirt. It was the last clean one he had.

On his way back to his desk, he glanced into the hall at the brawl in progress. Two men were trading blows while a woman stood nearby, screeching at the top of her lungs. In the midst of it all, he got a glimpse of red hair and a dark blue uniform, and grinned. Delancey, a beat cop and a nineteen-year veteran of the force, had it under control. The complainants just didn't know it yet.

As Stone reentered the room, he paused in the doorway, taking careful note of the man sitting at his desk. He was lean and looked unnaturally pale. His blond hair had recently been cut. His jeans and shirt were unremarkable in style, but clean. As Stone neared his desk, the man suddenly stood, and the cold blue intensity of his gaze, as well as the way he waited without moving, gave Stone an impression of military bearing.

"Have a seat," Stone said.

They both sat, and Stone took a last sip of his coffee before shoving aside a stack of papers to make room for his cup.

"So, what can I do for you, Mr.—?"

The man shifted nervously. "You can call me Smith. Martin Smith. However, I seriously doubt that it's my name."

He had Stone's attention. "Excuse me?"

The man took a deep breath. "I don't know who I am. My entire memory consists of the past few days. I don't remember anything before Friday evening, when I wandered into the emergency room of your local hospital."

Stone gave him another glance, this time more thorough. "Were you injured?"

Smith shook his head. "Yes, but not much. They guessed I probably suffered a blow to the head. I had some cuts and bruises, but I've had worse." The moment that came out, he looked startled. "How did I know that?" he muttered, then sighed in frustration.

Stone picked up a pen and started making notes. "Friday. That would be five days ago."

"There was a blackout."

Stone nodded. Another set of troubles to add to the mess they were already trying to unknot.

"And you hadn't been in an accident?"

Smith shrugged. "I don't know. All I remember is that

my head hurt. I'd been walking for some time, and the streets were dark. Everything was dark. And then I saw lights in the distance and headed toward them."

Stone remembered what Vanderbilt Memorial had looked like that night. The lights had been weak and flickering, but the security they represented had been comforting, even to him.

"So, what do you want of me?" Stone asked.

Smith hesitated briefly, then his jaw squared and he leaned forward. "Maybe you could check missing persons reports. And I want you to fingerprint me. See if I have an identity on record. See if I'm—" He paused and then looked away, unable to finish the horror of what he was thinking.

Stone finished it for him. "See if there's a warrant somewhere for your arrest?"

He looked up. "Yes. No matter what, I want to know."

"Okay," Stone said, and turned a fresh page on the pad. "Let's talk. We might get some answers from you that you didn't know you had."

Smith began to talk while Stone asked the occasional question, making notes in between and trying to make himself heard above everything else that was going on.

A short while later, he looked up from his desk to realize that in the midst of the turmoil in which they sat, he was hearing Jessie Hanson's voice. Before he could turn around, he heard her take a deep breath. He wasn't prepared for what she said.

"Detective, I think I witnessed a murder."

He reacted with a jerk, which sent his chair scooting on the floor beneath him. Martin Smith was still waiting for Stone's next question, but Stone's mind had scattered. He couldn't think. Couldn't move. Couldn't focus. All he could do was listen.

Jessica Hanson took the chair at Detective Chang's desk as she'd been instructed to do, nodding her willingness to wait while he finished a call. Her nerves were on edge, and she couldn't believe she was actually here. As she sat, she gazed around the room, curious as to the jumble of people and sounds. But when she realized that some of the people at whom she was staring were in handcuffs, she gasped and dropped her gaze, unwilling to be caught gawking at a felon.

Still in shock, she kept her eyes on the floor, trying to tell herself it would be all right. In the middle of her personal pep talk, she began to focus on one particular voice out of the crowd. One that was all too familiar and, to her dismay, right behind her.

Flea bites, it's Stone. She should have known he'd be here.

Jessica was at the point of walking out when Chang hung up the phone. His smile was friendly as he looked at the note on his desk, and then at Jessica.

"Miss Hanson, is it?"

She nodded and wrapped her fingers a little tighter around the strap of her purse, wishing someone was holding her as tightly as she was holding the leather.

"So, what brings you here?" he asked.

"Detective, I think I witnessed a murder."

The legs of a chair squeaked on the floor behind her and Jessica groaned inwardly. Stone had to have overheard what she said. She thought of Olivia and took a deep breath, refusing to be swayed by Stone's presence. He wasn't why she'd come.

Chang sat up straight and picked up a pen. "Murder? Whose murder?"

"Olivia Stuart's."

The expectation on his face smoothed away into one of disbelief.

"I'm sorry, Miss Hanson, but you're mistaken. Olivia Stuart died of a heart attack."

"I know what they say, but I also know what I saw. She didn't have a heart attack. She was stabbed in the back of the leg with a hypodermic needle by a tall woman dressed in black. I saw it happen.''

Chang frowned. ''Why have you waited so long to come forward?''

''Well, I spent the night in the hospital the night of the blackout, and after that...'' She hesitated, unwilling to admit that she'd doubted herself.

Chang had already noticed the bandage beneath her bangs. ''Yes, I see that you hurt your head.''

Jessica nodded. ''I work at Squaw Creek Lodge. I was in my office and working on payroll when the lights went out. I tripped and fell, hitting my head on some file cabinets. When I came to, I saw a light. I turned toward it and saw Olivia Stuart. She was wearing a teal dress and smiling at a picture she held in her hands. At first, I thought she was in my office. I called out for help, but she didn't come. The scent of gardenias was suddenly all around me, and then I saw someone come up behind her and stab her in the back of the leg with a hypodermic needle. It was a woman. She was dressed in black and I'm not sure, but I think she had blond hair.''

Chang interrupted. ''Wait a minute. Are you telling me you had some sort of vision? That what you saw happened after you fell and hit your head?''

Jessica bit her lip.

Chang dropped his pen and leaned back in his chair. ''Miss Hanson, were you in the hospital when Olivia Stuart was brought in?''

She bit her lip and held her ground. ''I don't know. I don't remember much about my accident until the next day, but I know what I saw when I came to in my office.''

''And that was before they took you to the hospital.''

''Correct.''

By now, Chang's frown was obvious. ''Look, Miss Hanson. I appreciate what you're trying to say, but you've got to look at this from my standpoint. You suffered a head injury. You wake up smelling flowers and hallucinating about…''

Jessica stood up. Her eyes were shiny with unshed tears as she clutched her purse to her belly like a shield.

"I didn't imagine a thing. I saw Olivia Stuart being attacked. I saw her drop the picture she was holding. I saw a woman stab her in the back of the leg with a hypodermic needle. I saw her clutch her chest then fall forward, across the table and then onto the floor.''

"Well, thank you for coming. I'll check out your story.''

"No, Detective Chang, I don't believe that you will. And I'd appreciate it if you wouldn't lie to me, because I didn't lie to you.''

She was gone before Stone could get out of his chair. He glared at Chang in disbelief. "Why did you let her leave like that?''

Chang grinned. "Are you kidding? That lady's a little off plumb. She needs to see a doctor, not a cop.''

Stone's instinct was to go after her, but he had a man with no memory sitting at his desk, waiting for answers Stone couldn't give. He glanced at Martin Smith, then back at Chang.

"I'll tell you what. You take Mr. Smith here up to Fingerprinting, then run his info through NCIC. See if there are any wants or warrants out on him.''

Chang looked startled. "But…''

"Also, it's highly unlikely that Martin Smith is his real name, because he's claiming amnesia.''

Stone glanced at Stryker, who was still on the phone. He remembered Stryker telling him that Olivia Stuart had still been alive when they'd gotten her to Vanderbilt. Supposedly, she'd whispered the word "coal" before she died. It was common knowledge that the mayor had been vocally opposed to a strip mining consortium that was trying to renew leases in their area. What if…?

He wouldn't let himself go past the thought, because

that would be giving credence to Jessica's claim to have *seen* a murder without actually being present, and that made no sense. Still...

"Chang, when Stryker gets off the phone, tell him I'm following up on a lead."

Chang frowned. "That's no lead. That's just a pretty woman who needs to go to bed." And then he grinned. "Or maybe that was your plan all along."

"Shut the hell up and do as I asked," Stone said, and then left.

A few minutes later, he pulled out of the parking lot and onto the street without giving himself time to back out of what he intended to do. He didn't know why, but he had a hunch he needed to hear more. And then his car lurched and began to list to one side, making enough noise, as it did, to garner unwanted attention. He pulled over to the curb and got out. It was just as he'd feared. He had a flat tire.

When Jessica opened the door, she had on blue jeans shorts and a T-shirt, and was clutching a wad of tissues. The fact that she was barefoot and crying made Stone reach for her, but when she saw who was on her doorstep, she took a wary step back.

"What are you doing here?" she asked.

"I want you to tell me what you told Chang."

She frowned. "Why, so you can make fun of me, too?"

"Am I laughing?"

Her gaze went from the somber expression on his face to the breadth of his shoulders beneath his sport coat, to his jeans and boots, and then back up again, lingering one last time on his mouth. Slowly she stepped aside.

He walked in, shutting the door behind him, then stared at her, waiting for permission he wasn't sure he would get.

"Please?"

She bit her lip and wished the very sight of him didn't make her weak at the knees. "Oh, why not? I've already made a fool of myself once. It shouldn't be any worse the second time around." She gestured toward the living room. "Do come in, Detective. Make yourself comfortable. Would you care for some coffee?"

"Is it better than your food?"

She glared, resenting his seemingly innocent remark. It was a less-than-subtle reminder that he knew a lot more about her than the fact that she wasn't much of a cook. But she'd stopped off at the market after leaving the precinct. At least the milk she had to pour in the coffee was fresh.

"Beggars can't be choosers," she said, and strode toward the kitchen.

Stone ignored her offer to wait in the living room and followed her.

Stone glanced up at the clock on the wall, then took a last swig of coffee, telling himself that he'd had worse, although right now, he couldn't remember when. He flipped his notebook shut and slipped it into his pocket, surprised that they'd been talking for nearly two hours.

"So, is that all you can remember?"

Jessica stared at his chin, unable to meet his gaze as she asked, "Do you believe me?"

Stone sighed. "It isn't about *me* believing you. It's about *you* believing what you saw. I know you're not trying to pull a fast one, Jessie. But…"

"But you think I'm nuts."

Stone frowned. "Jessie Leigh, we are no longer at a point in our relationship where I'm going to tell you *what* I think about you. However, I will admit that I *do* think about you."

Her lips parted in shock as the insinuation of what he'd just said soaked in.

Stone leaned back in his chair, rocking on the two back legs, when something occurred.

"Hey, Jessie."

"What?"

"Do you… I mean…besides the attack on Olivia, have you had any other, uh…" A little embarrassed, his voice trailed away.

Jessica sighed. "You mean, have I had any other *flashes of inspiration?*"

"Yeah, something like that."

"Actually, I have."

It wasn't what he'd expected her to say.

"Brenda lost her keys, and then I *saw* where they were." She folded her arms across her chest. "And, I was right."

He listened, saving whatever he was thinking for later.

Some of the bravado went out of her as she added, "And I knew that Sheila Biggers's house was on fire."

The legs of his chair hit the floor with a thump.

"You what?"

Unable to look at him, she looked down at the table, instead. It was almost more than she could handle to admit what was happening to her to a man who'd seen her naked body. It felt as if the telling of these incidents was stripping her right down to her soul. Her voice lowered, and her hands began to tremble.

"Monday I was at the lodge. I'd just finished payroll and picked up the phone to call Sheila. She's the manager's secretary. I wanted to tell her the checks were ready to be signed, but when I looked down, I didn't see my desk. Instead, I saw fire eating up a kitchen wall. I heard myself shouting to her that her house was on fire."

"What did she do?" Stone asked.

Jessica looked up, meeting his gaze with a cool, unblinking stare. "Hung up on me. But when I went into the boss's office later, she was gone. I found out that I'd been right. That my phone call had saved her house from being destroyed."

Stone frowned.

"You can check it out," she said. "But when you do,

don't tell her it was me who called. I have to work there, you know.'' She shoved her hands through her hair in frustration, carefully missing the bandage at the hairline. ''They already think I'm weird. This would probably get me fired.''

Stone glanced at her hair and then arched an eyebrow, trying to come to some kind of terms with the fact that the long blond locks he'd wrapped in his hands as he'd buried himself in her body were no longer there. ''You're not weird, Jessie Leigh. I'd say you're kind of cute...and definitely unique.''

Jessica refused to admit that he'd just made her day.

''But, you still think I'm guessing lucky, don't you?''

He spread his hands. ''I don't know what to think. But I do know it's easy to lose things. We all do. And there are only so many places they can be, right?''

She didn't answer, and he kept trying to make his point.

''Take this morning. I wrote a check for my rent, then couldn't find the darn thing anywhere. It was there one minute and gone the next. I wound up voiding it and writing out another. It'll turn up eventually. It has to.''

One minute Jessica was hearing Stone's voice, and the next thing she knew, the air had shifted. She was seeing a place where she'd never been, and somebody else's things.

Paper. Fingers—clutching a pen. Writing in dark, bold strokes. A cabinet top. Water. Plastic wrap next to a bright blue coffee cup.

A familiar scent yanked her out of the past and she jerked.

''Cheese.''

Stone grinned. He'd expected her to call him something worse, like dog breath.

''Now, Jessie, I didn't mean to hurt your feelings.''

She jumped to her feet and started to pace. ''No! I mean your check is stuck to some cheese.''

He flashed on writing his check—and the omelette he'd

been making. Suddenly, his skin crawled. *No way,* he thought, then glanced at his watch and stood up.

"No matter what happens, on behalf of the Grand Springs Police Department, I want to thank you for coming forward as you did. If more people would be willing to get involved, it would make my job a whole lot simpler."

Jessica began to relax. It was the best she'd felt since getting up this morning. In fact, she almost smiled.

"You're welcome," she said. "I'll walk you to the door."

Stone resisted the urge to kiss her goodbye. The last time he had, he'd been here in the capacity of a friend, and even then the kiss had been an overstepping of bounds. They were no longer lovers. Hell, from the way she behaved when he was around, he was even pushing his luck to still think of her as a friend. No more kissing. Not now. Maybe not ever again. This time he was on the job. He had rules. Then he looked down. Lingering tears shimmered on the surface of her eyes. He groaned.

"To hell with rules."

Before she could move, or he could talk himself out of the act, he leaned down.

Lips met, surface to surface. One of them sighed, the other one groaned.

Turn her loose before it's too late!

Stone did as his conscience demanded, but the moment he let her go, he wanted her back.

She stood before him, wide-eyed and motionless, her fingers pressed against the place on her lips where his mouth had been. The last thing he wanted was to leave.

"Jessie, honey..."

She blinked, and it broke the spell between them. Stunned by what she was feeling, and well aware that this kiss was as far as her dream would go, she slipped back into her usual prickly self.

"I told you, Stone, I'm not your honey. Not now, and if I was honest with myself, not ever. I've already been down that road with you once, but my coming back to Grand Springs doesn't mean I'm stupid enough to set myself up to be hurt again.''

He frowned. ''I never meant to hurt you the first time.''

She turned away, refusing to give away any more of her emotions. Reluctantly, Stone let himself out the front door.

The phone was ringing as Stone opened his apartment door. He thought about letting his answering machine pick it up, then rejected the notion. But he knew when he ran to answer it that he was simply delaying the inevitable. He'd come home for one reason and one reason only, and now that he was here, he was afraid to see if Jessie had been right about his lost check.

''Hello.''

An all-too-familiar female voice grated against his nerves.

''Well, well. So you *are* still in the land of the living.''

Cursing himself for answering the call, he shifted the phone to his other ear. Talking to his ex-wife was the last thing he needed, especially now.

''Hello, Naomi. What's the occasion?''

Her chuckle was familiar, but he couldn't remember why he'd ever thought it sexy.

''Didn't they tell you I called the other day?''

''Yes.''

When there was no other explanation forthcoming, Naomi chuckled again, only this time, with resigned understanding.

''So, you didn't want to talk to me?''

''Didn't have anything to say.''

She sighed. ''Look, Stone. I'm sorry everything was so—''

Stone glanced toward his refrigerator. He had more on his mind than discussing the past with a woman who'd been unable to love him enough to accept who he was.

''Let it go, Naomi. I have. Hell, it's been five, no, nearly six years since our divorce. We're way past the apology stage. Why on earth are you calling now?''

She sighed and wondered a little about that herself. ''I heard about the blackout. I guess I just wanted to make sure you were all right.''

Startled by her excuse, he had to laugh, and in doing so, freed himself from whatever uneasiness he'd felt in talking to her again.

''You've got to be kidding,'' he said lightly. ''We just lost a little power, not our minds.'' And then he thought of Jessie and the smile slid off of his face.

''Okay, okay. Maybe there was another reason I called,'' she said.

He tensed, fairly certain he wasn't going to like what she said.

''And that was—?''

''I got married.''

The grin returned, but this time in full force. The end of alimony! He didn't have to fake his delight.

''Hey! Congratulations!''

''Aren't you curious as to whom it could be?''

His drawl was cutting, for the most part, ending her dramatics. ''Naomi, I lost my curiosity and everything else pertaining to you when I signed the divorce decree. I hope that you're happy as hell. Thanks for calling. I'm fine—in fact, I'm going to be six hundred dollars finer every month than I was before you called.''

The allusion to the end of his alimony payments didn't sit well with the ex–Mrs. Richardson. Naomi slammed the phone down in his ear. Stone grinned to himself as he hung up the phone. *Well, maybe this day isn't so bad, after all.* And then he remembered why he'd come home. There was no use putting it off any longer. He walked to the refrigerator and opened the door.

He knew before he picked up the cheese that Jessie had been right. Already he could see a corner of blue paper stuck to the back of the package. Cool air wafted against his face as he picked it up, and as he peeled off the check, he started to shake. The writing was blurred, like black, fuzzy tears, but all he could think was, My God, she was right!

He tossed the cheese back into the refrigerator and closed the door. For several long minutes he stared at the check before tearing it into pieces and dropping it into the trash. And then he looked up, uncertain what to do next.

A clock on the wall was ticking away the seconds of his life. Down the hall, he could hear a faint but steady drip. Even though he'd called the landlord twice about the problem, the shower still leaked. Those were facts. But Jessie was dealing in visions. He was a cop. Cops dealt with facts, not fantasies.

Yet the implications of finding the check, coupled with everything else she'd told him earlier, were too vast to absorb. He needed another opinion besides his own to validate what he was beginning to believe. But who could he talk to? Who did he know that would listen with an open mind, and not react with disbelief and disdain as Erik Chang had done?

A name, along with a face, suddenly popped into his mind. It was the face of a man who lived and worked in the real world, while his roots bound him to another. Stone glanced into the trash at what was left of his check, and then headed out the door.

The outer room of the *Grand Springs Herald* was packed with customers and complaints. Stone stepped aside to hold the door open for a woman who was carrying what was left of a wet, soggy paper. The look on her face said it all. A careless paperboy's neglect was about to become the *Herald*'s problem.

Just past the front desk, reporters sat before their computer terminals, pounding out stories in an effort to make deadlines. Stone started past the desk when a young woman stopped him.

"I'm sorry, but no one's allowed past the front desk."

He flashed his badge. "I need to talk to Rio Redtree. Is he here?"

Her cheeks turned pink with embarrassment. "Sorry, sir. If you'll wait, I'll get him for you."

Moments later, a tall, dark man came through a doorway at the back of the room. When he saw Stone, a slow smile broke the somberness of his expression, and he hurried forward with an outstretched hand.

"What brings you to the world of ink?" Rio asked.

Stone glanced around, frowning slightly. "Is there someplace quiet where we can talk?"

Without questioning the need for privacy, Rio nodded. "Follow me."

Sunlight caught them full in the face as they went out a side door and started down an alley toward the back of the building. Stone squinted against the glare, eyeing a cat that was digging through the garbage cans, then glanced at Rio, who seemed oblivious to their surroundings.

"Nice conference room," he said.

Rio smiled and pointed.

Stone's eyes widened as they came out of the alley and into a walled-in garden. He'd lived in Grand Springs nearly all of his life and he hadn't known this was here.

"When did this happen?" Stone asked.

"Years ago," Rio said. "It's for the employees. It's a real nice place to eat lunch or take a break." He glanced at Stone and added, "And sometimes a good place to hide."

Startled by Rio's intuitive remark, Stone stuffed his hands in his pockets and looked away, staring at the scene before him.

Trees abounded, their thick, verdant branches shading the decorative stones that formed a meandering path through the garden. Benches in varying shapes and sizes rested beneath the trees, beckoning the viewer to come.

"Walk with me," Rio said, and led the way.

A cardinal flew across their path on the way for a drink at a nearby birdbath. High up in a tree, Stone could hear a squirrel scolding them for coming too close to his world. On the path beyond, in a wide patch of sunlight, a garden of flowers had burst into bloom, charming the butterflies and bees that dipped into their nectar.

"It's been a rough few days, hasn't it?" Stone asked.

Rio nodded. Stone didn't come to talk about the blackout, so he saw no need in wasting words, and it would seem, neither did Stone. Yet Rio was surprised at Stone's question when it came.

"Rio, have you ever worked with a psychic?"

It wasn't what Rio had expected to hear, but being the man that he was, he took the change of subject with his usual Native American aplomb.

"Have you?"

Startled by the conversational ball Rio threw back in his court, Stone paused, and then grinned. "I asked first."

Rio's eyes twinkled, but he treated his answer with respect.

"No, but I've known those who have."

"Do you believe them?"

"Believe whom? The people who worked with them, or the psychics themselves?" Rio asked.

"The psychics, or seers, whatever you choose to call them. People who see the future—or into the past. Do you believe in them?"

"Yes."

Stone sighed. Rio's brief but confident answer made it seem so easy.

"Okay, then let's say…if someone you trusted told you something that was very difficult to believe, what would you do?"

"You've answered your own question," Rio said. "If you already trust, then there would be no question of believing. Am I right?"

Stone didn't answer. He couldn't find a way to voice what he was feeling.

Rio glanced at his friend, and then motioned for him to sit.

"Look, Stone. You are my friend. Whatever you tell me now is between us. I give you my word it will not wind up in tomorrow's edition."

Stone had already known that, but it was hearing Rio say it that made him relax. He stared at a patch of sunlight on a nearby rock. The tone of his voice was low and steady as he continued.

"What would you say if I told you I know a woman who recently suffered a head injury and has begun having visions? Except for that change in her behavior, she's healing fine. I'd like to think of her visions as flashes of insight, but I'd also be wrong."

"Does she see into the past or into the future?"

Stone looked startled. He thought of Olivia—and of Brenda's lost keys. He thought of a fire—and of a lost check stuck to a package of cheese.

"I don't know, she just sees."

Extreme curiosity sparked the darkness of Rio Redtree's eyes, but he answered as truthfully as he knew how. "I believe that there are things in heaven and on earth that we will never understand."

It was what Stone had been waiting to hear.

Rio glanced at his watch, then stood. "I've got to get back to work or I'll miss my deadline. I don't know what's going on, but I'm guessing you've told me all you're going to. However, just remember, if something big breaks, I get the scoop, right?"

Stone grinned. "Ever the reporter."

Rio's eyes glittered, cat eyes of jet in a warm, brown face. "And you, my friend, are ever the cop."

Stone entered the front doors of Vanderbilt Memorial with a mission. He strode up to the receptionist and flashed his badge once more.

"Would you please page Dr. Noah Howell? If he's not in surgery, I need to see him immediately."

A few minutes later, Stone looked up just as the elevator doors opened. Noah Howell emerged, his lab coat flapping around the back of his thighs as he came toward Stone with a frown on his face.

He shook Stone's hand. "This better be good."

"What's up, Doc?" Stone said, and then grinned. "Sorry. I've always wanted to say that."

"Now that it's out of your system, how about telling me why you're here. Do we need to go to my office? It's just down the hall."

Stone glanced at his watch, then around the waiting area. It was virtually empty. "No, this will do."

And then Stone took a deep breath, aware that he was about to open a huge can of worms.

"Is Olivia Stuart's body still here in the morgue?"

The question seemed to catch Noah by surprise, but at least he knew the answer. "Why, yes, I suppose so. The funeral homes had no power, you know. Because we had the facilities and the room, we volunteered to keep the deceased here in our morgue until they were fully operational again."

"Did you perform an autopsy?"

Noah frowned. "No. There was no reason. Olivia died of cardiac arrest right before my eyes, and when asked, her son, Hal, refused the request." He gave Stone a considering glance. "It's not unusual, you know. Families usually consider it a desecration of their loved ones' bodies."

Stone shifted his stance and lowered his voice. "During your examination of Olivia, did you, at any time, see anything that would indicate she'd died anything but a natural death?"

This time, Noah could not hide his surprise. "She had

a heart attack, Stone. Both Amanda Jennings and I did all that we could to save her, but she died before our eyes.''

But Stone wouldn't quit. "I need you to do me a favor. I want you to go to the morgue and take another look at Olivia Stuart's body. I want you to look at the backs of her legs.''

"Exactly what would I be looking for?" Noah asked.

"If she'd been stabbed with a hypodermic needle, what would you find?''

"Probably some sort of bruising, and if it was a vicious wound, possibly a noticeable puncture or torn flesh, as well. But I assure you, there was nothing like that on her when they brought her in.''

"Did you look?''

Noah looked startled. "Well, not exactly, but—''

Stone took Noah by the arm. "Come on, Doc. Do me a favor. Just look.''

Noah rolled his eyes and then sighed in defeat. "Fine. I'll look. But I don't have all day. I have to be in surgery in less than an hour.''

"I'll wait here," Stone said.

"Like hell," Noah said. "This is your party. Come see for yourself.''

Stone cursed beneath his breath. He hated morgues.

The air was refrigerator cold and smelled of formalde-hyde, disinfectant and death. A pathologist sat at a nearby desk, staring into a microscope, while a series of instruments hummed and blinked beside him as they performed their functions.

"Hey, Dewitt, don't bother to get up. We're just passing through," Noah said, and chuckled at his own bit of hospital wit.

Stone gave the odd man a nervous glance. The fewer who knew why they'd come, the better off he would be.

They passed through another set of doors, entering a

room in which all the occupants resided behind numbered doors and slept an eternal sleep on cold, metal slabs.

Noah glanced at a chart, then moved toward door seventeen. He reached in and pulled Olivia Stuart's corpse out of the drawer. The slab and the sheet-covered body slid into the conversation without a squeak.

Stone swallowed. He'd liked Olivia Stuart. She'd been a good woman and a damned good mayor. It seemed an invasion of her privacy to be doing this, but if there was the remotest chance in the world that Jessica had been right, it would be a travesty of justice to let someone get away with her murder.

Noah reached for the sheet.

"This is it, my friend. May the truth prevail."

Five

"**W**ell, I'll be damned."

There was little else Noah Howell could think to say about the small dark bruise he found on the back of Olivia Stuart's leg.

Stone forced himself to focus on the tiny portion of bruised flesh, and not on what was left of the woman she'd been.

"So, Doc, without an autopsy, give me a *best-guess* scenario. What do you think could have caused that bruise?"

Noah looked up at Stone in disbelief. He still couldn't believe what he was seeing, then he looked back down, staring intently at the small purple spot. Even through his surgical gloves, he could feel the cold morbidity of Olivia's flesh. He shook his head and pulled the sheet back over her body.

"Without actual proof, it would be hard to—"

"Damn it, Doc, I asked for a guess, not a thesis."

Noah looked up. "I'd probably guess it was a needle mark."

Stone had been expecting him to say it, and yet when it came, he reeled backward in shock.

"Son of a bitch."

Noah pushed the body back into the drawer, then shut the door. He shivered. "I'll inform the coroner's office and order an autopsy immediately."

Stone stared at the wall of drawers. Olivia Stuart awaited her disbursement into the earth behind door seventeen. Knowing her as he had, he was certain her spirit was already in a better place, but what was left of her body deserved more than it was about to receive.

"And I'll handle it from my end," he said, then turned toward the door without waiting to see if Noah followed. "Let's get out of here. This place gives me the creeps."

Only after they were in the elevator on their way up to ground level, did Stone speak again.

"I need a copy of the autopsy report on my desk within twenty-four hours."

Noah shook his head. "No way. We're so behind now that—"

Stone put a hand on the doctor's shoulder. "Listen, Doc, if what we suspect is true, someone already thinks they've gotten away with murder. I don't want to wait a minute longer than necessary to start an investigation. Understand?"

Noah nodded, his shoulders slumping. "I'll do what it takes to get the job done, even if I have to do it myself."

The elevator doors opened and Stone stepped out. "Coming?"

Noah shook his head, pointing to the floors above. "I'm late for surgery as it is."

Stone paused in the door of the elevator, bracing his hands against the doors to keep them from closing.

"Doc, I need you to do me one more favor."

A wry grin spread across Noah Howell's face. "Why am I not surprised."

Stone's expression darkened. "Keep this quiet. I don't want speculation to supercede facts."

"Of course."

Stone stepped back and the doors closed immediately, taking Noah to the floors above.

A few minutes later, Stone slid into the seat of his car and then stared blindly out the window in disbelief. How had Jessica known this? And because she had, another, more serious problem dawned. In a way, she was witness to a murder. If word got out, she could be in danger herself. And with that thought came still another. Thinking of Jessie in danger made him sick with fear. He wiped a shaky hand across his face and closed his eyes, trying to remind himself that he had no claims on her other than the fact that she was just another innocent citizen he'd sworn to protect. But he kept remembering the way she laughed and the way she made love. As he broke out in a cold sweat, he groaned.

"Damn it," he muttered, "I don't need this," then he started the car and headed back to the station.

He'd already decided he wasn't saying anything to anyone but Sanderson until the autopsy report was in his hands. And he could just imagine how the chief was going to take the news. How does one tell the chief of police that some woman had a psychic vision and Stone had decided to act upon it? He shook his head. It sounded crazy, even to him.

Jessica was a morning person. Usually, she got up with a buoyant attitude that stayed with her through the rest of the day. But today, as she stepped out of the shower and glanced at herself in the mirror, she frowned.

In spite of doctor's orders, she had removed her bandage and washed her hair. Shoving back her ragged bangs, she turned her head, first one way, then another, looking intently at her wound before reaching for a towel. The way she looked at it, it was a toss-up as to which was worse—her homegrown haircut, or the bald spot that was sprouting new growth.

"I don't care," she told herself as she dried. "I don't have to go to work. Who's going to see?"

And then the phone rang. She dropped the towel and bolted, flopping across her bed as she reached for the phone beside her pillow.

"Hello."

Stone's voice rolled over her senses like warm honey on hot bread.

"Jessie, it's me."

In spite of the fact that she was safe from prying eyes, she instinctively reached for a sheet, then realized he wouldn't know she was naked. An odd little smile came and went as she dropped the sheet and moved the phone a little closer to her mouth. It was a decadent feeling to be talking to this man without wearing a stitch.

"I called to see how you were feeling," Stone said.

She rolled onto her back and closed her eyes. The air from an overhead fan was blow-drying the lingering moisture from her skin and she imagined that it was Stone's breath instead. She was so into her fantasy that her nipples suddenly peaked and hardened as her body tightened with longing.

She sighed. "I'm feeling fine. Just fine."

Stone frowned. She sounded strange, almost drugged.

"Did I wake you?" he asked.

She answered before she thought. "Oh, no. I've been up for ages. I just got out of the shower."

Stone gripped the receiver until his knuckles whitened, and he tried, without much success, to concentrate on something besides the thought of Jessica, wet and nude.

"Uh—" Realizing that he'd totally lost focus as to why he'd called, he gave himself a mental kick in the butt and shifted the receiver to his other ear.

Jessica was woman enough to hear Stone's confusion. And just when she could have taken heart from the fact that he could be remembering their past, she edited her thought. Yes, a naked woman might do wonders in getting some attention from Stone, but what about one with a bald spot and stitches? Aware of the dampness beneath her head, she abandoned her fantasies and sat up.

"Stone, hang on a minute, will you?" Without waiting for his answer, she dropped the phone and rolled off the bed to get a towel for her wet hair. It was dripping all over the bed.

Moments later, she was back. "Thanks," she said. "I was getting everything wet."

He groaned and covered his face with his hand.

"Stone?"

He jerked. At last. A reason to focus. "What?"

"Was there a particular reason you called?"

His mind was a blank, and then he remembered the autopsy in progress, and that he had wanted to warn her about talking to anyone other than him.

"Oh! Yeah! Uh, you know yesterday, when we talked about what you saw?"

She tensed and sat up.

"Yes, what about it?"

"You might have been right."

She'd known it, and yet hearing it said aloud gave her chills.

"About Olivia and the needle?"

"Yes, well—maybe yes about Olivia, maybe no—but you were right about my lost check. And, I think you should know that they *are* performing an autopsy on Olivia Stuart. We'll know more soon."

"Oh, Lord."

Stone heard her panic. And the fact that she'd been unable to come up with one of her colorful comments was proof of how rattled she must be.

"Jessie, I need you to do something for me."

She felt sick to her stomach, and took a deep breath, trying to calm her nerves.

"Like what?" she asked.

"Don't talk about this to anyone else. At least, not until I tell you it's all right."

"Why?"

He had to tell her. Her life could be on the line.

"Because, if you're right, then that means Olivia was murdered. And if she was, then that means there's a murderer who will be very unhappy to learn there was a witness...of sorts.''

There were aspects of this mess that kept going from bad to worse. She started to shake.

''But I'm not really a witness. At least not the kind that will help you solve the case. I saw Olivia being stabbed, but I never saw the woman's face who did it.''

Stone frowned. For some reason, he'd been expecting her to furnish recognition as to the attacker's identity.

''Then, how do you know it was a woman?'' he asked.

She closed her eyes, doing a mental playback of what she'd seen. ''Because...''

She paused, trying to focus. *The hands. Those long, tapering fingers. And the polish. She was wearing red nail polish!* Suddenly it dawned.

''She was wearing nail polish. Red nail polish. And I think maybe perfume. Every time I see it happening, I smell gardenias.''

Stone's frown deepened. ''What else, Jessie? Think.''

''That's all,'' she said. ''I didn't see her face, I swear. My focus seemed to be entirely on Olivia.''

''Okay, don't worry about it,'' Stone said. ''The main thing is, keep what you saw to yourself.''

Jessica nodded, and then remembered. Brenda! She'd told her sister, Brenda.

''Uh, Stone...''

''Yeah?''

''Brenda knows.''

His stomach tied itself into a miserable knot. ''Damn.''

She frowned. ''Well, I had to tell someone, and she *is* my sister, remember?''

In spite of the fact that no one could overhear their conversation, a flush heated his face as he glanced over at Stryker's desk. The accusation in Jessie's voice had been no accident. He'd dated one sister and made love to the other. It was a mess he could have never foreseen. What he had to remember was to keep his personal life out of his job.

"Okay, so she knows," Stone said. "But tell her to keep her mouth shut about everything, okay?"

If it hadn't been so awful, Jessica might have laughed. "I already disappoint and embarrass her on a daily basis. There is no way she's going to shoot off her mouth about what I said."

Stone spoke before he thought. "You're wrong. I know she used to feel responsible for you, but you were never a burden."

Jessica was stunned. "But I'm a grown woman. I'm responsible for myself," she muttered.

"Maybe you are now," Stone said quietly. "But when your parents died, you were what…seventeen?"

Sudden tears burned Jessica's eyes. "Just about," she said softly.

"Well, then, did you ever think that it might be difficult for her to change how she thinks a big sister should act?"

Jessica was speechless.

"Jessica?"

She sniffed. "What?"

"As soon as I know something final, I'll let you know."

"Thank you," she said, and hung up the phone.

The quiet in her house seemed threatening. With a shaky sob, she rolled herself into a ball and pulled the sheet up over her shoulders. She would call Brenda, but later, when she would be able to talk without crying.

Jessica was on her knees in the dirt, pulling weeds from her flower bed when a car pulled into her driveway. She braced herself on one knee and turned to see Brenda getting out of the car. From the way she was dressed, she must have come straight from work. But it wasn't what Brenda was wearing that concerned Jessica the most. It was the expression on her face. In that moment, Jessica thought, *She knows about the autopsy.*

Jessica stood, and then pulled off her gloves and tossed them on the front porch step. Waving a hello, she tried hard to smile, but her chin quivered instead. Moments later, she was in Brenda's arms.

"Oh, honey." It was all Brenda could think to say.

"Stone called you, didn't he?"

Brenda stepped back and cupped her little sister's face with her hands.

"Yes, thank goodness, but it should have been you. Why didn't you tell me, Jessie? I shouldn't have had to hear this from him."

Jessica led her up the steps to the porch swing. "Want something to drink?" she asked as Brenda plopped down in the swing.

Brenda caught her by the hand and pulled her down beside her in the seat.

"I want you to talk to me."

Jessica sat down in a slump, staring at a swirl in the wood beneath her feet.

"I already told you what I saw. You didn't believe me then, why believe me now?"

Guilt fell hard on Brenda Hanson's shoulders as she looked at her baby sister's face. The gamine features. The ragamuffin hair. That smudge of dirt on the side of her face. Mentally, she knew Jessie was a grown woman, but in her heart, she would forever see her sister as younger, and weaker, and waiting for someone to carry her over the rough spots in the road.

"Be reasonable, Jessie. Would you have believed me if the situation had been reversed?"

Jessica sighed, then looked up, grinning an apology. "Probably not."

"Then, am I forgiven?"

Jessica threw her arms around her sister's neck. "Of course, and I'm really glad you're here."

Brenda returned the hug. "Get dressed. I'm taking you out to dinner."

Instinctively, Jessica's hand went to her hair. "Oh, I don't know. I'm pretty tired. Maybe we could just—"

Brenda grinned. "Stuff the excuses, baby sister, and quit worrying about your hair. You know…in an odd, disheveled sort of manner, it suits you."

Jessica made a face and got up. "Where are you taking me?"

"You get to pick," Brenda said.

"Oh, good. I've been hungry for Mexican food for days."

Brenda rolled her eyes. "Just what I need! You know I can't resist that stuff, and those cheese enchiladas go straight to my thighs."

"You can diet tomorrow," Jessica said, and headed for the house. "Make yourself at home. I won't be long."

Brenda followed her inside, thankful that their relationship was back on level ground.

The autopsy report was in a folder near Stone's left hand. The conference he and Jack Stryker had just had with the chief was still ringing in his ears. He'd already read the report. Not once, but twice. And even though he'd more or less prepared himself for the positive results, what Noah Howell told him had stunned him.

Potassium. Olivia Stuart had been murdered with potassium. Enough to induce immediate cardiac arrest. They were guessing at least forty milliliters. And tracing it was going to be next to impossible, because it wasn't a controlled drug. Hospitals didn't even keep the stuff under lock and key.

He kept staring at the folder, knowing he was going to have to give Jessie a call. This changed everything. He could no longer ignore the truth. Olivia Stuart had been murdered. And, as of fifteen minutes ago, there was an official investigation under way.

Stone looked up as Stryker came out of the washroom, drying his hands. He glanced at Chang, who was on the phone at a nearby desk. Stryker had all the facts as Stone knew them, but Chang was a wild card in this mess. Jessie had talked to him first. Stone had to make sure that there had been no inadvertent leaks to the media about Jessica Hanson's so-called powers. He waited until Chang hung up, and then walked over to his desk and tossed the folder containing the autopsy report in front of him.

When the folder landed between his hands, Chang looked up, startled by the abrupt interruption to his work.

"What's the big deal?" he asked.

Stone pointed. "See for yourself."

Chang opened the folder and started to read. Halfway down the page, he stiffened. When he had finished, he handed the file back to Stone.

"Son of a gun! Who would have thought?" And then an odd, startled expression crossed his face.

Stone tensed. Chang had remembered.

"I want you to keep quiet about what you know," Stone said.

Chang stood up. "She was right, wasn't she? But how could that be? How did she—?"

"I don't know," Stone said. "And for that matter, neither does she. However, the fact remains that a woman was murdered, and, for all intents and purposes, Jessica Hanson is a witness." He lowered his voice. "Which means…we keep quiet about how we found out. What matters now is finding out who did it—and why."

Chang shook his head. "I just didn't believe her. It was such a far-fetched—"

Stone interrupted. "Stryker and I have the case. I'd appreciate it if, for the time being, you forget everything Jessica Hanson told you. The less said about what's happened, the better. We've already lost our mayor. We don't need to put any more people in unnecessary danger, right?"

Chang kept shaking his head as he dropped back in his chair. "I can't believe it. Who would have thought?" And then he slapped the side of his head and groaned. "Oh, man!"

"What's wrong?" Stone asked.

"This morning, I was at the doughnut shop, and Canfield and I were talking about all the weird things that have been happening since the blackout."

Stone braced himself. Already, he knew what Chang was going to say. "Damn it, Erik. Tell me you didn't blab it all over the place."

Chang's shoulders slumped. "It was so far-fetched. How could I have known she was telling the truth?" He looked up. "I never said her name. I swear. All I said was some woman."

"Son of a—" Stone pivoted, resisting the urge to hit out, yet in a way, he also understood Chang's reaction. He'd known Jessie Hanson for years. Hell, he'd even made love to her. And he'd doubted her, too. Well, the fat was in the fire, so to speak, and someone had to let Jessie know.

"Hey, Stryker."

Jack looked up.

"Want to take a ride?"

Understanding dawned. "You going to see her?"

Stone nodded.

A slight smile crossed Stryker's face. "Something tells me she'd rather hear it from you. Besides, I'm going to swing by the mayor's house on my way home. They've already taped it off as a crime scene, although I hate to think of what valuable clues have been lost. I just hope to hell her cleaning lady was as delayed by the blackout as we've been."

Relieved that he was going to see Jessie alone, Stone added, "I'll meet you there as soon as I've talked to Jessie."

Jack grinned. "I won't hold my breath."

"Well, for goodness' sake," Brenda said as they pulled into the driveway of Jessica's home from their evening out.

"Look! Someone's here."

Stone's wine-colored car looked black under the street-lights, but Jessica recognized it just the same. And when she saw him get up from her porch swing and start down the steps to meet them, she started to panic.

"Why, isn't that Stone Richardson?" Brenda asked.

When Jessica didn't answer, Brenda turned to tease. But the thought died as she saw Jessie's expression.

"Honey, what's wrong?"

Jessica undid her seat belt and got out of the car without answering. Stone met her halfway.

"It's bad, isn't it?" she asked.

Stone nodded.

Jessica covered her face with her hands and moaned. Brenda was there within moments, her voice trembling as she took Jessica in her arms.

"Jessie, honey, talk to me. Tell me what's wrong."

Stone answered for her. "Olivia Stuart *was* murdered. The autopsy report proved it without a doubt."

Brenda's arms tightened around Jessica's shoulders. She heard him, but she just couldn't believe it. Even when Jessica had warned her what was taking place, she hadn't really believed it would prove to be true.

"Oh, my God," Brenda whispered.

Jessica tore free of her sister's grasp and started toward her home. It didn't make sense, but she had an overwhelming need to get inside. There, she'd be safe.

Stone grabbed her as she started to run past him. His hands were firm upon her arms, but his voice was gentle as he did what he could to ease her panic.

"Let me go!" Jessica cried.

"Jessie, look at me," Stone urged.

She glanced over her shoulder at Brenda, her eyes wide with shock. But Brenda hadn't moved.

"Jessie..." Stone's voice was calm, his warning less

than urgent. It was more a tone one would take with a child who wouldn't listen.

She took a deep breath, telling herself that it would be all right, and looked up. Stone was watching her. Waiting.

"I'm all right." She stepped backward out of his grasp. "Sorry. For a moment there, I guess I just panicked."

A car turned the corner of the block. The headlights swept across them, then it continued up the block to a house at the end of the street. Stone held out his hand.

"Let's go inside."

Jessica started up the steps, with Stone and Brenda right behind her. Her hand was on the doorknob when she remembered that it was locked. Muttering beneath her breath, she began to dig in her purse when Stone appeared at her side, the trusty lock pick in his hands.

"Allow me," he said with a grin.

Once more, the lock gave to his skillful intrusion, and he stepped aside for the women to proceed. Brenda eyed him thoughtfully as she passed by. Stone managed a smile, but couldn't bring himself to fully meet her questioning gaze. When he'd been learning about police protocol, they had left out the part about wooing women of the same family. Now he knew why.

Jessica flipped on the lights as she entered. Stone shut the door behind him. They were inside. Together. And it seemed that no one knew what to say or where to start.

Finally it was Jessica who broke the ice, and her question ended the odd stalemate by bringing the true problem to the fore.

"Am I in any danger?"

"I don't think so," Stone said. "However, there's a possibility that the word has already been leaked about someone having a premonition about Olivia being murdered instead of dying from a heart attack."

Jessica glanced at Brenda.

"Don't look at me," Brenda said quickly.

"It wasn't your sister," Stone said. "It was one of ours."

"That detective," Jessica said. "The one who laughed in my face."

"He didn't exactly laugh," Stone reminded her.

"Well, he did everything but laugh," she said, and then sighed. "It doesn't really matter, I guess. What does matter is finding out who killed Mrs. Stuart. I always liked her."

"Everyone liked her," Brenda said.

"Someone didn't," Stone said.

Jessica blanched. That panicked feeling was coming back, and she needed to change the subject. She glanced at Brenda and tried to smile. "Who wants coffee?"

"I'll make it," Brenda offered.

"That's a relief," Stone said, and was rewarded by Jessie's offended glare. He grinned. Right now he would have done anything to get her mind off the business at hand.

Brenda disappeared down the hall, leaving Stone and Jessica alone.

"So, what are you thinking?"

In her typical straightforward manner, Jessica gave him an answer he wasn't ready to hear.

"That you could have called to give me this information."

He looked startled. "Well, yes, I suppose I—"

"Then, why didn't you?" she asked.

Stone froze. Why didn't he call? His gaze swept her face, then her body, trying to find an answer she would believe.

There was a smudge on the leg of her slacks, and her hair was as flyaway as the expression in her eyes. Along with the stitches just visible beneath her bangs, the small, bare spot surrounding them made him ache to hold her. She was so small, and looked so fragile and afraid. And as he stood, caught within the power of a blue, megawatt stare, he knew.

"Because I wanted to see you."

He'd shocked her. He could see it in her eyes.

Startled, Jessica took a small step back.

His voice lowered and he followed her retreat. "Because I wanted to hold you."

Her heart started to pound. How dare he tell her these things now?

"You've said all this before. Besides, you know it's easy to say when my sister is just down the hall."

He paused in midstep. At that moment, he realized he'd completely forgotten Brenda was even in the house. But it didn't stop him long. He started after her.

"I don't care if the Mormon Tabernacle Choir is in the next room, and if you'll stand still long enough, I'll prove it."

She froze.

A wry smile spread across his face. "That's what I like best about you, honey. You always know when to call a man's bluff."

His arms slid around her shoulders, and then he was pulling her close—and closer still.

She wound her arms around his neck. "I'm not your honey," she whispered. "You didn't want me, remember?"

He kissed her slowly. He tasted the edge of her lower lip, then moved past the gasp she'd just made to the sweet curve of her upper lip where it dipped downward in the center like the bud of a rose. He felt a shudder rip through her, and answered with a sigh of his own as he took her in his arms, lifting her off her feet until she was dangling in his grasp, several inches off the ground.

His whisper was soft near her ear. "You know what, Jessie Leigh?"

She opened her eyes and got lost in that dark, gray gaze. Only after he'd kissed her again then set her back on the floor did she remember he'd asked her a question.

"What?" she said with a sigh.

"I never said I didn't want you."

"But you let me go. It's all the same thing."

"I tried marriage and failed…miserably. I'm not stupid. I don't intend to make the same mistake twice."

She blinked through tears.

"But I'm not Naomi."

He looked down at her tousled hair and tear-filled eyes and pulled her close, pressing her face against the center of his chest. For a moment, he neither moved nor breathed as a longing for something more than they'd had before hit him deep.

"I know who you are, Jessie Leigh. I remember the feel of your skin beneath my fingers. I—"

Brenda's shout echoed down the hall.

"Coffee's done!"

Startled by her sister's untimely intrusion, she made a face and then sighed. "Rusty nails. Why wasn't I born an only child?"

Stone stepped back, grateful that he'd been saved from making another serious mistake. It didn't matter—couldn't matter—how much he wanted Jessie, or how much he cared for her. He'd been down that road before, and there was nothing at the end of it but trouble.

Long after Stone and Brenda were gone, Jessica lay in her bed, imagining she could still feel the imprint of Stone's mouth upon her lips and his breath upon her face. She closed her eyes, cuddling a pillow against her breast because she needed to be held and it was the closest thing to comfort she was going to receive.

Six

It Was Murder!

The glaring headlines of the *Grand Springs Herald* on Friday morning were causing an uproar all over the city. Gossip abounded as the news of Olivia Stuart's death was given a new and macabre twist.

It was common knowledge that the mayor had been publicly and vocally opposed to a strip mining consortium that was trying to establish backing within the community so they could renew their lease. Fingers of suspicion could be pointed in any number of directions, but there was no proof linking the naysayers to Olivia Stuart's death.

Other than the autopsy report, the detectives assigned to the case had few clues, and none that would stand up in court.

And, to Stone's dismay, although it had yet to appear in the paper, he'd already heard whispers on the street about a secret witness having a psychic vision about the murder.

If Jessica Hanson was to be believed, and Stone had no reason to doubt her now, then the killer was a woman who preferred red fingernail polish and the scent of gardenias. For a man trained to deal in physical facts, it was one hell of a pitiful lead with which to start a case.

Jessica Hanson was one of the few people in the city who should not have been shocked by the morning headlines, yet when she picked the paper up off her front lawn and opened it on the way to the house, she saw the headline and stumbled, stubbing her toe on a crack in the concrete.

Ignoring the pain, she stood barefoot on her walkway, with the tail of her robe trailing in dew-damp grass, and read—from the headline, to the byline, to the last period that ended the piece.

"Isn't it awful?"

Startled that she was no longer alone, Jessica looked up in surprise. Tinee Bloom, who lived in the next-to-the-last house at the end of the block, was standing at the edge of the path with her dog, Barney, on a leash. True to her name, Tinee Bloom favored clothing with vivid floral designs, and the green-and-purple, knee-length float dress she was wearing this morning was no exception.

Jessica eyed the oversize beagle who was sniffing beneath her best oleander bush and stifled a glare. Now she knew why that bush's flowers had such an unusual scent. It wasn't the flowers she'd been smelling, it was Barney the beagle's daily duty.

"What did you say?" Jessica asked.

Tinee pointed to the paper Jessica was holding. "The headlines. I saw you reading the headlines. I said...isn't it awful?"

Jessica nodded, then winced as Tinee's dog began to dig. When Tinee Bloom showed no signs of regret for what the stupid pooch was doing, she pointed.

"Miss Bloom, please...your dog!"

Tinee glanced down at the dog who was now taking the proverbial "dump" at the edge of Jessica's shrubs. She grinned widely and clapped her hands, totally missing the point of Jessica's remarks.

"Oh! Good Barney. Good doggie. That's my boy." Tightening her hold on the dog's leash and fluffing her henna-rinsed hair, she smiled.

"Well now. I suppose we'll just be going. You have a nice day," she said, and waved over her shoulder as she started down the walk.

Jessica was fuming as she glared at the woman's flower-bedecked backside. For two cents, she'd...

The thought faded as another slipped into place. The paper fell from Jessica's hands. A sensation of urgency swept over her and she felt an overwhelming urge to cry, then she shuddered and blinked as the world moved back into focus.

Tinee Bloom and Barney the beagle were almost at the corner. Jessica knew that, within moments, they would be crossing the street to make the return journey toward home. And she also knew that unless someone stopped them, it would be the last walk either one of them would take. Jessica grabbed the hem of her robe and started to run, screaming Tinee's name as she went.

Barney stopped to sniff at a lizard at the edge of the grass. Tinee smiled to herself. Silly old puppy, still playing with critters. She tugged at his leash, and he obliged by ambling on ahead. Tinee's stomach grumbled. There was coffee and Danish awaiting her arrival back home.

Four steps. Three steps. Two steps. One. At the stop sign, turn.

Tinee knew the corner by heart. With her head in the clouds and her hand on the leash, she started to step out into the street when a bloodcurdling scream sounded behind her. Startled, she yanked on Barney's leash and spun around. Jessica Hanson was running toward her at an all-out sprint and screaming something she couldn't understand.

"What's that you say?" she called out.

"The car! The car! You're going to get hit by that—"

It came out of nowhere. A sleek, gray bullet of a car that shot out of an alley, aiming at the curb on which Tinee Bloom and her dog were standing.

"Run!" Jessica screamed.

A look of pure horror spread over Tinee's face as she pivoted. The car was nearly upon them, making no attempt to swerve. In a move that would have made an Olympian proud, Tinee leaped toward a nearby tree, taking Barney with her. Seconds later, the car hit the curb, taking out the stop sign, as well as a section of a nearby hedge, before swerving back onto the street.

Jessica spun as the car sailed past. She had a brief glimpse of what appeared to be an underage driver behind the wheel before the car sped away.

Moments later, Tinee Bloom came out from behind the tree on tottering legs, clutching Barney to her breasts and gasping for breath.

"We would have been killed," she cried, and plopped Barney down at Jessica's feet. "If you hadn't called out, we would have been killed!"

People began coming out of their houses just as she threw her arms around Jessica's neck in thanksgiving.

"Oh, thank you, thank you," she said, hugging Jessica over and over in wild abandon. "You're a true heroine, that's what you are."

Several of Jessica's neighbors began to clap. It was a scattered sound that echoed within the small area in which they were standing, and it pierced Jessica's heart with sudden fear. This was serious. She had to find a way to stop this before it was too late.

"Of course I'm not," she said, and tried to lighten the moment by laughing lightly. It went nowhere. And to her dismay, Tinee Bloom was just winding up.

"Did you see that?" Tinee cried, pointing toward the broken stop sign and the damaged portion of hedge. "If Jessica hadn't warned us, we would have been killed."

Jessica felt the blood draining from her face. *I've got to get away. I've got to leave before it dawns on her that—*

Tinee suddenly clasped her hands to her mouth and turned back to Jessica, staring and pointing at her in a disbelieving manner.

"But how did you know?" she said.

Jessica started backing down the sidewalk as the gathering neighbors began to stare.

"Well, I saw it, of course," she said quickly, pulling her robe that much tighter around her. "But I think someone should call the police. I'll bet that was a stolen car. The driver looked far too young to be—"

Tinee wasn't about to be swayed from having her say. "You screamed before there was anything on the street. You were running toward me and shouting a warning before there was anything there to see."

Jessica groaned beneath her breath. This was getting worse by the minute.

"No, Tinee. You're mistaken."

"I'm not!" Tinee announced, and pointed to a nearby woman. "Did you hear her scream?" she asked.

"Why, yes, as a matter of fact, I did," the woman said, staring at Jessica in a puzzled manner. "That's why I came to the window." And then she added, "But there wasn't anyone in sight except Tinee and her dog. I know, because I looked, trying to see what would have made her scream."

Jessica paled. *Toe jam. I've been made.* She could see the words coming out of Tinee's mouth, yet when she heard them, she still reeled from the sound and the shock.

"You saw my future, yes, you did, Jessica Hanson. You saw into my future and changed my fate."

"I think someone should call the police," Jessica said, pointing toward the broken sign and the uprooted hedge. Then she looked down at her robe and bare feet. "I'll be going now," she said, and started back to her house, limping as she went while the voices behind her began to buzz like a nest of angry bees.

By noon, it was all over town. Jessica Hanson had seen into the future and saved Tinee Bloom's life. By three o'clock, it was being said that ten people owed their lives to Jessica Hanson. By five o'clock, she'd saved an entire busload of senior citizens on their way to a church picnic.

By nightfall, someone had heard they were going to make a movie out of Jessica Hanson's life, beginning with the day she'd started school and peed in her pants because she'd been afraid to tell the teacher she needed to go. And before the next day, it would be all over town that Jessica Hanson must have been the mystery woman who'd alerted the cops to Olivia Stuart's murder.

But for now, Jessica was holed up in her house and had quit answering her phone. Except for her first day of school when she'd peed her pants in front of seventeen of her peers, it *was* the worst day of her life. Brenda had come and gone, filled with dismay for what had occurred, yet agreeing with Jessica that there was nothing else she could have done.

And if Stone hadn't been too tired to cook when he got off work, and if he hadn't stopped to pick up a hamburger and fries to take home, it might have been morning before he learned that Jessica Hanson was really the child of an alien who'd been put here on earth for the good of mankind, and was now working full-time with the Grand Springs Police Department to help them solve crimes.

At that point, he had only one thought and it was unprintable. Now the idea of food made him sick. He tossed the sack in the seat beside him and spun out of the drivethrough, resisting the urge for an all-out run with lights and siren. If even a fraction of what he'd heard about Jessie was true, then she'd called all the attention to herself that she would ever need.

Jessica's phone was off the hook. Her door was locked. The lights were out. And she still felt like a bug on a pin. This morning, when she'd read the headline, she'd had a feeling it was going to be a bad day. Snorting lightly to herself, she rolled over in bed, pulling the covers up over her head. That was a fact she could have taken to the bank. Somehow, she drifted off to sleep, unaware that her day of disasters had yet to come to an end.

* * *

Stone was stuck at a traffic light behind a trucker who didn't seem to know the meaning of emission control. Coupled with the scent of a cooling hamburger and greasy fries, the diesel fumes were about to do him in. He glanced at his watch. It was a quarter to ten. He frowned. What if she was already in bed? He reached for the phone, hesitating briefly as he recalled her number, then made the call.

It was busy. Twice more, he tried to get through, and each time, all he got was that familiar buzz, buzz, buzz.

His frown deepened as he tossed the phone on the seat beside him. A few minutes later, he turned the corner leading onto her block. As he did, his car lights swept across the broken stop sign and the gouged-out portion of someone's hedge.

Someone must have had an accident. He pictured Jessie passing out cold on the floor of her manager's office and looked back at the hedge. What if the gossip he'd been hearing had upset her so much that she'd tried to drive and passed out again? His mind was in turmoil as he pulled into her driveway.

Her car was in its usual place. He circled it on foot, breathing a slight sigh of relief. It was dent-free. If only Jessie could claim the same state.

He glanced up at her house. It was in total darkness. Being the cop that he was, he turned, surveying the surrounding area with a judgmental stare, searching for something...anything that might be out of place. Satisfied that all was as it should be, he went up the steps and knocked.

The sound was a muted thud against the backwash of neighborhood night sounds. A radio blared from a passing car. He heard a man's angry voice and then the shrill, uneven cry of a woman returning the anger. The interchange reminded him of his last months with Naomi before their divorce. She'd gone from begging, to crying, and then screaming at him in fury, accusing him of putting his job before their lives. What she'd failed to understand was that his job was a part of who he was. He couldn't have a life with a woman who wouldn't let him be himself. And then he thought of Jessie. God help him, but even when he'd known it was futile, he'd let her get too far under his skin to forget. It was all he could do just to keep her at arm's length.

Disgusted with himself and what he viewed as a weakness on his part, he knocked again, only this time, louder, calling out Jessie's name as he did. All he got for his trouble was silence.

The tension of the moment was getting to him in a very big way. A fleeting image of Olivia Stuart laid out on that slab in the morgue came and went, along with the knowledge that Jessica's life could be in danger if anyone was to believe the gossip on the streets.

Trying not to let his imagination run rampant, he reached for his lock pick. To his dismay, he came away empty-handed, and remembered tossing it on the dresser last night, right next to his gun just before he'd gone to bed. This morning, he'd picked up his gun. He didn't remember seeing the lock pick at all.

"Damn it. Just when I need it most."

He doubled his fist and pounded on the door. Somewhere within the house he heard a sound, not unlike the thud of an overturned chair. Frowning, he moved to a window and peered inside.

At first, he saw nothing. Then, down the hall and to the right, he saw a small, pencil-thin beam of light moving along the edge of the floorboard like the tip of a blind man's cane.

Someone was in Jessie's house!

He froze. What if her phone hadn't been busy? What if a burglar had taken it off of the hook? Even worse, what if the hit woman had come to do away with the only witness to her crime? And that light! If it was Jessie, she wouldn't be sneaking around in her own home in the dark.

He ran back to the door and drew his gun, then kicked, centering his size-twelve boot right beside the lock.

The wood frame splintered, and the door swung open with a mighty slam. Something fell off the wall. Glass shattered as he bolted inside, his gaze fixed on the small beam of light. And when it suddenly dropped and rolled upon the floor, he got a highlighted glimpse of a foot and a leg as someone started to run.

He bolted toward the motion like a linebacker slipping through an unexpected hole in the defense, tackling the intruder knee-high and sending them both skidding down the hallway. The gun slid out of his hands and clattered against a nearby wall. Stone cursed beneath his breath. He had the runner. But he'd lost his gun.

A scream shattered his eardrum and someone kneed him hard in the groin. He gritted his teeth as pain shot through his body. Before he could think to react, he heard sirens and the sound of running feet. And then there were lights everywhere and he was looking down at the intruder he'd caught just as a man's loud shout broke the silence.

"Police! Don't move! We've got you covered!"

He groaned. He hadn't caught a burglar. He'd caught Jessie. And from the expression on her face, she might just let the cops who'd come to her rescue cart him off to jail.

Jessica had been sound asleep, and with the next breath, wide awake, sitting up in bed and listening, trying to discern what it was she'd heard.

There! She heard it again. Someone was pounding on her door. After the day she'd had, there was no telling what nut had decided to come calling. And then she panicked. What if it was the hit woman, coming to get rid of the only witness to her crime? It was a dumb assumption, but she'd just awakened and hadn't time to sort out the fact that hit women probably didn't bother to knock.

Careful not to make her presence known, she started down the hall on bare feet, skipping the board to the left of the bathroom door. It sometimes squeaked. The urge to turn on the lights was overwhelming, but she felt safe from disclosure within the darkness, and crept into the living room.

The sound came again, only this time louder and more forceful. She reached for the phone, and then in a panic, she knocked over a chair as she bolted for her bedroom. At least there, she could talk without giving herself away. Once there, she squatted down beside her bed as she dialed the phone in the dark. Her heart was pounding, her hands trembling as a man's calm voice echoed in her ear.

"This is 911. What is your emergency?"

Everything came out in a panicked whisper. "This is Jessica Hanson at 53 Broyles Lane. I think someone is trying to break into my house."

"Are you alone in the house?"

"Yes. Please hurry," she begged, and then jumped in fright as the pounding on her front door increased.

"Try to stay calm," the dispatcher said. "Officers have been dispatched to your address. Where are you?"

"In the back of the house...in my bedroom."

"Is there a place you can hide?" the dispatcher asked.

Jessica's gaze swept around the room. "The kitchen. I can hide in the kitchen."

The dispatcher was still talking as Jessica reached for the penlight in her bedside table and started back down the hall. She was listening to his orders, but moving within her own desperation. From where he was sitting, his advice might be sound, but from where Jessica was standing, it didn't hold water. Instinct told her that the burglar would be inside long before a patrol car could ever arrive.

And she knew just where to hide. The space beneath her sink was large. Plenty large enough for her to crawl inside. The way she figured, it was the least obvious place in which a burglar would meddle. There wouldn't be anything to steal beneath a kitchen sink, therefore they shouldn't think to look there.

Her reasoning was sound, but her timing was off. She was halfway down the hall when her front door flew back against the wall. When glass shattered, she dropped the light and started to run.

Hit from behind, she fell screaming, flattened beneath an unbelievable weight before being rolled onto her back. Her knee came up, and she grunted in painful justification as she connected with a delicate part of her attacker's anatomy. His hold tightened, and just as she was accepting her demise, she was suddenly blinded by a flood of lights. When she could see without blinking, she looked up, right into the disbelieving gaze of the man of her dreams. He rolled off of her with a groan.

"You!" she spluttered.

Officer Paul Turner was pumped. He'd caught the perp in the act. Everything had been crazy since the blackout had occurred. It felt good to collar one bad guy on the spot. He aimed his gun in the cornered man's face and shouted.

"Put up your hands! You're under arrest!"

"Wait," Stone said. "This is all a misunderstanding."

Turner's gun nudged the lob of Stone's ear. "Don't move!"

"I'm a cop," Stone said. "My badge is in my jacket pocket!"

Jessica was promptly yanked to her feet and shoved out of the way by another officer. Wearing nothing but a thigh-length pink T-shirt and a pair of briefs, she stood back, eyeing the situation with disbelief, while considering the wisdom of letting them haul Stone off just to prove a point. But then she thought of the consequences and changed her mind.

"He's a friend," Jessica said, and then she eyed her front door as the lights were turned on. "At least he was until he kicked in my door."

Stone groaned as he rolled to his feet. "Why didn't you

answer? I thought you'd been hurt. Hell, I even thought you were a burglar.''

She glared. "Where is that famous lock pick you so ardently carry?"

His shoulders slumped. "I couldn't find it."

Both of the officers were starting to grin. "Hey, aren't you Richardson from the detective division?"

Stone groaned. Talk about gossip. He was going to be the laughingstock of the department for years to come. He flashed his badge.

"She's a friend." He pointed toward Jessica's head. "She was hurt during the blackout. When she didn't answer her phone or her door, I got worried."

"Yeah, when I go check on my girl, I always roll her on the floor before saying hello." Officer Beamer snickered.

Turner guffawed, and then holstered his gun. "So, Miss...?"

"Hanson. Jessica Hanson."

"You sure you're all right with this?"

She nodded. "Yes. It was just as he said. All a misunderstanding."

They both started toward the door when Beamer stopped and turned.

"Hey, aren't you that woman who saved someone's life this morning?"

At that point Jessica paled perceptibly, and Stone decided it was time to step in.

"Look, boys. I'd consider it a great big favor if you'd keep this to yourselves. You see how it's upsetting her. The less said about it, the better."

"Yeah, sure," they both said. But Stone could tell by the gleam in their eyes that it would be all over the department before midnight.

"I'd owe you, big time," he said.

They paused at the door and then turned. Turner grinned. "Sorry, Richardson, but you won't make enough in your lifetime to pay out this debt."

When they shut the door behind them, it hit the facing and bounced back like a dangling yo-yo swinging in the breeze. Stone groaned, and then turned. Within seconds, he had Jessie safe in his arms.

"I'm sorry. So sorry." He carefully brushed the hair from her face, eyeing the healing stitches. "Tell me I didn't hurt you when we fell."

She looked up, her eyes swimming with tears, and knew then that the two years she'd absented herself from Grand Springs truly were all for nothing. She was hopelessly and desperately in love with this man.

"You didn't hurt me when we fell."

He groaned. "You're lying through your sweet little teeth."

Her gaze was fixed on his mouth, remembering what it felt like on her face—on her lips. Remembering how his breath felt on her eyelids—down the side of her neck—in her ear. She shuddered and swayed toward him.

"Am I under arrest?"

His heart was hammering against his ribs when he remembered why he'd come.

"Jessie..."

"Hmm?"

"What the hell happened to you today?"

Her face crumpled. "What do you think?"

"Did it happen again?"

She nodded.

He took her by the hand and led her to the couch. "Just a minute," he cautioned, then took one of her dining room chairs and wedged it beneath the front doorknob to hold the door shut.

Jessica watched him moving around her living room as if he'd lived there all of his life. She was afraid to blink. Afraid that she'd wake up to realize that this was only a dream. And when he came back and plopped down beside her, she wanted to throw her arms around his neck and beg him to make it all go away. Instead, she waited for him to speak.

Stone gauged the depth of Jessie's state of mind against his need to know.

"Are you okay?"

She nodded.

He covered her hand with his. "Then, tell me what happened."

This friendly, cop-to-citizen behavior wasn't what she'd wanted, but for now, it would be enough. She started talking.

Stone was still shaking his head in disbelief when she finished, and he leaned back on the couch with a sigh.

"And, I guess that's about it," Jessica said.

"Dang, Jessie, isn't that enough?"

Her shoulders slumped, and she thumped herself on the head. "I don't know how to turn this...this thing off." She looked up at him, her eyes wide and pleading for understanding. "I don't like it. I don't want it. But I can't bring myself to ignore what I see. Do you understand?"

His face mirrored his concern, and in a way, he supposed he also understood. But it was a hell of a time for her so-called "powers" to move into overdrive. He'd spent half the day making sure there were no leaks as to why an autopsy had suddenly been performed on a woman who'd been pronounced dead from a heart attack days ago. And now this. Because Jessie had seen an accident before it could happen, everything they'd done to protect her anonymity had been futile. And, there had been too many witnesses to this incident for her to ignore.

Jessica was getting nervous. Stone was too quiet. "So, do you think I've put myself in worse trouble?"

Sorry that his hesitation to answer had frightened her, Stone reached out and cupped her cheek with his hand.

"You did what you had to do, and I'm sure Tinee Bloom and her dog, Barney, are exceedingly grateful tonight."

Jessica shivered at the touch of his hand against her face, and then stifled a yawn.

Stone smiled. "It's been a long day, hasn't it, baby?"

If she hadn't been so tired, she would have given him a piece of her mind. How dare he talk sweet to her now? Two years ago, he'd been the one to step back from commitment. He hadn't trusted her enough to give them time, therefore, he no longer had the right to call her anything but Jessie. And then she sighed. Who was she kidding? From Stone, she would take anything he was willing to give. She looked away and then nodded. Yes, it had been a very long day.

Stone's stomach growled, and he remembered his hamburger and fries in the seat of his car. It wouldn't be the first time he'd eaten cold food, and it wouldn't be the last.

"My supper is in the car. Mind if I use your microwave to heat it up?"

"Help yourself," she said.

Stone moved the dining room chair aside and went out to his car, coming back moments later with a sack in his hand. At once, the familiar odor of fast food filled the room.

"Smells good," Jessica said.

He grinned. "Didn't you eat?"

She shook her head.

He handed her the sack. "Here, knock yourself out. I've got to lock up."

Jessica took the sack and headed toward the kitchen as Stone shoved a chair back beneath the doorknob.

By the time he got to the kitchen, she'd pulled several bowls of leftovers from her refrigerator. Stone's food was just coming out of the microwave. She handed it to him, then lifted a long, greasy fry from the plate and popped it into her mouth as he set the plate down on the table.

"What is in those?" he asked, curiously eyeing the size and assortment of dishes she was uncovering.

"Umm…" She took the lid off of one and peeked in. "This looks like some beef and broccoli stir-fry…and an egg roll," she added, then set it aside. She popped the lid on another one. "This is goulash. I made it yesterday." She looked up. "It's actually quite good. Really!" She continued on down the line, flipping lids and poking into the contents with less and less interest. "Here's some left-over fried chicken, and this one is… Huh! I thought this was all gone!" She showed him the bowl. "Spaghetti and meatballs."

He looked down at his plate and then back at the bowls.

Jessica looked at her bowls, then down at his plate.

Their gazes met. Their eyebrows arched questioningly.

"Trade you," they said in unison, and the deal was made.

Jessica reached for the ketchup and sat down at the table with Stone's burger and fries, while he got another plate from the cabinet and began loading it up. Her leftovers became his buffet, and he heaped his plate with hungry anticipation, before heading toward the microwave.

They ate in total silence until they were down to the last couple of bites. Stone laid his fork on his plate and leaned back in his chair, more than a little surprised by what had occurred. He'd just shared a complete meal with a woman without saying a word, and couldn't remember ever feeling as welcome, or as comfortable as he did right now.

"That was great," he said quietly.

Jessica had an overwhelming urge to hug something, namely him. Instead, she took her dirty plate to the sink, gave it a quick rinse and then stuck it in the dishwasher.

Stone kept staring at the long, slender length of her legs poking out from beneath her pink T-shirt and wished to God he had the right to take off the shirt and take her to bed. But he'd given up that—and everything else she'd been willing to offer. As he leaned forward, the thought crossed his mind that he could have been wrong two years ago. And then he remembered Naomi and the hell they'd gone through and shoved the thought aside as nothing more than a momentary weakness.

Yet, as he watched her work, he noticed that she kept glancing out the window over the sink, as if trying to see through the dark. He frowned. Thanks to his big foot, she didn't have a lock on her door. He knew she was going to be afraid.

"Uh, Jessie, about your front door. It will be tomorrow before I can have it fixed, so maybe I should spend the night here. What do you think?"

She shut off the water and turned.

There was a smile on her face that made Stone nervous.

She leaned against the counter, her voice low and sultry.

"I think you're a genius," she said. "And I will feel so much safer knowing there's a cop in the house."

Stone kept remembering everything about her, including the taste of her lips and the way she molded herself to him. *Oh, man.*

But Jessica had other plans. Her smile slid sideways as he stood up. "Come with me," she said softly.

He followed her out of the kitchen and down the hallway to her bedroom. The sexy sway of her backside was a turn-on, and that odd, sleepy smile that she'd given him was driving him wild. The hint of her shape beneath that baggy shirt was more enticing than if she'd been naked. He followed her, so close that he could feel the air moving as she passed. She was almost within his grasp, and he was at the point of forgetting everything but the joy of making love to Jessie.

Jessica paused, then opened her closet door and reached up, handing Stone a pillow and two blankets as she stepped back and closed the door.

"Here you go. You're a bit tall for my couch, but I'm sure you'll find a way to manage." Her hand was in the middle of his back as she walked him out into the hall. "Thank you so much for offering to stay. I just wouldn't have slept a wink if you hadn't."

Having said all she could without making a fool of herself, Jessica pivoted and walked back into her bedroom, shutting herself in and Stone out.

He looked down at the bedding he was holding and then back up at the door, wondering where he'd gone wrong.

He'd been so close, and it had ended with a feather pillow and two yellow blankets.

He ambled into the living room and tossed the stuff on a nearby chair, then sat down and pulled off his shoes and shirt before making himself a bed. A few moments later, he turned off the lights and crawled onto the couch, telling himself this was no more than he deserved. As his head hit the pillow, he sighed and then stretched, angling his long legs up on the end of the furniture where they dangled in midair.

Five minutes later, he was still wrestling blankets and cursing his height and her couch when he heard Jessica coming up the hall in the dark. He heard her pause, then take a deep breath.

"Have everything you need?" she asked.

Everything but you. "Sure do."

"Well, okay, then. Good night, and I'll see you in the morning."

Stone listened until she was gone, then gave the top yellow blanket a vicious yank, which instantly uncovered his feet. He looked down at the decorative border lying across his shins and rolled his eyes.

Yellow ducks with little orange feet and beaks stared back at him from a strip of white satin. He kicked, trying to cover himself back up, and then gave it all up as a lost cause.

"Son of a miserable—"

Ignoring the fact that his butt would be hanging over the edge of the cushions, he rolled over on his side with his knees doubled up toward his chin and closed his eyes.

And then a hinge squeaked down the hall and he heard Jessica call out again.

"You sure you're all right?"

"Yes, I'm sure," he answered. Her door slammed shut as he was hammering at a place on his pillow. "Everything is just plain ducky."

Seven

Jessica woke to the sound of hammering and the feel of lips feathering the edge of her cheek. Her eyes popped open as she rolled over in disbelief. Stone was lying beside her.

"Stone Richardson, what *are* you doing?"

Tracing the edge of her lower lip with the tip of his finger, he leaned over and blew in her ear.

"Trying to make time with this crazy girl I know."

She pulled the covers up to her chin. "Get off my bed," she muttered. "I need to take a shower."

His eyebrows arched as a wry grin tilted the corner of his mouth. "That sounds good. I'm game."

He rolled over on top of her, pinning her to the bed, and wondered what the hell he was doing here. He'd only meant to wake her up, not crawl in bed with her, but one look had led to a few extra steps, and before he'd been able to stop himself, here he was, wanting and wishing and telling himself it was lust, not love, that he was feeling for Jessie.

The hammering noise kept getting louder. She glared. Between that racket and the thunder of her own pulse, it was all she could do to think.

"I am not taking a shower with a man who does not trust his own judgment, let alone mine."

A little angry that she'd called his hand so neatly, he feathered a kiss on the side of her neck and then muttered against her lips, "I never said I didn't trust you."

She started to give him a piece of her mind...at least, a

part of it that she knew she could trust, when she met his gaze. In spite of his bawdy, teasing manner, she saw something that gave her real hope. She would have sworn there was more than lust in his eyes. Her voice softened—slightly.

"Oh, so you're handing out remedies, are you? If you ask me, you're too old to be playing doctor."

"Well," he drawled, and slipped a hand on either side of her face. "If I promise it won't hurt a bit, could we—"

The hammering stopped. "Hey!" someone shouted, and the sound echoed down the hall and into her bedroom.

Jessica jerked as if she'd been slapped, and then kicked and rolled, tumbling Stone off of her and onto the floor.

"What the hell did you do that for?" he yelped, staring at her in disbelief.

"Someone's out there!" she hissed, pointing toward the doorway.

"Well, yes, Jessie Leigh, someone sure is. A carpenter has been fixing your door. Who in blazes did you think was doing all that hammering...a giant woodpecker?"

"Hey, in there! Is anybody home? I'm through out here!"

Stone crawled to his feet, brushing at the seat of his jeans.

"Be right there!" he yelled, then glared back at the mop-haired waif standing at the foot of the bed. "You may as well get dressed. I'd say the mood is pretty much broken."

She stared at the button fly of his jeans and arched a brow.

"What a shame! I hope it doesn't hurt."

A slow flush spread across his cheeks as he pivoted sharply and stalked out of the room.

Jessica jumped out of bed and slammed the door behind him, turning the lock to punctuate her mood.

"Fly specks," she mumbled, and stomped toward the

bathroom with single-minded intent. She needed a shower, and the colder, the better.

A short while later, she emerged wearing clean white shorts and a nearly new baby blue shirt tucked in at the waist. Barefoot, she paused in the hall before following the scent of fresh-brewed coffee.

Stone was standing in the kitchen, nursing a steaming cup of the brew and staring off into space.

Something about the loneliness of his stance made her hesitate, and the sharp-edged remark she'd been saving disappeared from her mind. She sauntered across the floor and took a cup from the cabinet, reminding herself to stay calm.

"Good morning," she said.

He grinned wryly and toasted her with his cup.

"So, my timing was off. I see I should have waited until after the shower. You're a whole lot friendlier after you've gotten wet."

Her face reddened as she pointed her empty cup like a fat, accusing finger.

"Listen, buddy. I'm trying to be sociable here. And I'm trying to forget that someone I thought I could trust was right there in my bed when I opened my eyes this morning, invading my space!"

Stone set his cup down, pretending great dismay.

"And I didn't see a thing! Well, damn, Jessie Leigh, where's my gun? I'll call headquarters right now and put out an APB."

In spite of herself, she started to grin, but Stone wasn't through playing the game. He took her grocery list from the cabinet.

"I'll need a description. Did you get a good look at his face?"

"You're funny," she said, and poured herself some coffee. "Ha. Ha. Ha."

Stone grinned and took away her coffee, then took her in his arms. In spite of her huffing and puffing, as always, she melted against him. This time, he didn't waste a breath on a warning. He just dipped his head, nuzzling the curve of her neck.

"You smell so sweet," he whispered, trailing his lips up to the lobe of her ear.

Jessica sighed. *Any minute now, I will tell him what I really think of men who can't make up their minds.*

He shifted his embrace, moving his hands from the middle of her back to the curve of her hips. When he pulled her close against him, then closer still, he groaned and then sighed, resting his chin at the top of her head.

"Ah, Jessie. I missed you, more than I care to admit."

Her mouth twisted wryly as she pressed her nose against the breadth of his chest. *He missed me? Dear Lord, I nearly died from doing without this man in my life, and he missed me?*

And then she sighed. Held fast against the man that he was, she couldn't move. In fact, she didn't want to move— totally forgot she should have moved. There was an unexpected measure of comfort and safety in being held so dearly.

It was way past time for Stone to go. He was already late for work, and he knew when he got there that word of last night's fiasco would have already preceded him, yet he just didn't care. He had a little unfinished business with a tousled-headed sprite. He brushed his lips near her stitches, then reluctantly turned her loose.

"Hey, Jessie."

Mesmerized by the moment they'd been sharing, Jessica swayed, then looked up.

"About this morning."

She blinked. Was he about to get serious again?

"You know...when we were in bed together?"

She nodded.

"I didn't forget myself or where I was or whom I was with—or the fact that the carpenter was here."

A frown split the middle of her forehead. What on earth was he getting at?

"Then what was it all about?" Jessica asked. "You made it perfectly clear two years ago that I wasn't what you wanted."

Stone's belly knotted as he stared into her face. "I never said I didn't want you, Jessie. I said, I'm not making the same mistake twice. Being a cop and being married don't always go hand in hand. I tried it, remember?"

But not with me. Yet Jessie couldn't bring herself to utter the words and suffer the humiliation of rejection. She pushed out of his arms and took several steps back, putting some distance between them before she spoke.

"I never asked you for anything, Stone Richardson, and I'm getting damned tired of trying to defend myself."

Stone wouldn't admit she was right, but he couldn't admit he was wrong. Instead, he made himself focus on the reason he was even in her house.

"Speaking of defenses, there's one more thing I'm going to remind you of before I leave. Try to stay out of trouble today, okay? And if you don't want to answer the phone, just turn on your machine. Busy signals give me the creeps."

He winked, and then he was gone.

Jessica was still trying to think of a scathing comeback when she heard him backing out of her driveway. She dashed into the living room and then came to an abrupt halt.

Her door! He'd replaced her whole door. A new set of keys and an advertising flyer were on the hall table next to a note addressed to her.

Dear Jessie,
Thought you'd appreciate the precaution, just in case some nut ever tries to kick in your door.

"Precaution? What precaution?"
She glanced at the door. It was white, just like her old

one had been. He'd even matched the beveled design. She stepped closer, peering along the surface. There was something about it that didn't seem quite—

She reached out and touched it, then frowned. "What on earth?"

She picked up the flyer beneath the keys, scanning the text. Once more, she looked back at the door, shaking her head in disbelief. Not only had Stone replaced her lock, but if the literature was to be believed, while she'd been sleeping, a carpenter had installed a genuine, guaranteed-against-break-in, Colonial white, exterior steel door.

Jessica couldn't quit staring.

"Why do I feel like I've just been incarcerated?"

Stone walked into headquarters and headed for his desk. To his relief, everyone seemed busy, too busy to bother with him. But the closer he got, the more certain he became that something was up. They were busy, all right. Too busy.

He glanced at his partner, who had kicked back in his chair and was grinning broadly. Stone paused at his desk and stared at a football helmet sitting upside down on top of his files.

"What the hell?"

As he picked it up, dozens of condoms fell out at his feet. Taped inside was a big red sign that read Play Safe!

The men in the room erupted in a loud round of laughter. Coupled with the rude innuendos they were tossing about, Stone knew he'd been had. He sighed. It had been too much to hope that the news wouldn't get around.

"Heard you got busted last night in the middle of a little slap-and-tackle session," Stryker said, and then chuckled at the play on words, as well as his own wit.

"Well, you heard wrong," Stone said, and started picking up condoms and tossing them back into the helmet.

Stryker laughed aloud. "The hell you say."

Stone grinned and tossed a condom on Stryker's desk. "Here, we're partners. Share and share alike."

"Does that mean we share everything?"

Stone threw a handful of condoms at Jack's head. "No way. Find your own woman. Jessie is mine." And then he froze. *Where the hell did that come from?* A little frightened by the intensity of his feelings, he began digging through the files on his desk and tried to pretend the words hadn't been spoken.

The smile slid off Jack Stryker's face. He hadn't seen Stone this involved with a woman since his divorce. "So, it's like that, is it?"

Stone refused to comment. After all, what could he say? *I don't want her, but I don't want anyone else to have her, either?* That sounded lame, even to him.

Frank Sanderson stepped out of his office. "Stryker! Richardson! If everyone is through playing, I want you both in my office—on the double!"

Stone tossed the last of the condoms into the helmet and glanced wistfully at his coffee cup. He'd already been thrown out of a bed on his butt, and now the chief was calling them on the carpet before he'd even sat down. The start to his day was looking less and less promising as the hours went on.

"Close the door," Sanderson said as they walked into his office.

"What's up, chief?" Stone asked.

Sanderson dropped into his chair and leaned back. "Where do we stand on the Stuart case?"

"Right now, pretty much in left field. Olivia Stuart's house had already been cleaned, and the room in which they found her had been restored to its natural order, although I talked to the maid who'd done the cleaning. Other than some things having been knocked off a table, which she thought had been done when Olivia fell, she'd noted nothing out of place. And there's no evidence of a break-in, although no one really thinks robbery was a motive. Burglars aren't in the habit of poisoning their victims."

Sanderson didn't like the news and glanced at Stone. "So, does your psychic stool pigeon have anything new to add to the pot?"

Stone bristled. "If it wasn't for her, someone would have gotten away with murder," he said shortly.

"Sorry," Sanderson said. "But so far, the facts we have are based on one woman's so-called vision. Exactly how much of what she's said can we count on?"

Stone leaned forward, bracing his hands on the chief's desk.

"We could ask a woman named Tinee Bloom. Yesterday, our little stool pigeon had one of her 'visions' and saved Mrs. Bloom's life. Now half the town thinks Jessie Hanson is an alien, and the other half thinks she's God's gift to Grand Springs."

Sanderson frowned. "I don't like this. Someone could ask a couple of the wrong questions and link her to the discovery of Olivia Stuart's murder."

"Well, I don't like it, either," Stone said. "But right now, there's not much we can do. She's trying to play it down, although it's pretty much a lost cause. The gossip around town is that it was probably her, anyway. We've let the fact be known that Olivia's body was still in the morgue, alluding to the supposition that medical personnel spotted the suspicious bruising and got curious, but from the gossip on the streets, it's going to be a miracle if anyone buys the theory."

Sanderson frowned. "I guess you're right." Then he stood up, a sense of purpose in his step as he circled his desk. "Okay, so here's what we're going to do. The mayor's funeral is later this morning. I want both of you to attend on behalf of the department. And while you're there, I think it would behoove us to watch the behavior of those who've come to pay their last respects."

"So you think the killer might show up to gloat?" Stryker asked.

Sanderson shrugged. "Stranger things have happened. At any rate, I want you both present."

"Yes, sir," they echoed.

"Then, that's that," Sanderson said. "Go catch some bad guys."

They started out the door when the chief called out. "Hey, Richardson."

Stone turned.

"Heard you made a pretty good catch last night."

Stone grinned. "Why, thank you, chief. Does this mean I'll be getting a raise?"

Sanderson grinned and threw something, hitting Stone on the side of the head. He looked down at the small foil packet lying at his feet, grinned wryly, then bent down and picked it up. Even the chief had been in on the joke.

Most of the town was expected to be at the funeral. And from the things Jessica had heard, everyone wanted to go. Partly because Olivia Stuart had been a well-respected member of the community, and partly because she'd been murdered.

But Jessica was the exception. Last night, she'd had no intention of going. And then, while Stone slept peacefully on her couch, she'd had the same dream again. This time, she'd been aware it was happening, and had tried with all of her might to focus on the killer's face. It hadn't happened.

She'd awakened, teary-eyed and full of guilt. If only she'd seen who committed the crime, then maybe Olivia could rest in peace. And because she now felt duty-bound to make every effort to bring Olivia's killer to justice, she'd made a sudden decision to go to the service. Maybe just being in the same room with Olivia's body would evoke a vision she had yet to experience. And maybe, if she got all the answers to the questions, then this thing that kept happening to her would stop. There was nothing that would make Jessica happier. Then she amended that thought. Stone Richardson could tell her he loved her. *That* would make her happy. Extremely happy.

Jack Stryker tugged at his necktie and leaned over to whisper in Stone's ear. "I've never looked for suspects at a funeral before. I don't know about you, but I feel like I'm trespassing when I should be paying my respects."

Stone nodded and shifted in his seat. It had been their plan to sit at the rear of the church, hoping it would give them a better view of everyone who came inside. But a city councilman had seen them and insisted they sit next to him. Not wanting to make a big scene, they'd done so. Now the pews at St. Veronica's were filling up at record speed and it hardly mattered where they were sitting. Within a few short minutes, the majority of attendees would be standing in the back of the church, as well as out on the steps and onto the lawn.

Ornate sprays of flowers were everywhere: hanging on walls, mounted on stands, draped upon the kneeling rails surrounding the pulpit. A massive spray of white roses adorned the closed lid of the casket, upon which was a silver ribbon with the word *Mother* spelled out in an elaborate scroll.

Stone winced. Jack was right. Today, Hal and Eve Stuart were burying their mother and he was here looking for a killer among the mourners. It was obscene.

Jack elbowed Stone as a man took a seat in the pew directly across from them. "Who's he?"

Stone glanced to his right, recognizing the well-dressed man who'd been seated next to one of the bankers. "That's Maxwell Brown. He's a businessman here in town."

"Oh."

Just as the minister stepped up to the pulpit, Stone became aware of a change in the pattern of voices behind them. The hushed whispers were moving to a level of twitters and gasps. Curious as to who, or what, could have caused such a stir, he turned to see, and then his belly gave a nervous pitch.

"Oh, no."

"What is it?" Jack whispered.

"See for yourself."

Jack turned just as Jessica Hanson slipped into a vacant seat near the back of the church. He glanced at Stone, who seemed stunned by her appearance.

"So what's the big deal?" he asked.

"Didn't you hear them?" Stone asked.

"Hear who?" Jack muttered.

"Them." He angled his head toward the rest of the congregation. "Look at them whispering among themselves. They'll probably be expecting her to go into some psychic trance in the middle of the service."

"Oh, yeah, I see what you mean," Jack said, and then shrugged. "Look at it this way. She's got just as much right to be here as the next person, and she can't help what everyone thinks."

Stone refused to be swayed. His gut instinct told him that Jessie's appearance at the funeral was not a smooth move. He turned just as the minister lifted his arms as a signal for the congregation to stand. Stone girded himself for the oncoming service. The family was coming into the church.

Jessica had parked on a side street a couple of blocks from the church, and counted herself lucky to have found a space so close. It looked as if half the city had come to pay their last respects to Olivia Stuart. She smoothed the wrinkles from her plain blue suit, ran her fingers through her hair, fluffing it into a semblance of order, and started toward the church. Halfway down the block, someone called her name.

"Yoo-hoo! Jessica! It's me, Sheila. Wait up!"

Oh, no. Jessica increased her pace, hoping that Sheila

Biggers would give up the chase. Her hope was in vain as Sheila came up behind her, grabbing her elbow to slow her down.

"Jessica! Didn't you hear me calling you?"

Jessica managed a smile. "Sorry, I guess my mind was a million miles away."

"Yes, I suppose it was," Sheila said.

Jessica gave the woman a sidelong glance. What did she mean by that?

"Say, there's something I've been meaning to ask you," Sheila said, all but running to keep up with Jessica's stride.

"Wow, do you believe the turnout?" Jessica asked, trying desperately to change the subject.

"Monday at work someone called me and told me my house was on fire."

Jessica kept walking. "The boss told me. I'm really sorry. Was much of it ruined?"

Sheila grabbed Jessica's arm. "Hey, slow down a minute, will you? Your legs are longer than mine."

Jessica tried a change of subject. "If we delay much longer, we won't get a seat."

"It was you, wasn't it? The woman who called."

Jessica remained mute.

"I heard about you saving that woman's life and all," Sheila continued, as if Jessica had already answered. "And you saved my house from burning down, too. Even if you don't want to admit it."

"Don't you think that's a bit far-fetched?" Jessica asked.

Sheila's gaze moved to the stitches just below Jessica's bangs. "How do you do it? See the future, I mean? I've read about people who get psychic after suffering a blow to the head. Is that what happened to you?"

Jessica wished that she'd never left home.

"Look, Sheila. The only thing I've done is take time off from work until my stitches come out. I do not *see* into anyone's future. I never have. I never will."

It wasn't an actual lie. Except for Tinee Bloom's near meet with death, most of what she'd seen had already happened.

"Look at the crowd. We'd better hurry," she added.

Sheila gave her co-worker a curious glance. "You go on ahead. I'm supposed to meet my husband, Don, outside the church."

Thankful to be off the hook, Jessica smiled and waved. "It was good to see you."

But Sheila wasn't quite through with her yet.

"Hey, Jessica."

Jessie paused and turned.

"You scare me a little, but thanks all the same."

Jessica made straight for the doorway before someone else made comments she was in no mood to hear. And yet, the moment she walked into the church, she heard the whispers. Lifting her chin, she began looking for a seat, putting a calm face on a situation that threatened to explode.

Oh, cat scratches. What was I thinking?

Centered between an elderly man and a middle-aged woman, she gave them both a polite nod as she sat, purposefully fixing her gaze upon the pulpit at the front of the church and the rose-covered coffin in front of the altar.

Poor Olivia. I'm so sorry for the tragic end of your life.

"I say…Miss Hanson, isn't it?"

Jessica turned. "Yes, I'm Jessica Hanson."

Geraldine Mylam nodded. "I thought it was you."

Jessica turned toward the minister, who was about to take his place behind the pulpit.

Not to be deterred, the woman continued the conversation without a pause. "My name is Mylam. Geraldine Mylam, but I suppose you knew that."

Once again, Jessica turned. "No, ma'am, I don't believe we've met."

"Oh, I know that," Geraldine said. "But I just figured

since you were psychic and all that you would know who I was without my having to say.''

Distracted by the woman's comments, she looked up just as Stone Richardson looked back. Their gazes locked and Jessica's heart skipped a beat. His expression was not that of a happy man. *Barf bag!*

Geraldine Mylam continued as if Jessica was still paying attention, which she was not. ''You know, I lost my dear Terrance nearly five years ago. I was wondering if you could ask him something for me.''

Stone glared, then turned around to face the front, and the link was broken. Jessica jerked like a fish that had been tossed back in a pond.

''Excuse me,'' she muttered. ''I didn't hear what you said.''

''Terrance. I asked you if you could talk to Terrance for me.''

Now Jessica was completely lost. ''I'm sorry, but who is Terrance?''

Geraldine patted Jessica's arm, as if she was a child. ''Why, he's my husband.''

''Why would you want *me* to talk to your husband?''

Geraldine leaned closer so that her request would not be overheard.

''I want you to ask him what he did with my grandmother's silver gravy boat. It's been in my family for generations, and I can't find it anywhere.''

Jessica stared at the woman as if she'd lost her senses. ''I'm sorry, Mrs.…''

''Mylam. Geraldine Mylam.''

Jessica sighed. ''Sorry. It's been a long day. But I don't understand. Why don't you just ask your husband yourself?''

Geraldine's eyebrows arched in surprise. ''Why, because he's dead. But I thought with your powers and all that you could—''

''All rise.''

The minister's voice resonated within the walls, breaking Geraldine Mylam's train of thought, and saving Jessica from having to come up with an answer that didn't sound like a lie.

Hal Stuart entered the church, accompanied by his sister, Eve, and her little daughter, Molly. Jessica looked, then looked away, feeling guilty for watching them in their time of grief.

Hal Stuart walked like a man going to a hanging. His face was devoid of expression, while his sister, Eve, could hardly see to walk through the tears streaming down her face. Molly clung to her mother's hand and ducked her head, looking uncomfortable at being the focus of everyone's attention.

Sympathetic murmurs sifted among the mourners as the family made their way down the aisle to the front of the church and took a seat on the very first pew.

"You may be seated," the minister said, and the sound of three hundred and fifty people sitting down at once was like a wave breaking against the shore, washing up and then over the breakers until all the power within it slid out in a whoosh.

The service began.

A short while later, Jessica watched as Eve Stuart made her way to the pulpit, leaving her daughter in her uncle Hal's care. Jessica's heart ached for the family. She knew what it felt like to lose one's parents. Her eyes teared as she tried to focus on something besides the heartbreak in the young woman's voice. It was an impossible task. Eve Stuart proceeded with a testimony that would have made her mother quite proud.

And while it was all Eve could do to get through what she wanted to say without sobbing aloud, Hal seemed to be dealing with his loss in a different manner. He spoke in measured tones without once looking up from the paper before him. After all, Jessica thought, he was the man of the family. It behooved him to be stoic.

And finally it was over.

Jessica breathed a sigh of relief. In a way, she was disappointed that she hadn't had a revelation that would have provided some much-needed answers. But on the other hand, she hadn't given full thought as to what would have happened if she'd flipped out in front of the entire congregation.

She glanced up. People were moving around at the front, and it dawned on her that they were going to open the casket for public viewing.

"No," she muttered, telling herself that she wouldn't—couldn't—go.

The elderly fellow to her right jerked, and Jessica realized that he'd nodded off.

"Excuse me?" he said. "What was that you said?"

"I'm sorry," Jessica said. "It was nothing."

Satisfied that he hadn't done anything wrong, he reached for his cane as the people in the pew in front of them rose from their seats.

"Oh, no," Jessica said, realizing that if she didn't do something fast, she was going to be swept along with the crowd. And she didn't need to go look at Olivia's body. She'd already seen her die.

Suddenly it was their turn to stand. She grabbed her purse and looked around behind her, searching for the best and least conspicuous manner in which to walk out, when someone took her by the elbow and shoved her into the line. It was the old fellow, who had been sitting beside her.

Now he pays attention, Jessica thought.

"After you, miss," he said.

She was trapped. Either she turned and walked out in plain sight of everyone here, which would probably cause even more gossip, or she went through the motions like everyone else and prayed that nothing untoward would happen. Reluctantly, Jessica opted for the line of least re-

sistance and moved down the aisle past the pew where
Stone was sitting.

Don't look at him. Don't look at him.

True to form, she ignored her instincts and looked.
There was a warning in his eyes she couldn't miss. She
frowned back, giving him her best "mind your own business" look, and then moved on. Yet the closer she came
to the casket, the more panicked she became. Her palms
were sweating and her heart was skipping beats like crazy.

Don't look at her. Don't look at her.

Again, her instincts were warning her against something
she couldn't see. All around her, people were sniffing,
some openly crying. She felt like a fake in a sea of pure
grief. She wasn't nearly as sad for Olivia Stuart as she was
afraid for herself.

Don't look. Don't look.

And then she saw the end of the casket coming into
view, and like a magnet, her eyes were drawn to the
woman within. In that moment, a rush of kindred spirit all
but overwhelmed her.

Olivia...Olivia...you weren't alone. I saw. I saw.

She took a deep breath, inhaling the unexpected but
overpowering scent of gardenias. She walked away, unaware of the steady stream of tears flowing down her face.

Outside the church, someone tapped her on the arm.

"Dear, are you all right?"

Jessica blinked, then looked up. It was the woman
who'd sat beside her.

"What? Oh, yes, I'm fine," Jessica said.

Geraldine handed her some tissues. "Didn't she look
nice? I always say, it's easier to give them up when they
go out looking so lifelike and all."

"Thank you for the tissues." There was nothing else
Jessica could think to say.

"You're welcome, dear," Geraldine said, and patted
Jessica once more before turning away.

In the brief moment when the woman's hand was on

her arm, Jessica suddenly saw in her mind, as plain as the sunlight that was up in the sky, an ornate but tarnished gravy boat sitting on a shelf. Beside it, a basket with a broken handle, and above it, three fly rods, with fishing line dangling and covered in spiderwebs and dust.

"Fishing," Jessica said suddenly, and Geraldine turned.

"Excuse me, dear? Did you say something to me?"

Jessica stared unblinking into the scene before her. "The gravy boat. It's at the cabin. He took it fishing."

Blind to the crowds of people moving past them, Geraldine Mylam's eyes widened as she realized what the girl had just done. In her own way, Jessica Hanson *had* talked to Terrance Mylam.

"Oh." She reached out and touched Jessica's hair, then her cheek, then her arm. "Oh, my."

Jessica took a step back, suddenly aware that something momentous had happened.

"I, uh…"

To her dismay, Geraldine Mylam made the sign of the cross then grabbed Jessica's hand and kissed it before scurrying away.

Still a little stunned by what had just happened, her muse was broken by an angry voice next to her ear.

"What was that all about?"

She turned around. It was Stone and his partner, Jack Stryker.

There was a shocked expression on her face. "I'm not sure, but I think I just had my first séance."

Stone snorted in disgust while Jack started to grin.

"What on earth possessed you to come here, anyway?" Stone asked, glancing nervously around as the people moved past, many giving them more than just curious glances.

Jessica looked at him, and then looked away. "Like everyone else…I just came to say goodbye."

Eight

Jessica walked away, leaving Stone and Jack outside the church. Stone's first reaction was to follow her, but he hesitated, and while he was debating with himself, Jack interrupted his train of thought.

"What did you think about the service?" Jack asked.

Stone gave Jessica one last glance, and then turned back to his partner.

"You want the truth?"

Jack nodded.

"I thought Hal Stuart was more nervous than grief-stricken."

A wry grin broke across Stryker's face. "That's why we make such good partners," he said. "We read people the same way."

Stone glanced at a man who was coming down the steps of the church. "Then, how do you read that one?" he asked.

Jack turned to look, and then whistled beneath his breath.

"Oh, him. He's in the dough."

"What do you mean by that?" Stone asked, watching as the man stopped to speak to several people along his way to a waiting limo.

"That's Alex Bennett. He could buy and sell everyone in this town a hundred times over. He's big on charities, always donating, always on the society page. At one time or another, he's probably worked on a dozen events with Olivia Stuart."

Stone wrote down Alex Bennett's name in his notebook.

"What are you doing?" Jack asked.

"Reminding myself to check him out," Stone said. "At this point, everyone is suspect, remember?"

"I suppose, but I don't think Bennett is dirty. I hear he's as straight as they come."

"Hey, look who's here," Stryker said, pointing toward a tall blond man just coming out of the door. "Isn't that the guy who claimed to have lost his memory? Wonder what he's doing here?"

Stone shrugged. "Who knows? At any rate, so far nothing has turned up on him through the system."

Stryker was glancing out across the crowd as Stone slipped his notebook back in his pocket and absently turned to check on Jessica's progress. An immediate panic hit him and he groaned.

"Oh, no."

Jack pivoted, following Stone's gaze to focus on a gathering crowd up the block.

"Wonder what that's all about?"

"It's Jessie. I think they've got her cornered," Stone said, and started to run.

Like the good partner he was, Stryker was right behind him.

"Come on, Miss Hanson. All you have to do is pick some numbers out of the air." Jessica tried to push past the man who was blocking her way and waving a paper beneath her nose.

"Please, let me pass. I can't see into the future, and even if I did, I wouldn't be playing the lottery," Jessica said.

"We'll split it fifty-fifty," he persisted.

She turned, frantically looking for an avenue of escape from the people who were gathering around her. All she could see were faces of strangers, coming closer—some smiling, some curious, some of them even seeming afraid of her. And yet they persisted, staring and pushing.

A woman who appeared to be in her early twenties grabbed Jessica by the arm. "I'm a singer. I'm going to Nashville next week to cut a demo tape. Tell me, Miss Hanson. Am I going to be a star?"

An elderly woman stepped out of the crowd. "My Tilly is lost. I've called and I've called but she hasn't come home. Her name is Chantilly de Plume. Please, Miss Hanson, help me find my Tilly cat."

And then a man in a long, dark coat shoved his way into the small inner circle of space where she stood. His clothing reeked of filth. His pale eyes glittered; his hair was long and unkempt. Clutching a Bible to his chest, he pointed a gnarled finger at Jessica and started to shout. "Cursed is woman…spawn of the devil…temptress of Adam in the Garden of Eden."

It was all too much for Jessica to endure. She started to run, pushing past the man and his Bible and into the crowd. Voices rose and fell around her in a jumble of pleas and promises. Fingers clawed at her clothing and at her skin, as if by touch alone some of her magic might rub off on them. Just when she thought they would pull her under, she heard a rough voice and an angry shout. It was Stone!

"Get back, all of you! Leave her the hell alone or I'll put you all under arrest!"

Jessica slumped against him as he slid his arm around her shoulders for support. With bulldog intent, he began moving her through the crowd. Behind them, she heard Jack Stryker ordering the people to disburse, reminding them they were at a funeral and not a fair.

And suddenly they broke free of the mass and Jessica started to shake.

"Hang in there, honey," Stone said softly, and kept moving her down the block.

She couldn't speak. It was all she could do to keep putting one foot in front of the other.

Stone kept his eye on her face all the way to her car. She was pale and trembling, and he was afraid to say more for fear she would burst into tears. And then they were there.

"Jessie, give me your keys."

She opened her purse, but her hands were shaking. Her fingers trembled so badly she couldn't grasp anything but air. In defeat, she handed Stone the purse.

He thrust his hand inside and, seconds later, pulled out her keys and unlocked the car. In her haste to get inside, she almost bumped her head on the door.

"Easy does it," he warned, and protected her forehead with his hand as she sat, then dropped her purse in her lap as she was reaching for a seat belt.

"Hurry," Jessica whispered, glancing out the windshield with a near-frantic look.

Stone slid behind the wheel and closed the door, shutting out the street noise and isolating themselves even further.

"Jessie, are you—"

Her voice was shaking, but the gaze she turned on him was wide-eyed and cold. "Take me home. I want to go home."

This time when they reached her front door, he didn't ask her for her key. He had it in his hand. The tumblers clicked, the lock turned, and the door swung open.

Jessica stepped inside. Sanctuary! And for the first time since the ugly incident outside the church had begun, she felt a semblance of her sanity returning. Silently, she dropped her purse on the hall table and started down the hall when Stone's voice stopped her intent.

"Jessie, honey—"

She turned around. If he hadn't been so close, she might have made it to her room without coming undone. But his hand was on her arm, and there was a plea in his eyes she couldn't ignore.

Her chin trembled, and her lips began to quiver. Stone cursed once beneath his breath and took her in his arms. She inhaled swiftly, then exhaled on a sob.

"Oh, Stone. Why? Why is this happening to me?"

He lifted her off her feet and into his arms. He had no answers to give her, but she could have everything else of him that she wanted. Right now, denying himself or her was impossible.

When he set her on her bed, she rolled to the middle and curled up in a ball. Although the day had been warm, she was shivering. Stone knew it was shock. He bent down and pulled off her shoes, then covered her with an afghan that had been lying at the foot of her bed. When she clutched at it in desperation and closed her eyes, his heart sank. If this didn't drive her crazy, then nothing ever would.

He glanced at the time. Jack would be along any minute to pick him up, but he didn't want her to be alone. He thought of Brenda and started out of the room to make a call when Jessica called out to him.

"Where are you going?" she asked.

"To make a couple of calls. I'll be right—"

"Don't leave me."

She didn't have to ask twice. He crawled into bed beside her and then rolled her, afghan and all, into his arms. She shivered and buried her nose against his chest. Long minutes passed, during which Jessica began to relax. Just when he thought that she might be falling asleep, she spoke.

"Stone?"

"What is it, honey?"

"Oh, Stone."

The quiet pain in her voice broke his heart.

He looked down, lightly brushing the ragged bangs from her forehead. His voice was as soft as the kiss he feathered across her brow.

"Ah, Jessie, I'm so, so sorry." And in that moment,

he'd never been more honest with himself. He *was* sorry.
For so many, many things.

She looked up. Any minute now she was going to wake
up and find out this was all a bad dream. Things like this
didn't happen to people like her. She was an accountant.
She was supposed to be keeping track of other people's
money, not their fates. And here she was, lying in the arms
of the man of her dreams, and it was for all the wrong
reasons.

"I'm sorry, too."

His eyes darkened and a frown creased his forehead.
"Jessie, in all honesty, the last two years have been lonely
without you, but I don't want to be part of your regret."

She touched the side of his face, feeling the strength in
his jaw and the tension in a muscle jerking beneath her
fingertips.

"Then, what do you want, Stone Richardson? Tell me.
I need something to get past all this hell. Is there a magic
word I don't know?"

He inhaled slowly as his mouth brushed the surface of
her lips.

"You want magic? Then, Jessie Leigh, all you have to
do is say please."

She put her arms around his neck.

His lips trailed the side of her cheek, then downward,
following the path of her heartbeat as it raced throughout
her body. When he paused at the base of her throat, nip-
ping at her skin with the edge of his teeth, she gasped and
then sighed. And when he tossed the afghan aside, cov-
ering her with himself, she moaned.

"Stone. Oh, Stone."

He lifted his head, staring straight into her eyes.

"Say it," he begged. "Say it, Jessie."

She was shaking, but this time, not from shock or fear.
It was need that was making her come undone. She cupped
the back of his head with her hands, urging him to come
closer. He didn't need a second invitation.

"Stone…"

"What, honey?"

"Please."

He said something soft beneath his breath that she didn't understand, and then she was lost to everything but the man above her.

The weight of his body was like an anchor to keep her from flying away. Sensations came, one after the other, filling her heart and her mind: the touch of his hand upon her face, the sweep of his mouth across her brow—beneath the lobe of her ear, upon her lips. The sweep of his breath against her eyelids was only less enticing than knowing and feeling how much he wanted to make love to her.

There was no thought, no hesitation, no sense of shame or guilt within either of them that could stop what was about to happen. There was nothing to stop them…except a knock on the door.

And it came, rudely shattering the moment between them. Stone tore his mouth from Jessie's lips and buried his face against her neck with a groan. Through one long, shuddering breath after the other, he held her until his heart ceased the race and hit a normal rhythm.

The knock sounded again. This time louder.

"Damn," he said softly.

Jessica covered her face with her hands as he rolled off her body. All she could think was how close they'd come to losing total control.

At the doorway, he stopped, unable to leave her this way.

"Jessie, don't. For God's sake, don't be ashamed."

She sat up on the side of the bed, then started straightening her clothes and smoothing her hair.

"Shame has nothing to do with it," she said shortly. "That's probably your partner. You'd better answer the door before he knocks it down."

Stone walked out, muttering beneath his breath. This wasn't the first time she'd come undone in his arms, but visions of his life with Naomi were starting to haunt him. He lived with too many memories of the fights they'd had, and all because he was a cop and she couldn't cope. He groaned. Dear God, please don't let this be happening again.

Stone opened the door. It was Stryker, and he had Jessie's sister in tow.

"I met her coming out of the church on the way back to the car. Figured your girl might need some TLC," Jack said.

Stone wondered if he looked as startled as he felt. He'd intended to call Brenda himself, but not in the middle of making love to her sister.

"Is she okay?" Jack asked.

"She will be," Stone said.

Jack nodded. "Then, I'll be in the car when you're ready to go."

"Just give me a couple of minutes," Stone said. "I need to talk to Brenda before I leave."

Brenda stepped in, shutting the door behind her. For several moments, they looked at each other in total silence. Finally, Brenda's lips firmed.

"I appreciate the fact that you seem to keep showing up just when Jessie needs you most."

Stone sighed and ran his fingers through his hair. "Why do I think there's a *but* coming next?"

She folded her hands in front of her and fixed Stone with a cool stare. "Maybe because you're such a good detective?"

A slight grin lifted a corner of his mouth. "Come on, Brenda. Spit it out. You didn't used to be hesitant—about anything."

She flushed slightly but held her ground. "Well now, that was years ago, wasn't it? And we all had our quirks and hang-ups back then."

This time, it was Stone's turn to flush. "Score one for you, kiddo."

Brenda relented slightly. "I'm not shooting for scores. I'm only concerned now because Jessie is my sister and I'm all she's got."

And that's all my fault. If Jessie had her way, we'd be together.

"I've got to ask this," she said.

He shrugged. "I have nothing to hide."

"Are you over Naomi?"

"Not only yes, but hell, yes," Stone said shortly.

Brenda wanted to relax, but that was only half of what she needed to know.

"Good. You're whole and healed. But that doesn't tell me where your intentions toward Jessie are going." She held up her hand before he could speak. "Don't answer that, because it's not really my business. All I'm asking is, just please don't hurt her." Then the expression on Brenda's face lightened as Jessica came into the room.

"Jessie, I—"

Jessica paused, looking at Brenda without expression. "Oh, it's you," she mumbled, and looked away.

Brenda frowned. This cold, casual woman wasn't the Jessie she knew. She glanced at Jessica and then at Stone, then back again, wondering exactly what she had interrupted.

"Look," she said. "If I've come at a bad time, just say so and I'll be gone, but you know—"

Jessica laughed, an abrupt burst of sound that held no joy. "Sister, dear, today has been hell. So if you came to say 'I told you so,' then I suggest you save it for another day."

She started into the kitchen, when Stone grabbed her arm. His grip was firm, but the tone of his voice was even firmer.

"Damn it, Jessie, just cut the bull. No one hates what's been happening to you worse than we do, so don't take your frustration out on us. We're here *for* you, not to take you apart."

She flinched, unable to meet his gaze. He continued as if she was paying attention.

"Now that Brenda's here, I'd better get back to work. However, I will come by tonight to check on you, so if you want something in between time, don't hesitate to let me know."

She glanced up, a wary, waiting look on her face. "You don't have to bother, you know."

He smiled, and Jessica shuddered.

"Oh, but I do," Stone said softly. "There's some unfinished business between us, and I'm not much good at sleeping when I've left something undone."

Before she could object, he bent down and pulled her into his arms. The kiss was brief, but there was nothing friendly about it. It held a hint of warning, as well as promise. And when he turned her loose, he didn't look back.

"Brenda...it was good to see you again," Stone said. "Lock the door behind me."

Without thinking, she did as he ordered. When he was gone, she turned toward Jessie with a look of determination.

"Sit yourself down, baby sister. I have many questions to ask you and I want answers now."

"As long as you don't ask me to look into your future, you've got yourself a deal," Jessica muttered, and dropped into a nearby chair in defeat.

It was almost time to call the day quits when Stone pulled up in front of the precinct.

"I'll start the paperwork," Stryker said. "You go talk to the chief."

"Thanks a lot," Stone said. "And what do I tell him? We don't know a damn thing more about the mayor's murder than we did this morning."

Jack grinned. "Then, I guess that's what you'll say."

Stone cursed beneath his breath. "Some partner you are. Just get your butt out of my car."

Stryker laughed. "See you upstairs."

Stone pulled around the side of the building to the parking lot, locking the car as he got out. His mind was in turmoil as he sifted through the events of the day. The only ongoing connection to Olivia Stuart's murder was the town's growing suspicion that Jessica Hanson knew more than she should about someone's death. In fact, the people of Grand Springs were giving Jessie far too much credit for far too many things. All Stone knew was that Jessie was lucky as hell that she could prove where she'd been while Olivia was being stabbed with a needle full of poison. His hand was on the door when a man stepped in front of him, impeding his progress.

"Just a minute, Richardson. I want to talk to you."

Stone stifled what he'd been about to say. Granted Hal Stuart seemed rude, but considering the kind of day the man had had, Stone was willing to give him the benefit of the doubt.

"Sure thing, Hal," Stone said. "Want to come inside?"

Hal glanced at his watch and then shook his head. "No. Besides, what I want to know won't take long."

There was something about Hal's manner that still didn't sit right with Stone, but he let the thought slide.

"How can I help you?" Stone asked.

Hal's face was tight with anger, his eyes glittering dangerously. "I want to know if there's any truth to the gossip I've been hearing about my mother's death."

Stone flinched. "I don't know," he said quietly. "What have you heard?"

"That Jessica Hanson claims she had some sort of psychic vision and saw my mother being murdered. Now, if that's so, then why isn't someone in custody?"

Stone glanced around. "Look, Hal, why don't you come inside where we can—"

Hal was shaking with anger. "Don't give me the runaround," he said. "This is my mother we're talking about. I want some answers, and I want them now!"

"Okay, then, I'll tell you what I know. Yes, we were alerted to the fact that your mother's death might not have been natural. And, while that proved true, there is little else we know that will help toward the apprehension of the killer."

Hal wouldn't let up. "Was it Jessica Hanson? Is it true what I've been hearing?"

Stone hid his frustration. "I don't know what you've been hearing, but I can tell you that it was Jessica, and while she claims to have seen your mother being attacked, she did not ever *see* the killer's face. All she *saw* in her vision was someone shoving a hypodermic needle in the back of your mother's leg."

Hal winced, and then paled.

"Sorry," Stone said. "But you asked for the truth."

It seemed as if all the fight went out of Hal at once. He slumped against the building and covered his face with his hands.

"My God," he muttered. "This is hell! Pure hell! Today I buried my mother, and the investigation into her death was spawned from some psychic's vision! I feel like I'm caught in the 'Twilight Zone.'"

Stone put his hand on Hal's shoulder. "Are you all right?"

Hal shuddered, then pushed himself away from the wall. "She's sure? I mean, Jessica... Is she sure she can't help find the killer?"

"Sorry," Stone said. "It seems she has no control over what she sees. What comes, comes, and then it's gone."

Hal's shoulders slumped. "Well, then," he mumbled, and glanced up at Stone with an apologetic look. "Sorry if I sounded abrupt. It's been a bad day."

"Don't worry about it," Stone said. "I understand...and for what it's worth, you and your family have my deepest sympathies."

Hal nodded. "I'll pass your condolences along to my sister."

With that, he walked away, leaving Stone with an empty feeling for having been unable to help someone in need.

And then he remembered where he'd been going before Hal Stuart had so rudely interrupted, and headed into the building. The day wasn't over yet. He still had to talk to the chief.

Brenda handed the pizza delivery boy his money, along with a generous tip, and then shut and locked the door before carrying the aromatic box into the kitchen.

"Dinner is served," she said, waving the box beneath Jessica's nose.

"I'm not all that hungry," Jessica said.

"That's what you always say, and then wind up eating mine and yours, too."

Jessica grinned. It felt good to be doing something normal, like arguing with her sister over slices of pizza.

"What do you want to drink?" she asked, holding two different cans of pop in the air.

Brenda pointed to the one on the left. "I'll have that one on ice."

Jessica reached in the cabinet for a glass just as Brenda started to add, "Oh, and Jessie, don't—"

"I know. I know," Jessica said. "Don't float your ice when I pour in the pop."

Brenda grinned.

"You're so weird," Jessica muttered.

"But you love me," Brenda reminded her.

All the teasing disappeared between them, and a second later, they were in each other's arms.

"It will be all right," Brenda said, holding her sister tight.

Jessica soaked up the brief taste of comfort and then sat down at the table.

"Oh, I know that." And then she amended, "At least I tell myself that it will. It's what keeps me going."

"Yeah, that and a big cop we both know," Brenda said, and lifted out the first slice of pizza onto her plate.

A little embarrassed at first, Jessica didn't answer. How does one admit to falling in love with a man your sister once dated?

"Want one or two?" Brenda asked, dangling a second slice of pizza over Jessica's plate.

"Oh, one for now," Jessie said, and handed Brenda a napkin.

"I need a fork," Brenda said.

"Not with pizza! And not in my house!"

Brenda laughed. "Some things never change."

For a time, quiet descended upon the pair as they sat in comfortable silence, eating and drinking and taking satisfaction in being together. Four pizza slices from finishing it off, both Brenda and Jessica shoved back their plates with a groan.

"I can't eat another bite," Jessica said.

Brenda gave the congealing pizza one last look and made herself get up.

"I've got to be going. I have an early appointment tomorrow." Then she rolled her eyes. "Got a client who wants her boudoir redecorated in pink and black. And she wants to discuss this on a Sunday. Can't you just see it?"

Jessica laughed. "No, thank goodness. That's one sight from which I've been spared."

Brenda's grin slipped. "Oh, Jessie, I didn't mean that the way it sounded."

"Well, I did," Jessica said. "I need to laugh about this or I will go mad."

She followed her sister to the door and then waited while Brenda began gathering up her things.

"Hey, sis."

Brenda turned.

"Thank you," Jessica said.

"For what?" Brenda asked. "You paid for the pizza."

"I don't know. For being my sister, I guess."

Brenda's smile wavered. "It's entirely my pleasure."

"Yes, well, drive careful," Jessica said.

Brenda started out the door, then stopped and looked back.

"Hey, Jessie, is there anything you should tell me about driving home?"

Jessica grinned. "Yes. Watch out for the stop sign at the end of your street."

Brenda gasped. "Why?"

"Because you always run it. One of these days you're going to get a ticket."

Brenda grinned. "Oh, you! I thought you were going to tell me something I didn't already know."

Jessica followed her out. When Brenda was at her car, she stopped again, and this time, there was a more serious expression on her face when she turned.

"Jessie...about Stone."

"What about him?" Jessica muttered.

"He's a good man. If there's something going on between you, then let it happen."

Jessica stifled an impulse to shriek. Something going on? Why, no! Nothing but an imminent explosion of passion and lust.

"There's nothing between us but his misguided sense of duty. Until I whacked my head, he'd written me off his list. When all this mess is over, he'll disappear out of my life because that's the way he wants it."

"I don't know," Brenda said thoughtfully. "I wouldn't be so sure."

Jessica frowned. "Then you know something I don't."

Brenda winked. "Of course I do. I'm your big sister, aren't I?"

Jessica stood on the porch and waved as Brenda drove away, wondering what that cryptic parting shot meant.

"Bee snot. I'm the one who's supposed to be psychic, not her."

Just as she started into the house, another car pulled up

the driveway. She made herself stand when she wanted to hide.

It was Stone. He'd come back as he'd promised, and it was that very promise that was making her nervous. If she remembered correctly, it was something about unfinished business and leaving things undone.

She held her ground as he got out and shut the door. But to her surprise, he stayed by the car. Jessica held her breath—waiting. She looked past his square jaw and broad shoulders to his eyes, trying to read what he was thinking. It was impossible. Another long moment passed, and Stone reached for the door handle.

"So, do you want me to go home?"

Muddy feet. He's making me choose! Jessica lifted her chin. "I have pizza."

A slow grin broke the solemnity of his expression. "Are you trying to bribe an officer of the law?"

"I don't know," she said, and when he started toward her, she took a defensive step back toward the door. "*Can* you be bribed?"

He came up the steps without slowing down. "Depends on how much pizza you're offering," he said softly.

Jessica was now inside the house, and he was still coming on.

"I have four slices."

He kicked the door shut, and then picked her up before she could run, whispering against her cheek. "That's just about enough."

"To do what?" Jessica said as she slipped her arms around his neck and held on.

There was a hot glitter in his eyes as he looked down at her face. "To get us in trouble."

Nine

Worry shadowed Jessica's expression. In the same moment Stone saw it, he felt the walls coming back up between them again. He stopped in the darkened hallway with her still in his arms. The doorway to her bedroom beckoned, and as much as he wanted to make love to her, he had to make sure she understood the rules. He stood her on her feet and then turned her loose, making sure that she felt no coercion from him.

"Jessie, I'm not going to lie to you. I want to make love to you, more than I'm even willing to admit. But it won't happen unless you're willing."

His face was shadowed, but Jessica didn't need bright lights to see past Stone's hesitation. Even the fact that she knew why he was stalling didn't help. They'd been down this road before, and she wondered why she was even contemplating a return trip when the first time had been such a disaster.

Her answer came to her out of the quiet, out of the darkness, and her honesty shamed him.

"But Stone, I was always willing. You're the one who didn't care enough to keep me."

Stone was stunned. "That's not true!" He reached toward her. "I've always cared about you."

She pushed his hand away. "You're a police officer. You're supposed to care about people. I don't want you to just *care* about me, Stone. I wanted your love…and your trust. From where I was standing, I got neither."

Shocked that she'd revealed so much about herself, she

tried to move away, but he wouldn't let her. Finally she sighed, and her voice fell to a whisper.

"I loved you, Stone, and it still wasn't enough."

He closed his eyes and pulled her close. "Damn it, Jessie, you don't pull your punches, do you?" She didn't answer, and he tightened his hold. "Do you want me to leave?"

She tilted her chin and cupped her hands around the back of his neck, pulling until their lips met—his hard and beseeching, hers soft and compliant—then she shuddered.

He increased the pressure of his mouth but broke contact when she started to tremble. His whisper was soft against her eyelids—his hands gentle as they traced the contours of her face.

"Talk to me, honey. Tell me. I don't know what else to say."

She looked up, and there was truth in her clear blue gaze.

"I want you to love me forever...not just tonight."

He groaned. "Damn it, Jessie, I can't promise you something I don't believe in."

Tears shifted the view she had of his face, but she wouldn't relent. "Then, if you don't believe in me, I suppose I will have to believe enough for the both of us."

Because she wanted it so badly, she ignored what was left of her fears. She went into his open arms without hesitation, and when they closed around her in an all-enveloping hug, she let herself believe he was telling the truth.

Her ear was pressed against his chest. His hands were in her hair and kneading the back of her neck in a gentle but sensuous stroke. She knew his shape and yet felt it changing as his desire for her became more and more obvious. She closed her eyes and gave herself up to the joy, knowing that within moments, she would know even more of this man who'd long ago stolen her heart.

"Stone..."

"What, sweetheart?"

"Don't make me regret this."

There was a pain in his heart as he swept her off her feet and into his arms. For Jessica, it was enough, and when Stone carried her into her room and laid her down on her bed, her heart swelled with longing.

He tossed his jacket on a chair.

Her gaze went straight to the gun and shoulder holster he was wearing, and when he slipped it off and hung it over the jacket, she didn't flinch.

He unbuckled his belt and pulled it out of the loops in one long, continuous motion. When it came free of his jeans, she bit the edge of her lip.

Yanking on one side of his shirt and then the other, Stone pulled it free of his jeans, and then, from the bottom up, he began undoing the buttons, one at a time.

Jessica gritted her teeth as his hard, muscled belly was slowly revealed.

He tossed the shirt aside and sat down on a nearby chair, yanking off his boots without wasting a motion. When he stood and reached for the buttons on his jeans, Jessica's fingers dug into the coverlet beneath her.

His eyes glittered wildly as he pulled. The button-fly opening gave way without complaint, revealing the front of his stark-white briefs.

As much as Jessica wanted this to happen, she wasn't brave enough to watch any longer. It had been so long since they'd been together, and yet all she could remember was the pain of leaving. She stifled a groan and closed her eyes. She didn't see the condom he took out of his pocket, but if she had, she would have known that he was still protecting her, in the only way he knew how.

When the bed suddenly gave beneath her, her breath caught at the back of her throat. He slid up, and then on top of her, and she wondered how long it would take to die from delight. And then his hands moved beneath her shirt, pausing at her waist, and she knew, before it happened, that she was about to be undressed. His hesitation, coupled with an uncertainty she hadn't expected, made her tense.

Stone felt her resistance and gentled her with a feathery kiss across the surface of her belly.

"Sssh…easy, easy, honey. Just stay with me on this."

She opened her eyes and tried to relax as he eased her shorts down her legs, leaving a trail of kisses behind with every inch of skin that was revealed. His dark eyes were filled with promises, and before she could panic, he'd moved to her shirt, slipping the soft knit fabric over her head. Except for her pale pink panties and a pink lace bra, she was bare to his sight.

"Beautiful," he whispered. "So beautiful."

She could feel him. Feel the thrust of his body against her stomach and against the inside of her leg, and still he didn't take her. A shudder of longing swept through her as the bra came away, spilling her breasts into his hands.

A flush stained her cheeks, as pale and as pink as the garment he'd just removed. Stone wanted so much, yet was afraid to take for fear of losing her before they had started. Her skin was satin to his touch. She felt fluid beneath him as she shifted to make way for him to come in. He cupped her hips, testing the shape of her as she filled his hands. With only one barrier between him and heaven, he removed her briefs and tossed them off the edge of the bed.

Her arms came up and then around his neck, and he laid his cheek against the pillows of her breasts, knowing that there was no place on earth to compare with where he was now. Her heartbeat hammered against his cheek with a constant rapidity, and he lifted his head and gazed down at her face.

"Jessie?"

She looked back at him with love, and he moved his hips in a gentle, thrusting way. When she shifted and then bit her lower lip, it was all he needed to see. Hard and aching and filled with such need, Stone took Jessie Leigh in the time-honored way.

In that first instant, when Stone filled her, Jessica had a sensation of coming home. This was what she'd been waiting for. This was the acceptance she'd been needing. She pulled him closer, holding him with every ounce of her being, wanting this feeling to last forever.

He leaned down, seeking further connection with the woman in his arms, and centered his mouth on her lips, drinking in her gasps and her sighs, as well as one small, unexpected sob.

"Jessie, look at me," he whispered.

She looked up, fixing him with a wide, stunned gaze.

He started to move and her eyelids fluttered.

"Don't close your eyes," he ordered.

And she didn't.

On a slow, deep thrust, her lips went slack.

Another slow, deep thrust and she dug her fingers into his hair.

Another slow, deep thrust and she broke out in a sweat.

A whimper came up her throat as the pattern changed. He timed his movements to the beat of her heart, following her lead. The more rapid her pulse, the faster he moved, until it became a race to the finish for both.

Stone lost track of himself—and lost track of her. There was nothing within him but what they had become. He reacted only to the feeling of her—and of him.

Movement triggered sensation. Sensation fed need. Need became greed. Impossible to stop. Impossible to ignore. And just when it felt like it would go on forever, they hit a brick wall, shattering the madness within them in the blink of an eye.

When he could focus, he became aware of her arms around his neck, heard her whispering something soft, something sweet, that made his bones turn to jelly. His arms tightened and he rolled, taking her with him until she was lying on top, no longer pinned to the bed by his passion and weight.

All he could think was *Ah, God.* And it was, at once, a

prayer and a plea. It was over, and the sensation of falling was still with him. Tumbling, tumbling, tumbling. Head over heels—over Jessie—in love.

She woke up with a scream, startling Stone to the point of reaching for his gun, when he remembered where he was and reached for her, instead.

"Jessie! What's wrong?"

Wide-eyed and panicked, she stared at him, then her gaze shifted to his chest and she flattened her hand against his shoulder, as if in disbelief.

The terror in her eyes was impossible to misinterpret.

"Jessie, talk to me, honey. Were you having a dream?"

She looked down at her hand and groaned, then rolled out of bed and reached for a robe, yanking it on as she bolted out of the room.

Stone cursed and grabbed his jeans, pulling them on as he ran. He caught her at the back door and, at the same time, hit the light switch. Whatever was wrong, he needed to see.

Her gaze was blank, her body still shaking. She looked at him, then covered her face and moaned.

Suddenly, Stone shivered, as if someone had walked over his grave. This was almost too much, even for him.

"Honey...it's me, Stone. You must have been dreaming, okay? See where you are? We're in your house." He slipped an arm around her shoulder and led her back to the table, pulling out a chair and then seating her gently.

"Oh, God. Oh, God."

Stone froze. The words sounded strange coming from Jessie's lips. Where were her funny epithets? Where were her cockeyed remarks about the state of her affairs? Not once in his entire life had he ever heard her call out God's name.

He dropped to one knee and then lifted her chin, forcing her to face him.

"I can't help you if you don't tell me what's wrong."

She looked up at him and then swayed. He steadied her with a touch and a kiss.

"Jessie, honey, you're starting to scare me, okay? Wait. Let me get you a drink of water. That will be—"

"Blood. You were covered in blood."

Stone flinched at the lack of emotion in her voice. She kept staring into a place he just couldn't see, and from the look on her face, he was damned glad he couldn't.

"But I'm not," he said. He gripped her shoulder, forcing her to look at him. "See? I'm fine. It was nothing more than a dream."

Her hands had clenched into fists, her body shivering with an unexplained shock. "There were people all around you, watching...but not moving...no one helping you...no one trying to save you."

Damn. It was his first thought, and with it came a dread he'd hoped never to have again. This just sounded like more of the same thing that had broken up his marriage to Naomi. Every morning when he had dressed for work, he'd had to endure her tears at the sight of his gun, and every time he'd gone out the door, she'd been convinced he would never return. It had killed whatever love that they'd shared.

His heart dropped as he glanced at Jessie's pale face and tear-filled eyes, and he knew that his instincts had been right. No matter how much they loved each other, she was obviously not going to be able to handle the gory aspects of his job. He stood up and backed off, unconsciously putting more than a mental distance between them.

"Look, Jessie, you had a bad day. You saw me take off my gun. You had a bad dream. End of story."

She stood up as well. "No. You're wrong. It wasn't a dream, any more than everything else that's been happening to me has been. I know what I saw, and I saw you bleeding and no one would help."

He cursed and started back toward the bedroom to get his clothes.

Jessica followed him into the room and then stood in the doorway, watching as he dressed in angry fits and starts.

"I'm not afraid of what you do."

Surprised by her perception, he glanced up. "Then, what the hell do you call this?" he asked.

"A flash of inspiration?"

He frowned. After all she'd claimed to have *seen,* now she was daring him to call her a liar.

Before he could think what to say, Jessica surprised him by shedding her robe and crawling back into her bed. Turning her back to him, she pulled up the covers.

"Would you please lock the door on your way out?"

The pain of her rejection hit him in the belly with the force of a kick.

"Look, Jessie, you have to understand where I've been."

She rolled over, and the tears in her eyes nearly dropped him where he stood.

"No, I don't," she said quietly.

He took a slow breath around the pain in his gut. She was right. He'd rejected what she saw as a truth. If she didn't want to, then she didn't have to understand a damned thing about him.

Stone raked his hands through his hair, combing the short, thick strands into unruly sprouts. Unwilling to leave her like this, he walked to the bed and leaned over, brushing at the bangs near her brows.

"I'll call you tomorrow, okay?"

Too full of misery to speak, she shrugged and pulled the covers tighter around her, trying to block out the sound of his footsteps as he walked down the hall, and then the loud, firm slam of her front door as he left.

It sounded so final. Like it was over.

Stone slammed his butt into the seat of his car and jammed the key into the ignition. He never had liked Mondays.

"Good morning to you, too," Stryker said.

"Buckle up," Stone muttered, but it sounded too much like "shut up" for Stryker to argue.

Stryker continued as if nothing was wrong.

"Okay, we know that the last word out of Olivia Stuart's mouth was 'coal.' And we've got a map detailing the area where the consortium's lease for strip mining is expiring. We've got an agenda—try and see if there is any connection between Olivia Stuart's last word and the business to which she was so opposed. Now all we need is an attitude adjustment."

Stone started the car, yanking it in gear and leaving rubber behind as he peeled out of the parking lot.

Stryker glanced at his partner, then down at his watch.

"So, it's gonna be like this, is it?" When Stone didn't answer, Stryker glanced at his watch and slid a little further into the seat. It was going to be a hell of a long, silent day.

"Easy does it, Miss Hanson. One more stitch and they'll all be out."

Jessica squinched her eyes shut, wincing against the tug to her scalp as Dr. Howell removed the last stitch.

"And that does it," he said, dropping the bit of stitch, as well as his instruments, into a nearby pan. Moving her hair aside, he swabbed alcohol on the area. Peering closely at the results of his handiwork, he gave her a pat on the arm. "Except for the haircut, you're good as new."

She blinked and thrust her hand into her hair in embarrassment.

"Oh, I didn't mean your new style. I meant the cut I gave you." Noah flicked the end of a straggly lock away from her ear. "Yours is quite fetching."

He stepped back and looked at her more closely as his nurse moved in, swabbing the healing wound with a last dab of disinfectant. "You know…that hairdo really changes your appearance. You remind me of someone, but I just can't think who."

The nurse looked up to see for herself. "Hmm, you know, Dr. Howell, you're right. It really did change her appearance."

Jessica resisted the urge to stick out her tongue. She already felt like a sideshow freak, and now they were speaking of her as if she wasn't even there.

Noah suddenly snapped his fingers and a smile spread over his face. "I know. I know. You remind me of that actress who was in that movie with Billy Crystal. I forget the name. She played that girl who ordered her salad in bits and pieces with everything on the side and then pretended to have an…uh…" He flushed. "Well, you know…she faked, uh…"

His nurse nodded, seemingly oblivious to the fact that Dr. Howell had faltered over every other word. "Meg Ryan. *When Harry Met Sally*. And the word is *orgasm*. She faked an orgasm."

He glanced at his patient, anxious that she not be offended by their choice of subject. When he saw the grin on Jessica's face, he glared at his nurse.

"I will get you for that," he muttered.

The nurse puttered around the room, cleaning up behind Dr. Howell and ignoring the threat.

Defeated by the past week's events, as well as by what had happened between her and Stone early yesterday morning, Jessica slumped where she sat.

"If only the rest of Grand Springs could see me like that. All they see is some crazy witch."

Noah frowned. He'd heard the gossip about Jessica Hanson, and while he'd like to think it was nothing more than that, he'd been far too close a witness to her first correct prediction to scoff.

"You know, an old professor told me something once that I've never forgotten," Noah said. "He said, as long as *you* know who you are, it doesn't really matter what the rest of the world thinks about you."

Jessica sighed. "I guess that's my problem," she said softly. "I don't know myself. Why would I expect the rest of the world to get a grip when I've lost my own?"

"I could recommend some therapy, if you think it would help."

She grinned wryly. "Unless your shrink has a crystal ball on his desk, I don't think we'd have much to say to each other."

He almost laughed. "You've got a good attitude. I'm sure everything will work itself out."

Jessica left the doctor, minus her stitches, but still carrying the wound Stone had left in her heart. And, after a week off at home, it felt strange to be going back to work. Her nerves tightened as she turned into the parking lot at Squaw Creek Lodge. Mr. Dolby knew she was due in today, but she dreaded the confrontation. Yet when she walked in her office, the familiar surroundings went a long way toward helping her relax.

As she hung her jacket on a hook, she couldn't help but glance down. One thing had changed, and for the better. The bloodstain on the carpet was gone. And it looked as if whoever they'd called in from temporary services hadn't moved a thing. There was no work stacked on her desk, nothing seemed out of place. She started to relax. Maybe for once, something was about to go right.

A bouquet of fresh flowers was on the corner of her desk. She lifted the card, a smile of appreciation spreading across her face as she read. It was a "welcome back" bouquet from the staff. She leaned forward, inhaling the aroma of sweet peas and roses and baby's breath, then looked up as the door suddenly opened.

It was Sheila, carrying a cinnamon roll and a fresh cup of coffee.

"Shoot," she said. "I didn't know you were already here. I was going to surprise you."

Jessica pointed to what Sheila was holding. "If that's for me, I'd be glad to go out and come in again."

Sheila giggled. "You better not. It smells so good, I might break down and eat it before you got back."

"Then, thank you," Jessica said as Sheila set it down on her desk.

There was a long pause as the two women looked at each other, each remembering what had last transpired between them.

Finally, Sheila waved her hand. "Eat. Drink. You'll need sustenance to prepare yourself for Dolby's new do."

Jessica thought of the manager's last hairpiece and grimaced. "Don't tell me he's changed it again."

Sheila arched an eyebrow. "I won't have to. When you see him, believe me, you'll understand."

It was nearly noon before Jessica had a chance to see what Sheila had been talking about, and when she did, she was heartily glad she'd been forewarned.

Jeffery Dolby was strutting as he came toward her. Jessica knew she was staring, but it was impossible to stop. He'd dyed his eyebrows to match the new hairpiece. Wiry and yellow, it sat on his head like a straw nest on the forked branch of a tree; firmly planted, but out of place. Jeffery Dolby had gone blond.

"Miss Hanson, welcome back, welcome back!" Dolby said, and thrust out his hand, engulfing hers within his grasp. "Sheila said you were here, but we've been so busy this morning, I haven't had time to welcome you personally."

Jessica bit the inside of her mouth to keep from grinning and fixed her focus on the bridge of his nose, rather than what was above it.

"Thank you, Mr. Dolby. It's good to be back. Oh, and the flowers are beautiful. Please give everyone my thanks."

He smiled and pointed to her head. "I see you got your stitches out."

She fingered the edge of her hairline and the small scar that would soon be concealed with a new growth of hair.

"Yes. This morning. And I can't say I was sorry to see them go."

He patted his hair and then did a little two-step, as if shifting gears before moving on.

"I trust all was in order in your office when you returned."

She tried looking at his chin instead of the fuzzy blond hair above his nose, but it was no use. No matter how hard she tried, her gaze kept moving back to the changes in Dolby's appearance. When she met his gaze, she realized he was still waiting for her reply.

"Oh! The office! Yes! Everything was fine, and thank you for giving me the week off to recuperate."

His eyebrows wiggled like yellow caterpillars on a fishhook. "Think nothing of it. If you find yourself with slack time, don't hesitate to take the occasional early day home until you feel you're back to normal. You're a fine employee. We'd hate to lose you."

She nodded. The idea of going home early now and then might be wise, especially until she got back in the swing of a regular routine.

"Well now," Dolby said, patting the front of his suit. "I've a luncheon meeting. I mustn't be late. Again, welcome back."

He strode away, leaving Jessica alone in the hall. Only after he was completely out of sight did she let herself react. She smiled, then chuckled, and then laughed outright. And she was still giggling to herself when she turned the corner and walked straight into Stone Richardson's arms.

"Oh!"

Her gasp was as much from surprise as from the unexpected contact. When his fingers curled around her arms to steady her, she found herself wanting to throw her arms around his neck and give him a welcome he wouldn't forget. But then she remembered the way that they'd parted, and all her joy in seeing him again was tempered with reserve.

Inside, Stone was scared half out of his mind. The last thing on earth he could face was losing Jessie Leigh.

"I didn't mean to scare you."

She searched the intensity of his gaze. He looked as miserable as she felt, and she reached out and touched the side of his face.

"And I didn't mean to scare you, either."

At that moment, both knew they were no longer referring to their near miss in the hall. They were talking about Saturday night and the unexpected way in which they'd parted early yesterday morning.

"Forgive me?" Stone asked.

"If you'll forgive me."

Stone kissed the side of her cheek, and then took her in his arms and stole the breath from her lips. Someone whistled at the end of the hallway. Stone groaned beneath his breath as he broke their connection, then smiled down at her, noticing as he did that something had changed.

"Your stitches are gone!"

"Out this morning. Now all that's missing is some hair and…" She hesitated. She'd almost said "a few brain cells," but after the other night, making jokes about her *dreams* was no longer funny.

Stone knew what she'd been about to say, and while he didn't like to think about the consequences, he knew better than to tell her she was crazy. She'd already proved them wrong on all counts.

"I won't forget what you told me," he said. "I'll be careful, I promise."

She laid her cheek against his heartbeat. Like Stone, it was steady and strong.

"I like a man who keeps his promises," she said softly.

He held her close, cherishing the trust, as well as the love, that she'd given.

"I hate to kiss and run, but Jack's waiting for me out in the car. We're on our way to Hal Stuart's office, and then out to run down some more leads."

Jessica ran her hand along the front of his jacket, and when she felt the bulge of his shoulder holster, she gave it a comforting pat.

"Call me." There was more question than request in her words.

Stone grinned. "No way, honey. When I 'reach out and touch someone,' I want to do it the old-fashioned way. I'll see you tonight."

He left her standing in the hall, which was right where Sheila Biggers found her.

"There you are. I've been looking all over. Do you still want to do lunch? I'm starving."

Jessica's heart was lighter as she followed Dolby's secretary out the door.

And the days crawled toward the end of the week.

It was Friday afternoon, less than thirty minutes to quitting time, and none too soon for Jessica. Nowadays, she lived for the nights and Stone's arrival at her house. While nothing more had been spoken between them with regards to their future or lack thereof, Jessica was holding on tight to the bits and pieces of himself that Stone *was* willing to share. And every time she thought of his ex-wife, she fought an urge to curse. That woman had done a number on him he couldn't seem to forget.

Tonight, though, the routine was going to change. Stone was going to cook, and at his apartment. She wasn't sure whether it meant he was tired of pretending her cooking was great, or if he was just being the gentleman and paying her back for all the meals he'd scrounged at her house during the week. All she had to do was drop the monthly reports by Mr. Dolby's office and she was through for the day.

Her steps were hurried as she started down the hall. Her

hand was on the doorknob to Dolby's office when the door suddenly swung inward and a woman started out.

"Oh, Jessica! I didn't see you there."

Jessica grinned at the tall, dark-haired woman. "That's because the door was closed."

Nina Lindstrom managed a smile. And Jessica returned it easily. She and Nina had known each other for years.

"I see you haven't lost your sense of humor," Nina said.

"That's about all that's still where it belongs," Jessica muttered, more to herself than to Nina, and followed the other woman into the hall.

Nina glanced at her friend, and Jessica could tell that she was wondering how much of what she'd heard was true, and how much of it was just gossip.

"So, how have you really been?" Nina asked. "I heard you were a victim of the blackout."

"That's a kind way of putting it," Jessica said. "But, enough about me. How are you doing?"

Nina's shoulders drooped. "Not so good," she said. "The diner has closed for repairs, and it's pretty common knowledge that the Olsens aren't going to open it back up."

Jessica frowned. She knew Nina's life had been tough since her husband's death, but losing her job as a waitress at the Olsens' diner would hit her hard.

"How are the kids?"

Nina smiled, although her voice sounded a bit shaky. "Exactly how you would expect three kids under the age of nine to be. Rowdy and loud."

"Were you applying for a job?" Jessica asked.

Nina nodded. "But there aren't any openings, and I need something now." She shook her head and looked away, unwilling to let on how desperate she really was.

"Maybe something will turn up," Jessica said.

"I don't know. Grand Springs is in such an uproar over the mayor's death, and businesses aren't doing so well right now." Then Nina put on a brave face and smiled. "If you hear of something, will you let me know?"

"Of course," Jessica said, and touched Nina's arm in what was meant to be a comforting way.

But at the moment of contact, everything changed. Images flashed in and out of her mind, like slides on a screen. One after the other, in rapid succession without any explanations in between. And with each one she saw, her impression grew that Nina Lindstrom would soon experience a drastic change of pace.

Nina tensed. "Jessica, are you all right?"

Jessica jerked, blinked, and then took a deep breath as her hand dropped to her side. She looked up at Nina with an angelic smile on her face.

"Don't worry. I have a really good feeling that something is going to turn up...and soon."

Nina sighed. "I hope you're right. I could use some good luck for a change."

Ten

Jessica stopped in front of the door to Stone's second-floor apartment, giving herself a final check before ringing the bell. Her dress was new, and although she felt a bit self-conscious in the flowing, old-fashioned style, it gave her courage the boost it needed. This thing that was between her and Stone was so powerful, and so unexpectedly sweet, she was afraid to trust it could last.

The aroma of burning charcoal and cooking food drifted into the hall. It was all the impetus she needed to let herself be known. With her hand poised to knock, the door suddenly opened, and Stone swept her into his arms and into the room before she could blink.

"How did you know I was there?" Jessica gasped.

"Honey, I'm forever psychic where you're concerned." And then he laughed and kissed her hello before putting her down. "And I was standing on the balcony when I saw you come through the courtyard."

She grinned. "You cheated."

"All's fair in love and war."

A little ill at ease at being here with him, instead of on familiar ground, she ran a nervous hand over her hair and then smoothed the front of her dress.

Stone watched her with open admiration, letting himself absorb the fact that she was in his home.

"You look beautiful," he said softly, fingering the gauzy fabric of her dress. "The blue matches your eyes."

Jessica blushed, but was determined not to let him get

ahead of her tonight. "You look pretty good yourself. And you smell good, too. What is it called? Eau de smoke?"

He laughed and pulled her close, nuzzling at a spot beneath her ear. "Damn, but you're sassy tonight."

Jessica wrapped her arms around his neck, leaning into his strength and smiling with satisfaction. Food was on the grill. She was in Stone's arms. What more could a sane woman want? And then the thought slipped. Dare she assume she fell under the category of sane?

Stone's heart was melting by degrees. This crazy tousled-haired woman was making him nuts. Once more, he nuzzled against the curve of her neck, then bit, not hard enough to hurt, just making his mark on her.

"Ow," she muttered, and slapped him lightly on the arm. "If you're that hungry, then I suggest you finish cooking our food. I'm not on the menu tonight."

Stone circled the jut of her breast with the tip of his finger, grinning when she blushed a shade of hot virgin pink.

"Not even for dessert?"

To Jessie's credit, she met his gaze without flinching. "I'll let you know later," she drawled, then pointed toward the patio door behind them. "Is that supposed to be smoking?"

Stone spun, took one look at the white clouds billowing out from beneath the hood of the cooker, and bolted.

"Obviously not," Jessica said to herself, and followed him outside.

"Everything's fine," Stone said, and handed her a plate. "Here, hold this."

Jessica took the plate and then stood and watched him work as several minutes passed. But when he made no move to put anything on it, she couldn't stand the suspense any longer.

Stone was poking a fork in the steaks with studied intent when she spoke.

"Stone?"

"Hmm?"

"Why am I holding this plate?"

He looked up and grinned. "I didn't want our food to burn, and I figured you would need something to hold to keep your hands off of me."

Stunned by the audacity of the man, all she could do was sputter. He laughed aloud and took the plate she was holding, setting it on a nearby table.

"You have real staying power, Jessie Leigh. I'd just come to the conclusion that you would have held it all night."

She arched an eyebrow and leaned against the railing in her sexiest pose. "There are some things I might do all night, but holding platters isn't one of them."

This time, she had the pleasure of seeing him dumb-struck. Finally, he turned back to his cooking, shaking his head and muttering something beneath his breath about needing his head examined.

Pleased that she'd gotten in the last word, she turned and gazed out across the courtyard and to the pool beyond. The apartment complex was a grouping of four separate buildings, but they shared the spacious area in between.

Flowering shrubs bordered the base of the buildings, while pebbled walkways linked them together in a maze of winding paths. Tables with colorful umbrellas dotted the grassy areas between the paths, and just beyond, the sparkling blue waters of the pool beckoned.

A couple walked hand in hand toward the building directly opposite, and as they opened the door to enter, a small boy, who appeared no more than three years old, darted out between them, making a break for the outside like a puppy gone wild.

Jessica grinned as the child rolled and tumbled around on the grass, jumping and hopping and waving his arms. Even though she was high above him, she could see that he was talking to himself. As the moments passed, she kept expecting a parent to join him. Although the courtyard itself was enclosed, there were far too many hazards await-ing a toddler alone.

When he darted toward their building, she leaned over the balcony, somehow convinced that she must keep him in sight.

Stone was taking up the last of the steaks and happened to look up as she leaned. Almost dropping the platter, he grabbed her arm half in jest, half in earnest.

"Easy, honey. You've already had one nasty bump on your head. You don't want to fall from up here."

"Stone, look." She pointed to the toddler who was daw-dling toward the fenced-in area around the pool.

He followed her direction and frowned. He'd seen the child and the mother before, but had no idea who they were, or where they lived. And while he was debating with himself about what he should do, Jessica suddenly gasped.

"He's going to fall in the pool."

Stone looked again. The child had turned away from the fence and was digging under some shrubs with a stick.

"No, honey. Look, he's playing by that bush."

She wrapped her arms around herself and started to shake. "No, no, no. Not there," she moaned.

In that instant, Stone realized what was happening. Jes-sica was seeing something that had yet to happen. Without looking back, he bolted through his apartment and out of the door, running down the stairs as if his life, and not the child's, depended on it.

When the door slammed behind Stone, Jessica jerked in shock, realizing he was gone. She gripped the balcony rail until her knuckles turned white. And even though she knew Stone must be on his way to the rescue, she feared it would not be in time. Already the child had made his way through an unlocked gate and was circling the pool with absent fascination.

When he drew back and tossed his stick in the water, she unconsciously reached out, wanting to stop the inevi-table and knowing it was an impossible feat.

The stick hit the water with a splash, and the child shrieked with delight. But when it began to float out to-ward the middle of the pool, Jessica saw a frown creasing the little boy's forehead. She held her breath, counting the seconds between the time the child leaned over, and when he tumbled headfirst into the deep end of the pool. At that point, her scream pierced the silence, and then she ran for the phone.

Jessica's scream was the first thing Stone heard as he burst out of the building. All he could think was, Don't let me be too late.

The child didn't even float, and was already sinking when Stone hit the water headfirst. Down, down, he dove, reaching out, stretching his arm to lengthen his grasp. And when he caught fabric—and then the tiny, limp arm—he encircled it fiercely, locking his fingers in a grip that only death would have freed, and began swimming up toward the lights dancing on the water above.

He broke the surface of the water with the child held high in his arms. Afraid to take time to look down, he made for the edge of the pool with the child in tow, and as he reached the side, the child was torn from his grasp.

Breathless and shaking, he pulled himself out of the pool just as Jessica initiated the first sequences of CPR. Her hands were shaking and her face was ghost white, but she wasn't missing a beat. It was just what Stone needed in order to catch his breath before he could help.

"Did you call 911?"

She nodded and continued to work.

Moments later, when he could breathe without gasping, Stone crawled to his knees and bent to the child.

"I'm okay," he said quickly, taking over the motions from Jessie without breaking the rhythm. Already the sound of sirens could be heard in the distance, and then soon, another, much sweeter sound came. The sound of a child choking, then coughing, then crying.

Jessica dropped to her knees and covered her face with

her hands, knowing if she never did another important thing during her lifetime, this would be enough to carry her through.

Suddenly, paramedics burst on the scene. When they got to the child, Stone gladly relinquished his role of rescuer and leaned back on his knees, still shaking from an onslaught of emotions.

And even as Stone was drawing in deep draughts of much-needed air into his lungs, the little boy was breathing on his own and asking for his mother.

Stone groaned beneath his breath as he got up. He would like to have a talk with her himself. What the hell kind of a woman would let a toddler out unattended in a place like this?

Someone touched his shoulder and he turned. It was Jessica. He grabbed her hand, and in that moment, the connection they had was as strong as when they made love.

"My God, Jessie." For the moment, it was all he could say.

"Mommy. Want my mommy," the child cried.

Stone squatted beside him, gently smoothing the wet mat of hair from his forehead while the paramedics began strapping him on the gurney.

"Where is your mommy, son?"

The little boy's gaze was frantic, his motions jerky as he tried to pull free of the restraints. "Sleepin'. Mommy sleepin'," he cried, and tugged at the strap across his chest. "Want my mommy!"

"He came out of that door," Jessica said, pointing to the back of the nearest building.

"He's plenty stable, and we'll be a couple of more minutes," one of the paramedics said. "If you could find her, it would speed up the process a lot when we take him in."

Stone got to his feet. "I'll find her."

Jessica was right behind him when he went inside. He started down the hallway, shouting aloud.

"Police! Open up!"

Doors opened and people peeked out, curious as to what was going on. Before he could explain what he was about, Jessica suddenly grabbed his arm and started running toward the stairwell. By now, he knew better than to ask why.

They exited on the third level. Jessica was out of breath and there was a stitch in her side that she kept trying to ignore. But she knew, as well as she knew her own name, that the drama of the evening wasn't over yet.

"Here," she said, pointing to a door on their right that was standing ajar.

Stone pushed his way inside and then stopped in the doorway, staring in disbelief at the young woman who was slumped on the floor, a hypodermic needle next to her hand.

"Son of a bitch," he muttered as he knelt at her side.

Jessica moved through the apartment as if she'd been there before, heading for the refrigerator with unerring intent. And when she opened the door, the small vials sitting high on a shelf only confirmed what she already knew. She grabbed one on the run, dropping back to Stone's side and shoving it in his hand.

"Stone. Look! She's not an addict, she's a diabetic!"

Ashamed of the fact that his first instinct had been to distrust, he thought of the paramedics already on hand.

"Stay with her," he ordered.

Jessica stayed, partly because he'd asked, and partly because she'd been led here by a power she didn't understand, and there was nowhere else to go.

Water stood in puddles from the front door to the bedroom beyond, marking the trail where Stone had walked as he'd gone to change his clothes. Their uneaten food was on a corner of the cabinet, while outside, the waning smoke from the grill dissipated into the night air.

Jessica sat huddled in her chair, rocking back and forth in mute defeat. While she was thankful beyond words that both mother and child would survive, the knowledge that she was no longer in control of her senses was more than she could bear. Trying to live with this thing was going to drive her insane.

There was a touch on her shoulder. She looked up.

Stone held out his hands and she moved into his arms.

"Here, sit with me," he urged, and sat down where she'd been, holding her safely in his lap. His voice was near her ear, and the quiet, confident tones went a long way toward calming the depression in which she'd fallen.

"You did good, honey."

Her lips trembled as she laid her head on his shoulder.

"I want this to stop."

There was such defeat in her voice that Stone panicked, and then held her that little bit tighter.

"I know, Jessie, I know. And I wish there was something I could do to make it all better."

"Oh, Stone. So do I."

Outside, the world went on as if nothing had happened, while they sat locked in each other's arms, wondering what else she would she see, and what else might go wrong.

A half hour passed, and it was moving on to the hour when Stone seemed to kick into gear. He kissed the lobe of Jessie's ear, then deposited her on her feet.

"You...stick the steaks in the microwave. I'm going to mop up my mess."

"But—"

"No buts," he said. "It's over. You're here. And I'm damned hungry. Feed me, woman, before I turn on you, instead."

A small smile tilted the edges of her lips, and he grinned.

"What? You don't fancy being my dessert?"

This time, Jessica heard herself laughing. It wasn't much, but it felt good just the same.

"I already told you about that dessert business," she said.

Convinced that, for the moment, he'd pushed her as far as she needed to go, he turned.

"I'm going to get a mop."

He had just stepped out on the patio to the adjoining storage room when the phone rang.

"Hey, Jessie, get that for me, will you?" he called.

She picked up the phone on the third ring.

"Richardson residence."

A very pregnant pause lingered after a near-silent gasp.

"Hello? Who's calling, please?" Jessica repeated.

"I want to speak to Stone."

The woman's voice was stilted, sounding almost angry as Jessica put her hand over the receiver.

"Stone, it's a woman. She sounds upset. Says she wants to talk to you."

Mopping at the puddles with manly disdain for neatness, he frowned, then shook his head.

"Ask who it is," he mouthed.

"May I ask who's calling?"

"Tell him it's Naomi, and I don't like this third-party interrogation one bit."

Jessica blanched. "It's your ex-wife, and she says she doesn't like this third-party interrogation one bit."

Stone grinned, and when he did, Jessica's spirits lifted.

"You tell her I'm busy, and unless she's been kidnapped or bleeding to death, I don't need to know."

Jessica's eyes were dancing. "He says to tell you…"

"I heard what he said," Naomi muttered. "And you tell him— No. Never mind. I must have been out of my mind to even call."

By now, Jessica was grinning widely. "She says, she must have been out of her mind to call."

There was a distinct click in Jessica's ear.

"She hung up."

Stone was leaning on his mop with a silly grin on his face.

"Then that means you can do the same."

Jessica hung up the receiver, and then stood, watching as Stone returned to mopping up the water he'd dripped.

"Umm...Stone?"

"What, honey?"

"Does that happen often?"

He glanced up. "What? You mean her calling like that?"

She nodded.

"Oddly enough, I hadn't heard from her in years and then she called a couple of days ago. That call was the second time this week. The first time she called to tell me she was getting married. Knowing Naomi, it didn't amount to anything but boredom or curiosity." Then he shrugged. "This time, who the hell knows."

"Do you still love her?"

There was such uncertainty in her voice that Stone dropped the mop and, within seconds, had her in his arms.

"Jessie Leigh, compared to the way I feel about you, I'm not sure I ever did."

Jessica bloomed as the microwave dinged. "I think the steaks are hot."

Stone lowered his head. "Oooh, honey, so am I."

Hours later, the digital dial on Stone's clock was registering 12:45 a.m. as they came up for air.

Stone brushed the hair from Jessie's eyes and then ran his hand possessively over her bare midriff.

"How do you feel about a midnight supper?"

Jessica stretched and then smiled, like a well-fed cat who had its owner right under its paw.

"But you've already had dessert," she said.

Stone got up and reached for his jeans, ignoring his nudity, as well as the interested look from the woman in his bed.

"I know what I've had," he drawled. "But it's my place. My bed. Here, I make the rules."

"Somehow, that doesn't seem fair."

He looked back, cocking an eyebrow as he gave her an appreciative stare.

"You know what, sweet thing? Tonight, lying there in my bed, all mussed and rumpled, you've come close to giving me heartburn. Now, I know my limitations as well as the next man, and I know if I don't get something substantial into my belly, I'm going to fade on you fast."

"Does that mean we can't do it again?"

He grinned. "Pretty much."

She rolled out of bed. "I guess I'm getting hungry, too."

He laughed. "I thought you'd see it my way."

It happened just as the day broke on the horizon. One minute she'd been lying still beneath the curve of Stone's shoulder, and the next she was moaning down deep in her throat and reaching out toward a horror she couldn't stop.

Stone came awake within seconds and knew it was happening all over again. Sweat broke out on his forehead as he watched her face grimace in some unseen pain. And when she screamed out his name and sat straight up in bed, this time he was ready for her panic.

"It's okay, it's okay," he said, grabbing her before she could run. "I'm here, Jessie, I'm here."

She looked at him with disbelief, and as before, her gaze slid to his shoulder, then down at her hands.

"Blood...so much blood."

"It was a dream. I'm here. I'm okay. It was just a dream."

Jessica started to cry, and he felt like crying along with her. God help him, but this was hell, knowing what she was capable of seeing and knowing that he could very well be the next victim to fall.

He pulled her down beside him, cradling her as she sobbed.

"Ah, Jessie, don't cry, please don't cry," he whispered, feathering kiss after kiss upon her face and neck, tasting tears and feeling her pulse as it raced beneath his lips.

"Oh, Stone, I'm so afraid of losing you."

He rose up on one elbow. "Jessie, look at me," he said, forcing her to meet his gaze. "What do you see?"

She didn't hesitate. "The man I love."

His voice broke. "Jessie Leigh, you do know how to take a man's breath away." He cupped the side of her face, wiping away tear tracks with the ball of his thumb. "I love you, too," he said softly. "So much that it makes me ache."

"Then, what are we going to do?" Jessica asked.

An odd grin tilted at the corner of his mouth. "The way I see it, we're already doing all the right things. What I want you to do is trust me to see danger coming. I'm a trained officer, and I'm damned good at my job."

Jessica shuddered on a sob as she blinked back more tears. "I know, but—"

"No buts," he said, planting a swift kiss near her nose. He looked at the clock and then frowned. "Dang it, the alarm is going to go off in exactly twenty-three minutes. What do you think we should do?"

Her fingers encircled his arms, digging into the flesh in a desperate attempt to hold him safe against harm. He was so beloved, and she was so very, very afraid.

"Oh, Stone... I don't know."

His hand slid down past her waist to the curve of her hip, and then he rolled, pulling her beneath him as he went.

"I have an idea," he said softly. "How about another dessert?"

She almost smiled. "For me, or for you?"

His head dipped toward her breast.

Later she would think this had been a good idea, after

all. Love had a way of removing the bad taste of the day's bitter beginning.

Brenda was sitting on the front porch swing when Jessica drove up later that morning.

Jessica muttered under her breath as she got out of the car, heading toward the house on the run.

"If you're going to gripe, then you're going to have to follow me around to do it," Jessica said as she unlocked the door. "I'm going to be late for work."

"Since you didn't come home last night, whose fault would that be?" Brenda asked.

Jessica threw up her hands and headed for the back of her house. Brenda followed right behind her, stopping at the bathroom door.

"Jessie, are you sure you know what you're doing?"

Jessica stripped as she ran, turning on the shower as she stepped out of the last of her clothes.

"No, actually, I'm not," she said. "But you told me to go for it, remember? And, the way things stand right now, I'm already gone."

Brenda groaned and slapped herself on the forehead. "Me and my big mouth," she mumbled as Jessica stepped in the shower and slammed the door shut behind her.

Brenda walked inside the bathroom and sat down on the closed lid of the commode. "Okay," she yelled, trying to be heard above the rush of water inside the stall. "Then, answer me this. Are you being careful?"

Jessica poked her head out of the door, sending a spray billowing up into the room and fogging the vanity mirror.

"Heel blisters, Brenda. What do you think I am, a fool?"

Brenda had to grin. Heel blisters, indeed.

"I had to ask," she said.

Jessica slammed the door shut again. "I don't see why," she yelled. "I never asked you that question."

A strange expression slid across Brenda's face. "Well,"

she muttered. And then took another breath and tried to be indignant, but it just wouldn't come.

Suddenly, she stood and yanked the shower door open, instantly showering herself and the floor with a fine, misty spray.

"I hate it when you are right," she said briefly. "Are we still renting movies tonight, or are you jilting me for that cop?"

"You're getting all wet," Jessica said, pointing to her sister's clothes.

Brenda's gaze never wavered. "You didn't answer my question."

Jessica leaned out of the door and handed her sister a towel. "Just don't bring some stupid horror movie. I'm not in the mood for blood."

The door slid shut, leaving Brenda standing in a puddle of her own making.

"Shoot," she muttered as she began to mop at her clothes. "I'm going to have to go home and change. I think this is going to shrink."

Eleven

As the hot summer days passed, the residents of Grand Springs began to move on with their lives. The Olivia Stuart murder case was ongoing, but few talked about it now, except those who were directly affected. And Jessica tried not to be one of them.

To her relief, her flashes of inspiration were becoming rare, and none life-threatening...except the one with regards to Stone. Every so often the dream came again, and when it did, she would wake up in tears. Although nothing had happened to him, in the back of her mind was always the fear that it could.

It seemed to Jessica that the city was healing, and most of the residents were looking forward to the upcoming Fourth of July celebration. There would be games in the park, a carnival at a nearby shopping mall, and a fireworks display after dark. Best of all, the children were going to be allowed to swim in the city pool at half price.

Summer. It was a time to stop and smell the roses, and Stone wanted to do that with Jessie, and more. The only thing that kept him from staking a permanent claim were old fears of a marriage gone wrong—that and the fact that Jessica's eyes were haunted by a dream only she had seen. He couldn't get past the idea that she was projecting subconscious fears of the dangers of his job into her dreams. If it affected her like that and they weren't even married, even though he loved her to distraction, he shuddered to think what the reality of a marriage with her might be like.

* * *

It was quitting time on Thursday. Jessica turned off the computer and leaned back in her chair, looking forward to the upcoming three-day holiday weekend. Although the lodge itself would not close, offices such as hers would not need to be open. Payroll was done and all the invoices recorded. The checks had been cut to pay vendors with which Squaw Creek Lodge dealt. All she had to do was put the paperwork on Jeff Dolby's desk and she would be free until Monday.

That meant three days with Stone at his cabin. Granted, she wasn't the biggest fishing fan in Grand Springs, but when hanging out with a man like Stone, fishing wasn't the only game in town.

A smile of anticipation crossed her face as she started down the hall toward the manager's office.

Maybe it will rain.

And then she remembered all of the festivities Grand Springs had planned and crossed out the thought.

Maybe the fish won't be biting.

She grinned to herself as she entered Dolby's office. At least that wish wouldn't trouble her conscience.

Sheila Biggers was still on vacation, and so the outer office was empty as Jessica walked inside. She knocked on the manager's door, and when he called out, she entered with the reports in hand.

"Well, well," Dolby said, smoothing his hand over the slick, shiny surface of his head. "I'll bet you're all ready for a good long weekend. I know I certainly am."

Jessica handed him the papers and smiled. Mr. Dolby had given up hair for a cooler, more stunning approach. Four days ago, he'd come to work bald. What hair he'd had left had been shaved, leaving nothing on his head but skin. No more combing for Dolby, although she wondered about the can of furniture polish on a table behind his desk. Was it there for the furnishings, or for Jeff Dolby's head?

"These all seem to be in order," he said. "I'll see to

the disbursement of checks myself. Run along now and have a great weekend.''

"Thank you, Mr. Dolby, you too.''

She left the lodge with a smile on her face and headed home to pack.

Jessica had been up since long before daybreak and the kitchen was a mess. Cookies in all shapes and sizes were cooling on the countertop, and dishes had been piled in the sink. Spilled flour trickled from the cabinet onto the floor where she had inadvertently tracked it from one side of the room to the other. Sugar was in her hair, and she had a smudge of chocolate at the edge of her mouth, a remnant of taste-testing the dough.

She stood at the side of the sink with an empty cookie sheet in one hand and a dripping dishrag in the other, staring at the room in disbelief.

How had this happened? She'd started out to make some cookies for the weekend trip and wound up with a mess that would take her hours to clean up. She glanced at the clock. It was nearly 7:00 a.m. Stone could show at any time, and she hadn't even started to pack. With a groan, she thrust the dishrag in the sink. It was as good a place as any to start.

Less than five minutes later, the phone rang and she tossed the dishrag back in the sink, glad to have an excuse to stop. A little breathless from her race to answer, her voice came out in a high-pitched squeak.

"Hello?''

"Jessie, is that you?''

At the sound of Stone's voice, everything she'd been stewing over faded into obscurity.

"Stone! You should see what I've done. The kitchen is a mess, but the cookies aren't half bad. If you don't want to eat them, maybe we can use them for sinkers or bait.''

He didn't laugh as she'd expected, and her smile faded just the tiniest bit.

"Look, Jessie, about this weekend..."

By now, her smile was completely gone. "What's wrong?"

She could hear him sigh and knew that it probably wasn't good.

"Come on," she said. "I'm a big girl. I can take it. Let me guess. You decided to take Stryker to the cabin instead of me. I can't say that I blame you. He's probably a better fisherman, although I can guarantee you won't have half as much fun."

"Hell," Stone muttered, while in the background, Stryker was calling for him to hurry. He motioned to Jack that he'd be right there. "Jessie, honey, we aren't going to be able to leave for the cabin until tomorrow. There's an APB out for some guy who escaped from the state pen, and the reports have him headed our way. The chief has taken everyone off of leave until the situation is under control."

Jessica slumped against the wall as she gazed around the kitchen with disgust.

"Okay. At least I'll have time to clean up my mess," she said, and then could tell by the surprise in Stone's voice that her reaction was unexpected.

"You aren't mad?" he asked.

"Only at the mess I made, and certainly not at you," she said. "Why on earth would I be mad?"

Stone's whole body went weak with relief. In the back of his mind, he'd been prepared for a tantrum similar to the ones Naomi used to throw.

"I don't know," he said softly. "I guess I just wasn't thinking."

Jessica's voice softened. "Oh, I think that you were... thinking, I mean. But I don't think you were thinking about the right woman."

Stone sighed. "Are you being psychic on me?"

"No, that's simply women's intuition. Take care of yourself. Find a brick wall to hide behind, and call me when it's over."

"You know what, Jessie Leigh?"

"What?" she asked, laughter rich in her voice.

"I love you so damned much."

She grinned. "Wait until you see my cookies, then we'll see how strong that love really is."

His laughter rang in her ears, sending shudders of longing up her spine.

"Look, honey, I've got to go. Stryker is having himself a fit. Oh...and if you don't have to, don't go anywhere tonight, okay? We've got roadblocks at every entrance into the city, but there's no telling where, or if, the escapee might show."

Stone's voice faded into a faint, husky buzz as she suddenly focused on a water tower near a wide, green field.

"Uh...Stone."

"Yeah, honey?"

"Are they setting up a roadblock at the highway near the backside of the high school, too?"

He tensed. "Yes, why?"

"That's good. You might want to tell the chief not to send out for doughnuts and coffee until after midnight."

Stone straightened, all the teasing gone from his voice. "Are you sure?"

"As sure as I can ever be," she said, and then hung up the phone.

The next morning, it was all over the news. Pictures of the roadblock in the morning paper. Bulletins on the local television newscasts. One disgruntled escapee back behind bars where he belonged, thanks to the fine work of the Grand Springs Police Department, and an anonymous tip from a conscientious citizen.

Jessica had the stereo on full blast and was doing a saucy little two-step in her T-shirt and panties to the tune of a Garth Brooks oldie. Yes, she thought as she tossed an extra pair of socks in her bag, like Garth, she had friends low places.

The music was so loud she didn't hear the knock on her door. And when it came the second time, and then the third, she was still unaware that her long-awaited suitor had arrived. Right in the middle of the last round of Garth's chorus, the music suddenly ended. Surprised by the cessation of sound, she walked toward the living room to see what was wrong, and then squealed in shock as she entered. Stone was standing in the middle of the room holding the plug in his hand.

"Stone! You nearly scared me to death," she muttered while her heart did a two-step of its own.

"Well, you would have never heard it coming," he growled. "It's a wonder you're not deaf." He waved the electric cord to prove his point.

She was still frowning when he scooped her up in his arms and began kissing a little mole near her ear.

"Good morning, sunshine," he said sweetly, kissing her again and again, until the frown fell away.

"You are so bad," she said, and wrapped her arms around his neck.

His eyes twinkled devilishly as he planted a swift, urgent kiss on her lips.

"Damn, honey, I thought you told me I was good. Really good."

She slapped at the hands sliding toward her hips and moved them back to her waist.

"That's beside the point. Now, are we still going fishing, or should I move my bag from the bed so that you can go play?"

He laughed, and then cupped her bottom before sending her off with a swat.

"Go get your pants on, woman. I hear fish a'callin'."

"Fish can't talk. There's coffee in the kitchen. Give me five minutes and I'll be ready to go."

His gaze raked the soft contours of her unfettered shape beneath the oversize shirt. "I'll give you four, and then I'm coming in after you."

Jessica had the bed cleared and was reclining against a pillow, waiting, when he came through the door. A cocky grin spread across his face.

"You think you're so smart, don't you?"

She stretched, and the motion pushed her breasts against the T-shirt in a provocative thrust.

"Unlike you, I don't need a tackle box full of bait to catch my fish. I've got all the bait I need, right here." She patted the bed beside her.

Stone started shedding clothes at the door, and by the time he joined her on the bed, he was naked and primed.

"Jessie, honey, you are a truly dangerous woman, and as an officer of the law, I feel it is my duty to subdue you in any way that I can."

Jessica shifted her legs as Stone slid in between them. Her body was already aching and heavy with want.

"Do you swear?" she whispered.

"Only when I have to," he said, and then slid inside.

The cabin was rustic, which meant the outhouse was out back and the water was in a nearby well.

"What do you do for baths?" Jessica asked, dubiously eyeing the spare double bed on which Stone had dropped their bags.

His eyebrows knitted thoughtfully, and Jessica rolled her eyes. "Oh, great. Don't tell me, let me guess. You guys don't bother, right?"

He grinned. "That's not so! When we get too rank, we wash. The lake's not too cold this time of year. It will be great."

"You bathe in the lake? What about snakes and fish and stuff?"

"You worry too much," he said.

Jessica flopped down on the bed and then winced as she bit her tongue upon the impact.

"Ow," she muttered, and felt in her mouth to make sure everything was still properly attached.

Stone looked up from digging through his tackle box. "What happened?"

"You tell me," she said, giving up on her injured tongue to poke at the bed's lack of springs. "I was expecting to bounce, not ricochet."

He grinned. "Yeah, it is a little hard, but you know what they say, a firm bed is good for your back."

She gave the cabin's interior a slow, thoughtful look. "I think I have been snookered."

His grin widened. "Well don't look at me. I never snookered a woman in my life. I have, however, sweet-talked a few."

She stifled a smile and threw a bag of rubber worms at his head. When Stone was in one of these teasing moods, he was impossible.

"We came to fish, so let's fish," she said.

"Don't you want to unpack?"

She eyed the accommodations once more with undisguised disdain, and then leaned over and unzipped her bag. "There, I'm unpacked. Now, are you going to put up or shut up?"

He handed her two tackle boxes, and then walked out with the fishing rods, assuming she would follow.

She did, stumbling across tree roots and dodging bramble bushes on their way to the water's edge. And as she ducked to go under a particularly low limb, it suddenly occurred to her that something was way off-key.

"Hey, you! Why am I carrying the heavy stuff and you're just carrying the poles?"

Stone grinned, but only because he knew she couldn't see his face. Once, a few months after he and Naomi had been married, he'd tried to take her fishing. Jessie had already made it farther than Naomi had. His ex had taken one look at the cabin and the accommodations and cried. He'd taken her back to town and given up the idea as a lost cause.

Underbrush crackled beneath their feet as they continued through the woods on their way to the lakeshore, and Stone sighed. He could hear Jessie muttering beneath her breath, but to her credit, she wasn't yelling. At least not yet.

He knew he was trying her in more ways than one, but the way he had it figured, if she was willing to put up with him during this, there was the possibility that she could handle just about anything.

"Hey!"

At the sound of Jessie's shout, Stone paused and then turned.

"What's up?" he asked, trying to ignore the twig stuck in her hair and the spiderweb plastered to her leg.

"I asked you a question and never did get my answer."

"Sorry," Stone said. "I guess I was enjoying all this natural beauty and didn't hear you. What was it you said, honey?"

Jessica thought about glaring. He had some nerve! Piling her down with all this stuff and then calling her "honey."

"I asked you why I'm carrying all the heavy stuff and you only have a couple of fishing poles?"

"Oh," he said, hiding a grin. "Why, it's because you're the apprentice and I'm the master. Apprentices carry. Masters mast."

At that, he turned and headed for the lake. Not because he was in that much of a hurry to start fishing, but because he was afraid if he stood there much longer, she was going to take a swing at him with the stuff in her hands.

"That is so much bull," Jessica muttered, but she continued to follow him right up to the lake's edge.

"Here you go," he said, handing her a rod and taking one of the tackle boxes from her.

"Here I go, what?" she asked.

"That's your rod. That's your tackle box. Pick a lure of the box and put it on the end of the line. Cast it into the water. Reel slowly. If something tugs on the line, give it a jerk to set the hook and then reel in your fish.''

''I can do that,'' Jessica said, and wiped her hands on the legs of her jeans, then opened the lid to the tackle box.

Inside were lures in all shapes and sizes, as well as a colorful assortment of plastic worms. She dropped to her knees and began poking around, actually taking pleasure in sorting through Stone's treasures.

''Don't take all day about it,'' he said as he made his first cast. The lure and line arched perfectly as the reel spun out line. The spinner bait he'd chosen dropped in the water with a near-splashless plop.

Jessica watched, mesmerized by the way he stood, the way he moved, the way he held his head cocked to one side, as he reeled the lure toward shore.

When Stone glanced her way, she was picking through lures with studied intent. He smiled. At that moment, he knew he'd never loved her more.

''Need some help, honey?''

''No, I've got it,'' she said, and rocked back on her heels to attach the lure to her line.

''Don't get too close to the trees, and easy on the cast or you'll get backlash,'' he warned.

She glanced over her shoulder, then down at the reel, and nodded.

Here goes nothing.

The tip of the rod moved in a beautiful, symmetrical arc. A perfect one-hundred-and-eighty-degree cast—that slipped out of her hands. She watched in openmouthed awe as the rod landed with a splash about ten feet away from the shore and started to sink.

''Oh, turkey feathers.''

Stunned by what she'd done, Stone gawked for no less than a second before wading in to retrieve his second-best rod. Luckily, the water was only waist high, and Stone's shirt was still mostly dry as he started back to shore. His color was a bit high, but Jessica attributed that to haste rather than distress.

"Sorry," she said as he handed her the pole. "I don't know what happened."

He managed a grin. "That's okay, honey. It happens to everyone...once."

She got the message, then dropped down to change the lure.

His shoes squished and his undershorts were in a wad, but it wasn't the first time he'd fished wet, and it wouldn't be the last. He picked up his own rod, then glanced back at Jessie.

"What are you doing now?" he asked.

"Changing the lure. That one was bad luck."

"Oh." He nodded as he made another cast, a little bit worried that what she'd said almost made sense.

This time, Jessica was determined to do it right. She tightened her grip on the handle until her knuckles turned white. By George, if the rod went in the lake this time, she was going with it.

Stone eyed her stance. The wind was blowing just enough to tousle that crazy haircut all over her head, giving her a childlike appearance. But there was nothing childish about Jessie. She was all woman, everywhere it mattered.

"Easy does it," he urged as she drew back again. And he knew it was wrong before the arc passed her nose. It looked more like a chop than a cast.

"Ouch!" she squealed, and looked down in dismay at the blue-feathered spinner she'd hooked in her jeans.

Stone dropped his rod and knelt at her feet, inspecting the lure caught near the hem of her jeans.

"Ooh, dang, honey. I'll bet that hurts. Here, let me see. Naw, you got lucky. It's not stuck in you, just your pants."

"Yeah, I'm lucky," Jessica muttered, and tried not to stagger as Stone hiked her foot on his knee to cut out the hook.

Now she had a hole in her jeans. Fishing was more expensive than she had first imagined. He handed the extracted hook to her, and she dropped it back in the box.

This time, Stone didn't have to ask. "Gonna change the lure again, are you?"

She nodded. There had to be one in here that could do things right.

A few minutes later, she was ready again, and this time, the glitter of the silver-and-white lure dangling from the end of the line made her smile. She stood and reeled it up toward the tip of the rod.

"Ready to try it again, are you?" Stone asked.

"If at first you don't succeed, and all that stuff," Jessica said.

"Good girl. Give it all you've got." But just to make sure he didn't become the next casualty, Stone took a couple of steps to the side and winked at her.

Jessica beamed and drew back the rod like a batter at the plate.

"No, honey, don't "

Stone's warning was too late. The line whirred, running out and then recoiling inside the reel. Next to losing the big one, it was a fisherman's worst fear.

Jessica looked down, wondering why the line hadn't flown out upon the water like Stone's always did. When she saw the tangle of line hanging out of the reel, she frowned.

"Oooh. Backwash."

"Backlash. It's called backlash."

She glanced up. He had a strange, fixed expression on his face. "Yeah, right," she said, then dropped down on the ground and started picking at the knots with an overdone sigh.

Stone's nerves were as shredded as the line on her reel. The wet socks in his shoes were causing blisters, and the leather belt he was wearing was starting to draw, drying like green rawhide. He looked back at the mirror-perfect surface of the lake and winced when a fish actually flopped in the water beyond. He sighed, looking down at Jessie and her woebegone face.

"Here, honey," he said gently, handing her his pole. "I'll cast it for you, and you can practice reeling it in while I untangle your line, okay?"

Her expression brightened as she jumped to her feet. "Oh, thank you, Stone."

He sighed. "You're welcome." Then he cast. The line slipped out of the reel, floating through the air in silent perfection. "Here you go, Jessie. Just reel it in slow, like I was doing."

She took the rod, almost dancing with delight as he dropped to the ground to stare in dismay at the mess she'd made of the line. There was no need in trying to untangle it. It would never be the same if he did. He took out his pocketknife and started to cut just as Jessica squealed.

"I've got one! I've got one!" she shrieked, and started running backward, with the line outstretched.

Stone jumped to his feet. "No! Don't run! Don't run! Reel it in! Reel it in!"

Jessie froze. "Oh! Yeah, right!"

She started to reel, and to his dismay, she pulled in a fish the size of his forearm. Stone was forced to watch her success while her tangled line dangled from his hands.

"Look!" she cried. "I caught a big one, didn't I?"

He managed a grin while thinking that if he didn't love her so much, he would pack up her troublesome little butt and take her back home.

"This is fun," Jessica said. "Let's do it again."

Stone dropped her rod at his feet. "Waste not, want not," he said quickly. "That fish is big enough for the both of us to eat." Then he glanced at his watch. "Wow. It's going to be dark in…oh…five or six hours. Are you ready to go to the cabin?"

"No way," Jessica said. "Take it off. I want to do it again."

Hell. I was afraid she'd say that. He reached for the fish to remove the hook.

The sun was dangling just above the horizon like bait dangles in the water. Still there, but close to sinking.

Jessie's line was intact once more, and during the afternoon, she'd had a couple of good strikes, but nothing like the fish she'd pulled in hours earlier. She was down on her knees, digging through the mess she'd made of Stone's tackle, still in search of that perfect lure, when he spoke.

"Jessie?"

She looked up. There was a smudge on her cheek, and her makeup had disappeared hours ago. She smiled just as the sun disappeared, and for a brief flash of glory, the sky showed vivid hues of pink, purple and gold. Stone stared at her, silhouetted by the heavenly palette, and knew she would never be more beautiful to him than she was right then. Unable to contain the love he was feeling, he laid down his fishing rod and dropped to his knees before her.

Jessica's heart surged. The expression on his face gave her more hope than she'd had in weeks. If she didn't miss her guess, that was love, true love, staring back at her. She rose to her knees and wrapped her arms around his neck.

Stone's arms enfolded her and he held her close, feeling her tremble as she leaned against his strength.

"Jessie, I very much want to make love to you."

The deep timbre of his voice raked across her senses, and she hid her face against the curve of his neck and sighed.

"Dare I assume this means yes?" he asked.

She lifted her head and got lost in the hope in his eyes.

"I'm sorry," she said softly. "But I've said yes so many times in my dreams that I guess I thought you already knew."

Even though he'd been pretty sure she would say it, he went weak with relief and pulled her forward, tasting the tears on her face.

"Thank you, Jessie."

"For what?" she asked. "I haven't done anything yet."

As he combed his fingers through the tangles in her hair, he glanced down at the hole in her jeans and the light in her eyes.

"On the contrary, Jessie Leigh. You've done something I would never have believed possible."

"What's that?"

"You've proved me wrong about the staying power of a woman."

The smile slid off her face as his meaning sank in. "All I asked for was a chance."

He sighed. If only he could believe their whole life would be like this. And then she shivered and he looked up, realizing it was getting late. The air was getting cooler. And, as much as he hated to move, they needed to be inside before dark. He kissed her once more, just because he could, and then got to his feet and held out his hand.

"Come on, honey. We'd better head for the cabin. It's going to be dark soon."

Jessica let him pull her upright, and then stood while he shut the tackle boxes, watching as he pulled the stringer out of the lake. Her fish flopped, and Jessica eyed it nervously as she picked up the rods before starting back the way they'd first come.

"Hey," Stone yelled when he heard her walking away. "What about your fish and the tackle boxes?"

She pivoted slowly. "I caught the only fish, right?"

"Well, yes, but—"

"Then, that would make me the master and you the apprentice...right?"

He started to grin. "Are you threatening me, woman?"

"Oh, no. However, once we get back to the cabin, I can promise you many wonderful things."

His grin widened. "That sounds like a bribe."

She spun on her heel and started into the woods. "Take it any way you like," she yelled back. "But I suggest that you hurry. I'm feeling terribly grateful for this day and for my daily bread."

His laughter followed her all the way back to the cabin.

Twelve

"**I** don't know how to clean fish."

Stone stood in the doorway of the cabin with the tackle boxes in one hand and the dangling fish in the other, grinning wryly as Jessie made her nervous announcement from the other side of the room. He dropped the boxes, then looked up. There was a thick drawl in his voice that made her nervous.

"Well now, I don't know about this. My daddy always taught me that if you catch it, you clean it."

Stone stifled a chuckle as she stared at the fish he was holding with complete dismay.

"Then put it back," she said. "I'll eat beans."

This time, he did laugh. "Ease up, Jessie. I was just teasing. I'll clean it, and if you don't mind, I'll cook it, as well."

She sniffed. "Are you hinting that I might ruin our meal?"

"No, ma'am. I'm pretty much saying it outright."

She dropped down on the bed and stared at her shoes, only now realizing that she'd come into a house—however dubious the distinction—with dirty feet.

"I'm not much good at the things that count, am I, Stone?"

He dropped the fish on the floor and pulled her off the bed and into his arms.

"On the contrary, Jessie Leigh, you are very, very good at what matters. You love and give love better than anyone

I've ever known. You're smart, and besides that, you're awful damn cute.''

When she blushed and grinned, he felt his heart swelling inside his chest to the point it might burst.

''The way I see it, anyone can learn to cook. But people don't learn what you already know. That comes from instinct, and from the heart.''

She felt a great sense of peace. ''I'll take cooking lessons.''

He smiled and hugged her to him, nuzzling his chin on the crown of her head as she laid her cheek against his chest.

''You do whatever makes you happy, Jessie Leigh. Just don't let anyone mess with your heart. It's already perfect.''

She sighed, hugging him to her. ''You know what?''

''What, honey?''

''So are you.''

For Stone, it was the best thing she could have ever said.

''Well now,'' he said, more touched than he could show, ''I guess we'd better get some light going in here. I'll bring in the gear and then clean your fish while you sort out the stuff, okay?''

''Okay.''

And that night, Jessie ate fish by lamplight, and made love by the light of the moon.

The case involving Olivia Stuart's murder was going nowhere. Stone and Jack Stryker were dealing with dead-end leads and daily frustration.

Before Stone and Jessica knew it, the month of July was almost gone, heralding August and the last carefree days of a Colorado summer. And while their Fourth of July fishing trip had pretty much been a bust, Stone was still determined to take her to the woods and make her like it.

And, because Jessica loved the man like there was no

tomorrow, she valiantly agreed to take a Friday off of work and give it one more try, with the following exceptions. No fishing allowed. No rustic cabin without indoor plumbing or electricity.

Stone couldn't wait for it to begin. Jessica was counting the hours until it would be over. But more than escape from a weekend in the woods, she wanted something from him that she was afraid she might never get. A commitment.

The phone rang just as Jessica was getting out of the shower. She answered it, dripping wet, and with a towel clutched beneath her chin.

"Hello?"

"Hi, honey, it's me. Are you ready to go?"

She glanced down at the puddle in which she was standing and then up at the clock.

"Just about."

"Great. I'm going to run by the bank and cash a check and then I'll be right there, okay?"

A shiver of foreboding suddenly swept through her, and she yelled, afraid that he was about to hang up.

"Stone, wait!"

"I'm right here, what's wrong?"

The sensation was gone. She had nothing but instinct on which to focus.

"Oh...nothing, I guess. Just that I love you."

His voice deepened. "I love you, too, Jessie Leigh. And I can't wait for you to see the cabin. You're going to love this one, I swear. It has running water and an indoor toilet and a real feather bed. Out back, there's a place where moss grows thick, right beneath a big tall pine. And at night, if you lie on your back and look straight up through the trees, you can see stars. And if you squint your eyes just right, it almost looks as if the stars are hanging on the ends of the branches like Christmas ornaments."

The image was beautiful, and with Stone in the picture, just about perfect.

"I can't wait to see it," she said softly.

"I'll be there soon," he promised.

"Be careful," she said, but he'd already hung up.

She glanced at the clock again and then swiped at the water on the floor before heading back to the bathroom to get a fresh towel. She didn't have much time to get dressed, but at least this time, she was already packed.

An hour had come and gone since Stone's call, and the sun was completely up. The day was getting hotter by the minute as Jessica sat in the porch swing, staring intently up the street, watching for him to turn the corner.

Bumblebees dipped in the flower beds below her, buzzing a warning in case anything came too close. Sweat had beaded on her upper lip, and the shaggy style of her haircut was raking the back of her neck in damp persistence. The longer she squinted into the bright light of day, the more strained her eyes became. She couldn't imagine what was taking him so long, but she was worried. With the beginnings of a nagging headache threatening to ruin her day, she finally gave up and went inside to get something for the pain.

For Jessica, the silence inside her house was unnerving, and after she'd taken her pills, she flopped down on the couch, picked up the remote and turned on the TV, unprepared for what she was about to hear.

"...Police. No word on the situation is available as yet, but we have it on good authority that several people have been taken hostage."

Jessica froze, watching the screen with a wide, blank stare. It didn't matter what they were saying, because in her heart, she already knew. The very thing that she'd feared most of all was happening. And even though she didn't know details, she knew that somehow Stone was involved.

"Again, for those of you just tuning in, word has reached the station that the main branch of the Bank of Grand Springs is being robbed as we speak. Over an hour ago, a silent alarm went off. Police responded by surrounding the bank, although no one has made any attempt to come out. For your information, the following streets have been blocked off to normal traffic for the protection of passersby. Please take an alternative route to work."

She groaned. *What about the protection of the people inside?*

The announcer droned on, having repeated the story several times already, although Jessica wanted to scream.

Tell me more. Tell me more. I'm just tuning in.

She glanced at the clock. It was a quarter to twelve. Almost noon. She covered her face with her hands and remembered her dream—and the blood.

Stone. Oh, Stone.

She got up from the couch and headed for the door. She had to be there. She had to see for herself. Someone would tell her that Stone was all right.

Stone glanced down at the check in his hand as he entered the bank. When he looked up, he found himself staring into the muzzle of a gun.

His first thought was *Oh, hell,* and his second was for the gun locked in the glove box of his car. Before Stone could move, a heavyset man with a pockmarked face jammed his gun in Stone's ribs.

"Get your hands in the air, and get over there with the rest of them!" he shouted, waving his gun toward the counter where at least a dozen people were crouched on the floor.

Stone did as he was told. Twice the gunman jabbed Stone in the back, and each time it happened, Stone flinched, half expecting the gun to go off.

Phones were ringing all over the building. A woman was crying hysterically, while two others tried to comfort her.

When Stone met their gazes, he knew they were as frightened as their friend, just too afraid to speak.

Another man was crouched on the floor, holding a handkerchief to his head, while blood seeped out from beneath the edges in a slow, steady stream. It was Bill Jackson, the vice president of the bank, and when he saw Stone, recognition flickered. Stone's instinct was to check Jackson's wound, but as he started to crouch, the gunman jabbed him in the side.

"Sit down over there and don't be a hero. If he'd done what he'd been told, that wouldn't have happened."

Stone sat. If any of the gunmen figured out he was a cop, he was in trouble. And as he sat, he began to focus on the man with the pockmarked face, and the way he kept waving his gun.

The man moved back and forth like a caged cat, all the while keeping his assault rifle aimed at the hostages' faces, while another man, smaller in stature and weight, kept darting from the windows to the hostages and back again.

Even though the big man seemed to be the one in charge, it seemed that he was nervous about something other than being caught. When the man suddenly yelled, it became all to obvious.

"Damn it, Scanlan, you and Cody hurry up back there!"

Scanlan? Cody? Then that meant there were four of them instead of two. Stone's muscles became tense as he continued to watch the pair in front of him, gauging their nervousness against the possibility of someone getting shot. And at the thought, he suddenly remembered Jessie's dream and his stomach knotted. *My God! What if her premonition about me is going to come true? What if I never get out of here alive?* Stone sat without moving, contemplating the times he and Jessie had wasted because of him—because of his inability to believe she wouldn't turn out like Naomi if he married her. He kept seeing her face, those eyes, that smile. And then the man they called Trigger began pacing in front of where Stone was sitting and he began to watch him, knowing that at any moment this situation could get deadly.

Trigger was a small man, nervous and wiry, with stringy blond hair and a thin, wispy beard. He kept looking toward the street and sniffing repeatedly as he danced from one foot to the other.

Stone didn't move, but his expression mirrored his thoughts. *Junkie. That one is a junkie.*

Trigger danced closer to his buddy in a nervous jerk. "Hey, Garrett, want me to go see what's keepin' Cody and Scanlan?"

Garrett. The name rang a bell in Stone's memory, but as he searched the man's face, no sense of recognition came.

Coldly, and without warning, Garrett pointed his rifle in the little man's face. "Damn it, Trigger, you do like I told you and nothin' else."

Trigger's attention shifted instantly, like a dog that had been given a fresh quarry to point, and he focused on the woman in tears, jamming his semiautomatic at her nose.

"Shut up!" Trigger yelled. "Or I'll give you somethin' to cry about!" Then he laughed, and it was a wild, crazy kind of shriek. "That's what my old lady usta tell me."

When the gun touched the woman's face, her eyes rolled back in her head and she slumped to the floor in a faint.

Stone watched her fall and knew a sense of relief. Fainting had probably saved her life. The little man was high as a kite. There was no telling what he might do.

And while they all sat, caught in a web not of their making, someone in the back of the room suddenly shouted, and there was a loud thump, then sounds of a scuffle. Stone guessed it was coming from the vault where the other two robbers had supposedly gone.

At the noise, Garrett pivoted, his eyes cold, his stance tense and crouched. Then he turned to Trigger.

"Go see what's taking them so long." Then Garrett

changed his mind and caught him by the arm. "Never mind," he said. "Here they come."

Stone eyed the two approaching men. One was short and stocky, with thinning red hair that looked stiff and dirty. While Stone didn't recognize him, there was something about his behavior that told Stone the man was an old hand at this game.

"Damn it, Scanlan, where's Cody?" Garrett snarled, his eyes darting nervously toward the back of the bank.

Scanlan yanked at the man standing beside him, then began to curse as he jabbed his gun in the middle of the man's back. "He's in the vault. This son of a bitch here locked him in the vault!"

Stone watched Garrett freeze. Unlike Stone, who'd come into this mess slightly late, everyone else was aware of the news, and they held their breath with great fear.

"What the hell are you sayin'?" Garrett whispered. "Where's my little brother?"

"That's what I been tryin to tell you," Scanlan yelled, and shoved the teller to his knees. He fell at Garrett's feet. "He locked him in the vault. Says he can't get it open again until eight o'clock tomorrow. Says it's a damned time lock." Then he aimed his gun at the man on the floor. "You know what I say? I say shoot him and let's get the hell out of here."

Garrett's face flushed, making the pockmarks look even deeper and darker. Momentarily speechless, he stalked around the lobby in a complete circle, and then yanked the young teller to his feet, shoving him up against a desk.

"What's your name?" Garrett asked.

"David Clark."

"Well, then, Mr. David Clark, you get back there and unlock that vault, and you do it now." He shoved the barrel of the gun beneath Clark's chin to prove his point.

"I can't," Clark said, and started to cry. "It's on a time lock and won't open until eight o'clock tomorrow morning. I swear!"

Garrett's eyes narrowed, and he reacted with cold precision, drawing back and hitting the young teller on the side of the head. Clark dropped like a poleaxed steer.

Garrett pointed his gun at each and every hostage individually. "You people better say your prayers and bed down for the night, because that's my brother in there, and I ain't leavin' here without him."

An elderly man suddenly moaned and slumped. The woman beside him screamed. "It's his heart! He's having a heart attack!"

Trigger started cursing, and Scanlan and Garrett were shouting in each other's faces.

Stone couldn't stay still any longer.

"Let me help him," he said, and at the sound of his voice, everyone, including the robbers, froze.

Garrett turned, his gaze fixed upon Stone's face.

"I didn't say you could talk," he said slowly, jiggling the rifle loosely in his hands, as if testing it for weight.

Stone pointed. "You can do time for robbing a bank, but they'll execute you if that man dies."

He never saw the blow coming. One minute Garrett was standing over him with a look of hate on his face, and the next thing Stone knew, his cheek was bleeding and the cut had gone straight to the bone. He took a deep breath and gritted his teeth—then looked up.

"You can beat the hell out of me, and it won't change a thing."

Stone started to get up, when Garrett jammed the gun in his belly.

"On your knees, pretty boy. You want to help him, you crawl."

Ignoring the blood dripping down his cheek from the cut, Stone took off on all fours, and moments later, he had the man flat on his back and was administering CPR.

Just then, at the entrance to the bank, a uniformed officer suddenly appeared out of nowhere and grabbed a woman who was starting into the bank, hustling her quickly out of sight. Trigger screamed and began waving his gun over the hostages' heads, then toward the door and back again.

"Cops! Cops! We've been made! Son of a bitch, we've been made!"

"So what," Garrett growled. "We ain't goin' anywhere, at least until tomorrow mornin'. I ain't leavin' Cody behind."

Stone continued the motions of CPR, and in the back of his mind, kept thinking that on a scale of one to ten in a worst-case scenario, this mess would be about a twelve. The only positive thing about the entire episode was when the old man's color began to improve. Suddenly he coughed and then moaned.

Stone leaned back on his heels, catching his breath as he checked for a pulse. It wasn't good, but it was there, and for now, it was the best he could do. The woman, who Stone supposed was the wife, started to sob, and he reached out to touch her.

"Try to keep him still," he said softly.

"His pills. They're in his jacket," she said, pointing toward her husband's pocket.

Stone took them out, read the instructions and slipped one under the man's tongue, then handed the bottle to his wife.

"Better hang on to these for him. Just in case."

Her fingers curled around the small plastic vial. "Thank you. Thank you," she whispered. "You saved Gordon's life."

"You! Dr. Kildare! Get back over here where you belong."

Stone gave the woman one last assuring glance, and then crawled back to where he'd been sitting, taking careful note of the situation as it now stood.

Trigger was scratching his skin and cursing without pause. Scanlan was huddled in a corner with his gun across his knees, and if looks could kill, they'd all be dead. However, it was Garrett who worried Stone most. There was a wild, hunted look in his eyes as he kept glancing toward the vault in the back of the room.

And the phones in the bank continued to ring.

Jessica was running. Every now and then she got a glimpse of herself as she flew past the plate-glass windows in the downtown district, and it was like looking at a stranger. She saw flashes of blue—her jeans and the sky blue shirt that Stone liked so much, the one he said matched the color of her eyes. She saw traces of white—the tennis shoes she was wearing, and the stark fear that had drained all the color from her face.

Wind whipped through the streets and into her eyes, raking through her hair and giving it a more windblown appearance than normal, and yet she ran without caution, dodging streets that had been blocked off—taking alleys to get where she wanted to go.

And then through the mouth of the alley just up ahead, she saw the stone edifice that marked the front of the Bank of Grand Springs. There, parked in front, just as she'd feared, was Stone's car. She burst out of the alley, straight into an officer's arms, and before he could stop her, she was screaming Stone's name.

Someone grabbed her from behind and she spun, her eyes filled with hope, only to see Jack Stryker's face, drawn from worry. She grabbed his arms, the plea in her voice no less urgent than the expression on her face.

"Jack! Where's Stone?"

But he didn't answer. Instead, he began dragging her out of the danger zone. When they were safe, he turned, his grip still firm upon her arm.

"What the hell do you think you're doing down here?" he growled. "You could get yourself killed, and then what do you think Stone would say?"

It was all she could do not to scream. "He's in the bank, isn't he?"

Stryker sighed. "We think so. I recognized his car the

moment I arrived. Our best guess is they've taken at least a dozen hostages, maybe more.''

She moaned, and he caught her as she swayed.

''Look,'' he added. ''We don't really know what's going on. They've made no contact. They don't answer the phone. No one's made any demands. Right now, it's simply a waiting game.''

''What if they don't know the police are out here?'' she said.

Stryker's face darkened. ''Oh, they know, all right. Our best guess is they've been in there at least forty-five minutes, maybe longer. And since they've made no move to come out—''

''They're going to shoot him,'' she moaned, and covered her face.

''No. You're wrong, Jessie. I've been here almost from the start and no shots have been fired.''

She clutched his hand, squeezing it hard enough to make Stryker wince.

''No, you don't understand,'' she cried. ''They're *going* to shoot him.''

Stryker blanched as the implication of her words finally dawned. He looked toward the bank in disbelief, and then back at Jessie, wanting to argue. But he knew more than most about her, and the doubt factor in this situation had to be ignored.

''Hell,'' he said softly, and then he heard his voice shake as he asked. ''Will he die?''

She paled and slumped to the street in a faint. Stryker reached out, but not soon enough to catch her. Her head hit the curb with a thump.

''Oh, man,'' he groaned as he lifted her up in his arms and carried her toward a parked ambulance that had been called to the scene. ''First casualty.'' He said a quick prayer as he laid her down on the grass.

Jessica woke up with a headache, and her first thought was that the painkillers she'd just taken hadn't worked.

And then she looked up and saw sky and the back of Jack Stryker's head, and she moaned. A cold pack shifted on her forehead, and she reached up to feel it with a shaky hand, wondering why it was there.

Jack turned, his face mirroring his concern, then leaned down and laid a hand on her forehead.

"How ya feelin', kid?"

Every ugly memory came rushing back, and she felt like crying. This was where I came in, she thought, only now it was the wrong cop leaning over her.

"What happened?"

"You fainted." He touched the side of her forehead lightly, and grimaced. "I didn't catch you in time. You gave yourself quite a lump."

Jessica reached for her head in a panic and then sighed. At least they hadn't shaved any more hair. Stone still teased her about the—

Her breath caught on a sob. Stone. Would he ever tease her again?

"Help me up," she said.

"I don't know if you should—"

"I won't faint again."

There was something about the tone of her voice that told Jack she was serious. He helped her get up.

"Tell me what happened," she begged. "I have a right to know."

Jack pointed toward a middle-aged man who was in the act of getting out of a car. "Nothing's happened. You didn't miss a thing, and a hostage negotiator just got here. Maybe he can make some headway into this mess."

She looked so lost, so small, so afraid, that Jack reacted before he thought. He put his arm around her shoulders and pulled her close, letting her lean against him for strength.

"It'll be all right," he said softly. And then more to himself than to her, he added, "It has to be."

* * *

Except for the steady stream of Trigger's curses and an occasional sob from one of the hostages, the bank was almost silent. The bank of phones had been quiet for at least a quarter of an hour, and that told Stone, more than anything else, that the police were taking control of everything within their power.

Garrett had been back and forth to the vault at least a half-dozen times, and each time he'd gone, they'd heard him shouting to a brother who was beyond his reach. Each time he would come back, his actions were a little more frantic, his control slowly slipping.

Stone watched, knowing it wouldn't take much to set the man off. Just a slip of the tongue, or a panicked hostage, and someone would die.

And while Stone was watching, a phone on a nearby desk started to ring. Everyone, including the cornered trio, jumped. The phones had been quiet for so long.

It rang. Seven times, then eight, and then Stone lost count of the number. Intuition told him a negotiator was probably on the other end of the line, waiting for someone to pick up the phone. They were trained to calm snakes like Garrett. Maybe with a little TLC, he would let some of the hostages go.

"Why don't you answer it?" Stone said. "It might be for you."

Garrett spun, a snarl on his face that would have stunned a lesser man. "So, hero, you're turnin' psychic now, are you?"

He drew back his gun to deliver another blow when the man they called Scanlan grabbed him by the arm.

"What if he's right?" Scanlan said. "We need to find us a way to get out of here."

Primed for violence, Garrett hit him instead, and Scanlan staggered from the unexpected blow.

"You bastard!" Scanlan shrieked, and reached for the assault rifle hanging over his shoulder.

For once, Trigger did something that actually made sense. He fired one round up in the air, and everyone, including Garrett and Scanlan, dropped to the floor.

"Well now," he said. "Now that I have your attention, don't you think it might be a good idea if we didn't shoot at ourselves?"

Garrett crawled to his knees, but the worst of his anger was over. Scanlan got up with his gun aimed straight at Stone's head.

"I saw you lookin', pretty boy," he said softly, and poked the gun at Stone's shoulder. "You want some of this? Huh? Do you? Do you?"

Stone didn't move. Didn't answer. And to his undying relief, Garrett finally picked up the phone.

"What?"

When Garrett remained silent, listening intently, Stone figured his guess had been right.

"No one's hurt," Garrett said suddenly, and then he looked toward the row of hostages. "I'll rephrase that," he drawled. "No one is dead...yet."

Silence again, and Stone watched Garrett's face, trying to read by his reactions what the negotiator might be saying.

"No, I ain't got no demands," Garrett said angrily. "Unless you got someone out there who can open the time lock on a vault, I ain't goin' nowhere, and neither are the good citizens of Grand Springs here who have decided to keep me company."

Silence again, only this time it was brief.

"No, I ain't willin' to let no one go. My brother is locked in that vault, and until he comes out, no one's goin' anywhere."

Then the look on his face shifted to the row of hostages on the floor. His eyes narrowed angrily as his gaze fell on the young teller who'd messed up their plans.

"And you all better be hopin' my little brother is alive when that vault comes open, cause if he ain't, I'm gonna start shootin' 'em down where they lay...startin' with the smart aleck who calls hisself David Clark.''

He slammed the phone down, and then turned around and took it off the hook.

"Negotiations are over," he said shortly. "Bed down, people. We got ourselves a wait."

"What did they say? What did they want?" Jessica asked as Jack came back to her side after talking with the negotiator at some length.

He frowned, and then shook his head. "It's not good."

Jessica grabbed his arm. "What do you mean? And what was that shot? Is anyone hurt?"

Jack refrained from telling her exactly what the negotiator had said. The way he figured it, Jessie was on a "need to know" basis, and right now, she didn't need to know it all.

"They said everyone was okay. The shot was supposedly some sort of warning. And as for what they want, I guess we'll have to wait till morning to find out."

Jessica paled and glanced down at her watch. It wasn't quite three o'clock. Morning was forever away.

"Morning? Why are they waiting till morning?"

"Because, somehow, one of them got locked in the vault and they say they aren't leaving without him."

Jessica paled. "Oh, Jack! Anything could happen between now and then."

He led her back to the shade. "Yeah, kid, and don't we all know it."

Thirteen

Breakfast was served in the lobby of the Bank of Grand Springs, compliments of four vending machines in the employees' break room. The vending machines, and the thirteen citizens of Grand Springs, would never be the same.

Last night had been the longest night of Stone's life, and he could only imagine how some of the older people had fared. The floor had been rock hard and cold, and the three bank robbers had fought among themselves right up until daybreak.

After that, Garrett, who still proclaimed himself the leader, had seemed to calm. Now Stone saw him watching the clock, as if willing time to fly faster to the eight o'clock hour. To the moment that the time lock and the vault would give up his brother.

The fact that the robbers had also had to deal with thirteen people and their bodily functions had added friction they could have easily done without. It seemed that at one time or another, someone needed a bathroom, or water to take medicine. Once, hysteria had played a strong-enough role with one of the women hostages that she'd clapped a hand to her mouth, and bolted for the bathroom without asking for permission.

Scanlan had swerved at the sound and taken aim with his rifle just as Stone lifted his hand in a shout.

"Don't shoot. Don't shoot. She's just sick."

The interruption stalled Scanlan's intent long enough for the woman to make it to the bathroom without being shot, and when the obvious sounds of retching filled the lobby of the bank, Garrett started to curse.

He kicked at the young teller responsible for the locked vault. "This is all your fault, you SOB. If you hadn't tried to play hero, we wouldn't be here, waiting for that damned vault to open. If anything's happened to Cody, you're gonna be the first to die."

Stone glanced at the clock, then toward the front of the bank. He could see nothing but vacant streets from where he was sitting, but he didn't have to see them to know that the entire force of the Grand Springs Police Department was somewhere nearby.

By now, he'd watched the hostages long enough to know which ones would endure, and which ones might break. And oddly enough, David Clark, the young teller who'd showed the first spunk by trying to lock both robbers in the vault, was the one he worried about most. Clark had tossed and turned all night, moaning and mumbling in his sleep, and now, since daylight had come creeping in through the windows, Clark's gaze was more often on that front door, only yards away.

"Hey! You!" Garrett yelled, and pointed his rifle. "Get up and go make us some more coffee," he ordered. "And don't pull no funny stuff or I'll splatter your old man where he lies."

The woman's gaze flew to the man beside her, then she looked back up at Garrett, got to her feet and started toward the back of the bank to the employees' break room. The man they called Trigger was right behind.

Stone breathed a quiet sigh of relief. One more injury-free incident behind them. He glanced at the clock. It was fifteen minutes until eight. He closed his eyes, letting his head fall against the back of the counter, and for the first time in a long, long while, he started to pray.

He prayed for himself, and for a chance at a life with Jessie. For the twelve other people being held hostage—

and for a stranger who'd spent the last twenty-two hours of his life locked up in a vault.

All he could think, was *God, don't let him be dead.*

When Jessica woke, she found herself stretched out at one end of a back pew in St. Veronica's Church, and as she struggled to sit up, she vaguely remembered coming in here sometime after midnight. Her head hurt horribly, and she tested the side of her scalp with her fingertips. The knot on her head was still there. Brenda was stretched out at the other end of the pew, her hand pillowed beneath her cheek, still asleep. Jessica sat up, looking at her surroundings in disbelief, then covered her face in despair.

Dear Lord, it's real.

Just for a moment, before she'd opened her eyes, she'd almost convinced herself it had been a bad dream. Last night, Jack Stryker had told her to go home and try to get some rest. She'd given him a look Stone would have recognized as total defiance, and walked down the street to St. Veronica's Church, instead. Brenda had found her there after dark, and together, they'd stayed in the church on their knees, praying for a miracle that had yet to occur.

Jessica glanced at her watch. It was only a little after seven. Almost an hour before the vault would open. And then what? she wondered. Would they let everyone go? Reason told her no. The hostages were their only bargaining power. A sick feeling of defeat swept through her, and she looked up to the altar for strength.

A priest was coming toward them down the aisle, and the compassion on his face was almost more than she could bear. When he touched her shoulder, she took his hand.

"Is there any news?" she asked.

"No, my child. Nothing has changed. Mrs. Daubish has just brought food and fresh coffee to my quarters. Won't you and your sister come eat with me? I would be honored."

Jessica glanced over her shoulder at the door. "I should go see if anything has—"

"Please," the priest urged. "Eat first. You must keep up your strength for what has yet to come."

Jessica's lips trembled. "And what will that be, Father? What's going to happen to Stone, and to all the other hostages inside?"

His touch was gentle as he urged her up. "I'm sorry, but I can't answer that. No one knows the future but God."

And as he spoke, something occurred to Jessica that she hadn't realized before. She wasn't sure, but it felt as if that thing—that *knowing* that had been plaguing her life for the past two months—was no longer with her.

She thought back over the past twenty-four hours. Not once had she had an inkling of foreboding, only fear. She'd had no flash, no image darkening her mind to warn her of upcoming danger. In a way, she felt empty—even cleansed. The priest was still waiting for her answer. She looked back at Brenda, who was already rousing.

"Thank you. I'll wake my sister and we'll be there shortly."

He smiled, and then pointed toward a door to the right of the altar. "My quarters are through there, and then to your left. Come when you're ready. I'll be waiting."

Jessica turned. Brenda was sitting up in the pew with a puzzled expression on her face. Jessica couldn't help but smile. Brenda's hair was flat on one side, and there was a red imprint on the side of her face where she'd laid on the hard wooden pew.

"For a moment I forgot where I was," Brenda mumbled, and then frowned as she ran her fingers through her hair. "Mercy, do I look as awful as I think I do?"

Jessica reached out and touched her sister's hand. "You look beautiful to me, and you will never know how much I appreciate you being here."

Brenda leaned over and kissed Jessica's cheek. Her heart

went out to her sister, and to the people who'd been taken hostage. "Has anything changed?" she asked.

Jessica stood. "I don't think so, but I'm anxious to go see. The priest was here moments ago. He asked us to have breakfast with him."

"Good," Brenda said. "I'm starved." And then she looked into Jessica's eyes and knew that food was the furthest thing from her sister's mind. She reached out and touched Jessica's cheek, and then pointed toward her head. "Are you all right?"

Jessica felt for the scar on the edge of her hairline, and then her fingers moved to the knot on her head. One injury had started it all, maybe this injury had *ended* her ability to see.

She nodded, a look of wonder on her face. "You know, sis, I think that I am. But I wish I was as certain of Stone."

Brenda smoothed at her hair and clothes, and then fiddled with Jessie, combing her fingers through her younger sister's hair and straightening the collar of her shirt. Not because Jessie's hair was a mess, but because she wanted to give her hope, and love was all she had to give.

Cody Garrett stumbled out of the vault, half laughing, half crying as his brother braced his fall.

"Oh, damn, Aaron, I knew as sure as my name was Cody Joe Garrett that you wouldn't leave me. All the time I was in there, I knew you wouldn't leave."

Voices carried in the near-empty lobby, and even though Stone was on the other side of the room, he heard the man's cries and his blood ran cold.

Aaron? Aaron Garrett?

He knew the name. The man was on the FBI's ten-most-wanted list, although his appearance was drastically changed from the picture on the wanted poster. He had a rap sheet as long as Stone was tall, and none of it was pretty. He'd been in and out of prisons most of his life, and for everything ranging from burglary, through gunrunning, to assault with a deadly weapon. The only thing Garrett hadn't been convicted of was murder, and Stone figured it wasn't because he hadn't done it, but rather, because he'd never been caught in the act.

Cody Garrett made a break for the bathroom, and when he came out, his brother was holding some food and two cans of pop. He bolted it down like a starving dog, hardly chewing, biting it off instead, in gulping jerks.

Finally, Cody wiped his hand across the back of his mouth and turned toward the front of the bank where the hostages were being held. He frowned, and the scar across his nose knitted like a purse string.

"Now, where's that little bastard who shoved me into that vault? I got a bone to pick with him."

David Clark started to whine beneath his breath like a cornered animal, and Stone shook his head in a warning manner, reaching out and gripping the young teller's shoulder, urging him to stay calm.

"They're going to kill me," Clark whispered, and then looked away, his gaze focusing on the expanse of floor between him and the bank's front door.

"I don't think so," Stone hissed. "Try to relax. Don't let them know you're afraid."

Nearby, the man they called Trigger heard their whispers and darted toward them in a quick, antsy hop.

"Shut the hell up!" he screamed, and jabbed the gun in their faces.

Stone silenced instantly. Ever since daybreak, he'd been watching the little man's feverish antics. From the way Trigger was behaving, Stone figured he was in desperate need of a fix. There was an old rule that cops always followed. A man with a gun was a dangerous man. A junkie with a gun was deadly.

Suddenly, Clark started to sob, his shoulders hunched where he sat, his face hidden against his knees.

"Oh, God. Oh, God. I'll never see my wife and baby again."

They were coming closer. Stone's hands curled into fists and he held his breath, willing himself to a calm he didn't feel.

"There you are, you little bastard!"

Cody Garrett's shout was all the warning Clark was going to get. Instinctively, he rolled into a ball, begging for mercy from a man who had none.

Clark's shrieks of pain were drowned out by the unexpected squeal and squawk of an amplified megaphone, and then words began echoing within the canyon of buildings outside and drifting into the bank.

"This is the Grand Springs police. We want to talk. Please hang up your phone."

David Clark was losing control. Prostrate before his captors, he clawed the floor on which he lay, begging and sobbing, pleading for his life.

Stone touched Clark's ankle. It was all he dared do. The last thing he wanted to do was aggravate Aaron Garrett any further. But the expressions on the hostages' faces ranged from hope to fear. Now that the brother was out of the vault, the obvious question was on everyone's mind. Would their captors be willing to negotiate, and if they did, then how? Since the incident had begun, they'd each lived with the knowledge that they might not survive.

Aaron Garrett cursed at the interruption, while Scanlan made a move Stone didn't expect. He stalked to the phone and slammed the receiver back down on the cradle, then glared, daring Garrett to argue. Within seconds, it started to ring.

"This heist was your idea, so you find a way to get us out of this mess," Scanlan said.

Garrett shifted the assault rifle into a lock-and-aim position, but Scanlan didn't flinch.

And the constant ringing of the phone punctuated the silence in which they stood.

Jessica came out of the church and started down the street toward the police barricades, Brenda right behind her. She could see Stryker standing in a huddle of men, talking and gesturing angrily, while uniformed officers crouched behind their cruisers, their guns aimed at the bank.

Then the town clock began to chime. It was eight-fifteen.

Someone pointed, and Stryker turned. He walked away from the group, meeting Jessica halfway.

"Jessie, go home." Then he looked at Brenda for support.

Brenda shrugged. "I tried, but I'm not leaving her here alone."

Jessica ignored them both. "Is there any news?"

"No. But if you go home, I swear I will call you the moment anything changes."

Although her knees were shaking, Jessica stood her ground.

"You can't make me leave," she said. "I need to be here. I need to know when it happens."

He cursed and turned his back on the women, unable to deal with the prediction Jessie had made about Stone. When he faced her again, he'd regained his composure.

"Then, come with me. And you've got to promise you'll stay where I put you."

She clutched his arm, her eyes wide and beseeching as she looked up at his face.

"You'll never know how much this means to me."

"Yes, I think I do," he muttered, and then managed a wry grin before escorting her and Brenda behind the SWAT unit.

"Gentlemen, this is Stone Richardson's…fiancée, and her sister. Treat them right, or you'll have to answer to me."

The men smiled, and then politely looked away, each of them well aware that the man in question was one of the hostages.

Jack turned, giving Jessica a last warning look. "I'll check on you from time to time and keep you updated, otherwise—"

"I know," Jessica said. "Stay put."

He shook his head. "I hope Stone knows how lucky he is."

Jessica's expression shifted. "Yes, actually, he does."

Moments later, Jessica was sitting on the curb beside her sister. Shoulders touching, heads leaning toward each other without speaking. Waiting for it to be over.

Aaron Garrett reached for the phone. When he did, everyone breathed a quiet sigh of relief, including his three cohorts, who wanted out in the very worst way.

"Yeah?" he growled. "Start talkin'."

Garrett's face flushed angrily as he listened to the man on the other end of the line. "I ain't got the problem. I got me thirteen of your finest citizens. Now, I want four parachutes delivered to the bank within the hour. Don't try no funny business with 'em, cause I'm gonna repack 'em myself. I want a ride to take me and my men to the airport. I want a plane standing by with just the pilot on board. I take one hostage to assure our safety, and after we jump, the pilot and hostage will go free."

After listening for brief seconds, Garrett screamed into the phone. "I'm callin' the shots. It's my way or no way. And I'm real inclined right now to just start shootin' people, starting with the son of a bitch who caused this whole mess."

David Clark jerked. In a move that no one expected, he was suddenly scrambling to his knees and then crawling, trying to get to his feet to make a run for the door.

Stone's heart dropped. Trigger was already screaming and taking aim. If one of them died, then the robbers would have no qualms about killing the rest. Before he could talk himself out of the notion, Stone leaped to his feet, shouting for Clark to stop.

Stone never heard the gun go off, but he felt the bullet's impact as it knocked him off his feet. He fell facedown on the floor, right on top of the hysterical teller who'd made a futile break for freedom.

Oh, God. Oh, God. It happened, just like Jessie said.

Stone rolled over on his back and tried to sit up, but the room kept tilting and spinning. His shoulder was burning, like he'd fallen into a fire. He reached up to touch it and his hand came away wet. He looked down at his blood. It was everywhere and still running—spilling out of his body and onto the floor.

A horrified silence followed the act, yet no one made a move to help, and in that moment, Stone was faced with the truth of Jessica's final dream.

Blood…everywhere…people looking…no one moved to help.

He groaned and put his head between his knees, afraid to pass out. To live, he needed to stay in control.

Garrett stared in disbelief while the phone lay on the counter beside him, forgotten in the shock of the moment. He stalked to where Trigger was standing and slapped him in the face. The blow popped loudly. "What the hell have you done?" Garrett shouted, and drew back again.

"They was makin' a break for the door," Trigger whined, holding his cheek.

"No. One of them was makin' a break, the other was tryin' to stop it. Now look what you done."

Trigger's little eyes bugged at the blood running between Stone's fingers.

"I didn't mean to—"

"You shot a cop."

Scanlan cursed beneath his breath and turned to hit the wall with his fist. Cody Garrett giggled, and when no one joined him, he looked down at the floor. Aaron Garrett turned red, then pale, then he started to curse. Trigger slunk quickly away.

"Who said that?" Garrett snarled, raking the line of hostages with the point of his gun.

The old man's wife held up her hand. "I did."

Garrett shoved his gun in front of her nose. "What did you say?"

Her face was lined, but her eyes were alive with a fire that belied her age. "I'll say it again. You shot a cop. Now they aren't going to give you a toothpick, let alone what you asked."

"You old bitch," Garrett snarled. "I oughta—"

"Go ahead," she said, acceptance for her fate in her voice. "Go ahead and shoot me, too."

"What if I shoot your old man, instead," Garrett snarled.

Tears filled her eyes, but her gaze never wavered. "It won't matter. He's already dead."

Stone groaned and then rolled, trying to get up. He got as far as his hands and knees.

"I'm not dead," he muttered. "Get back on the phone. Talk fast or they'll come in after the lot of you."

It was a bluff, but in the heat of the moment, it worked. Garrett picked up the phone.

The negotiator was repeating the same phrase, over and over. "Talk to me! Someone pick up the phone and talk to me!"

The burst of gunfire had been evident out on the street. To a man, every cop in the area went into a crouch, while the SWAT unit suddenly burst into action, running toward their captain to await further orders.

Jessica gasped, and then whispered a prayer as she got to her feet. But true to the word she'd given Jack, she didn't move a step farther. "Oh, God—dear God." It was all she could say.

Brenda's panic was evident as she slid her arm around Jessie's shoulder.

"That doesn't mean it was Stone," she said.

Jessica was mute, her face colorless, her mouth little more than a thin, grim line. She stared without wavering toward the door of the bank, as if by thought alone, she might see through the stone walls. She heard what they said, but she knew better. It *was* Stone who'd been shot. She knew, because she'd already seen it happen. In the past. In her sleep. In her dreams.

"Talk to me! Somebody talk to me!" Hank, the hostage negotiator, was shouting. He wiped a shaky hand over his eyes, then covered the receiver with his hand.

"I heard someone say a cop has been shot."

Stryker grunted as if he'd been the one to get hit, and he pivoted sharply, looking at the place where he'd left Jessie and stared in disbelief. She'd been right all along! He thought of his partner, and all the years they'd spent together on the force, and he exploded in anger.

"Get a medic in there," he whispered harshly. "Find a way to get a damned medic in there now!"

Hank started to shout, repeating the same phrase over and over.

"Someone pick up the phone and talk to me. Hello! Hello! Talk to me. Somebody talk to me!"

Suddenly the same man was back on the phone.

"What happened?" Hank asked, trying to maintain calm in his voice when he felt like cursing.

"It was an accident," Garrett growled, and then tried to carry it off with bravado. "And if I don't get what I want, someone else might be next."

"You broke faith, my friend," Hank said, his head spinning as he tried to work through his thoughts to what he believed might work. "You need to show some compassion so we can continue in good faith. We don't want anyone else to get hurt."

Garrett was starting to sweat as Hank's voice burned in his ear.

"I want you to let the hostages go, starting with the one you just shot," Hank said.

"I'll just bet you do," Garrett snarled, and then there was a commotion behind him and he spun in time to see the cop falling facedown on the floor. His heart plummeted and he kept telling himself that the damned cop wasn't dead, he'd only passed out.

"Let him go, and then we'll talk," Hank said.

"No one goes out. But you can send in a doctor. No cop. Just a doctor. He can fix up the guy that got shot."

Hank spun, frantically waving for the chief of police. Frank Sanderson was there within seconds. His remark was terse, his patience thin.

"What?" he barked.

"He'll let me send in a doctor."

Sanderson frowned. "And add another hostage to the situation. Hell, no! Make him send whoever's hurt out."

"They said it was a cop who got shot. Isn't Richardson one of yours?"

Sanderson blanched, and before he could think what to say, Erik Chang was at his elbow.

"Let me go in, chief. Before I was a cop, I worked as an EMT. I've got a black belt in karate, and Stone is my friend. Besides, I owe him."

Sanderson shook his head. "No way. I'm not going to give them two cops to shoot at instead of one."

"They've already got twelve other people for targets. One more won't make that much difference," Chang said. "Besides, I'm willing to take my chances."

"Hurry, damn it," Stryker said. "He doesn't have much time. He's bleeding bad."

They all stared at Stryker in disbelief. "How do you know that?" they asked.

Stryker pointed at Jessica. "I guess you could say a little bird told me."

"Someone get me an EMT uniform," Sanderson yelled, then pointed at Chang. "You get rid of your gun and ID. We're operating on a 'need to know' basis here, and they don't need to know squat.''

Hank took his hand off the receiver. ''We're getting a medic,'' he said quickly. ''Tell your men not to shoot. He's coming in.''

Jessie laughed and Stone reached out, wanting to capture the sound and the joy on her face.

''What's so funny?'' he growled as he pulled her close against his chest.

''Nothing,'' Jessie said, and snuggled willingly within his arms.

''Then, why the laughter?''

Her arms tightened around his waist as she looked up into his eyes. ''Because I'm so happy.''

Stone awoke with a jerk, and the pain that came with cognizance nearly blinded him. Just as he was opening his eyes, he remembered where he was and what had happened. The dream in his mind was just that…a dream. He groaned and looked up—right into the familiar face of Detective Erik Chang.

''Lie easy, sir,'' Chang said, hoping that his generic behavior and professional manner would alert Stone to the deceit he was trying to practice. ''I'm an EMT. You've been shot, and I'm tending your wound. The bullet exited your body, so there is no extraction necessary, but I'm applying a pressure bandage to alleviate the bleeding. I'm sorry if I hurt you.''

Stone lifted his hand toward the place on his shoulder where the fire continued to burn. Chang pushed his hand away.

''Don't move. Don't talk. Let me do all the work, okay?''

Chang's face was going in and out of focus, but Stone heard what was said and somehow understood. In lieu of nodding, he blinked. Once. Then took a deep breath and continued to watch as Chang went on with his work.

It was a small blink, but Chang breathed an inner sigh of relief. He was here and Stone was alive. For now, it was enough.

Stryker knelt in front of Jessica and touched the side of her cheek.

She looked up, stark misery on her face.

"We think Stone has been shot."

Jessica moaned. Even though she'd known it, hearing the words said aloud seemed too ugly to bear.

"Easy now," Stryker cautioned, looking to Brenda for help. "We've got a man inside. He's a trained EMT. He's doing all he can for Stone."

"And if it's not enough?"

He wasn't prepared to answer that. He stood suddenly and started to walk away.

"Stryker."

He turned.

"Thank you for letting me stay."

Fourteen

Ruth Dean had been right. Her husband was dead. Chang had been ordered to check the old man, but it was too late.

She'd been staring at her husband's face all along, but when Chang spoke, she stiffened, and then she looked up, straight at the men who were holding them hostage. To Chang's relief, they were talking among themselves, unaware of the animosity in her gaze.

"I'm sorry," he said softly.

She looked back at her husband. "Yes, so am I."

Behind Chang, Stone began to rouse once more, and Chang turned, his hand on Stone's shoulder, urging him to quiet. He leaned lower, making sure his words were for Stone's ears alone.

"Can you hear me?" Chang whispered.

Stone's eyelids fluttered, and then he looked up. "Yes."

"Don't open your eyes," Chang whispered. "Let them think you're still out."

But Stone gripped Chang's arm, for the moment refusing to give up to the overwhelming weakness.

"Do you have a gun?" Stone asked.

Chang shook his head, and then glanced back at their captors. "I was searched when I came in. I couldn't take the chance," he whispered, glancing over his shoulder to see where the men were.

Cody was nowhere in sight, Trigger was lighting up a smoke with shaking hands, and Garrett and Scanlan were still arguing.

Urgency was in Stone's voice as he continued. "Don't

mess with them, Chang. They're bad. The one in charge is Aaron Garrett, the young one is his brother. Don't know the others, but they call themselves Trigger and Scanlan.''

Chang recognized the Garrett name all too well. For the first time since volunteering to come in, he wondered if he'd made the wrong move. And then Stone tightened his grip, and the thought disappeared.

"Do you have anything in that bag that would knock them out?'' Stone asked.

Startled by the idea, Chang thought, and then nodded. "But there's no way to get it in all of them. I might be able to inject one, but that would leave three mobile, and it just wouldn't work.''

Stone could feel himself weakening again, but he'd had more than twenty-four hours to figure this out.

"Coffee,'' he mumbled, grabbing onto Chang's hand in a futile effort to keep from passing back out. "They drink coffee by the gallons.'' Then he closed his eyes and sighed.

Chang frowned. The idea had merit, but Stone was close to passing out. And then the old man's widow startled him as she grabbed his arm.

"Give it to me,'' Ruth whispered. "They keep making me do it...make the coffee, I mean. Give it to me. I'll make sure it gets in.''

Stone's eyes opened once again, and his head turned just enough to lock into the old woman's gaze. The cold look on her face was all he needed to see. He grabbed Chang by the wrist to get his attention.

"Yes,'' Stone whispered. "Let her do it.''

Although it went against Chang's training to involve the public in what should be police procedure, he dug through the paramedic's bag until he found what he wanted. With one eye on their captors, and the other on the bottle in his hand, he drew a syringe completely full of pure morphine.

"Ain't you about through over there?''

Stone closed his eyes while Chang froze—the syringe

still in his hand, his hand still in the bag. Masking his expression, he looked up. The man they called Scanlan was less than ten feet away.

"Just about," he said calmly, and let the syringe fall back in the bag.

Scanlan took a step closer. "What are you doing in that bag?"

Chang pulled out an empty syringe. "I was going to give him a shot of painkiller, but he's allergic, see?" He pointed to the Medic Alert chain hanging from Stone's neck.

Scanlan leaned over, frowned, and then poked Stone with the toe of his shoe. "Just don't let him die, you hear? I ain't willin' to go down for no murder."

As Scanlan moved away, Chang grabbed the loaded needle from the depths of the bag, capped it and quickly slid it across the floor. It came to a stop beside Ruth's ankle.

Out of the corner of his eye, he saw the old woman reach down and pick it up, then slip it down the front of her blouse. When she leaned back, there was a look of satisfaction on her face.

It was just after two o'clock, and Stone had been awake for at least a half an hour. With Chang's help, he'd even made it to the bathroom and back. Except for the dried blood on his clothes and a gray cast to his skin, one might think he was only exhausted from the ordeal and not from having been shot. Yet when Garrett suddenly yelled at the old woman from across the room, Stone's gaze went instantly to her face.

"You! Old lady!"

At Garrett's shout, Ruth Dean flinched, but remained silent. Stone held his breath.

"Go make some fresh coffee, and do it now," Garrett said.

She got up slowly, her knees and joints stiff and aching from sitting on the cold floor.

"Hurry up!" Garrett shouted.

She hobbled away, and Stone sensed the purpose in each of her steps. Minutes later, she slipped back in her place on the floor, and when Stone glanced her way, there was a light in her eyes that hadn't been there before.

Stone looked up at the clock, then away. Now they played the waiting game. And while they waited, he gathered mental strength for what was to come and prayed that he made it out alive. He had something to say to Jessie that wasn't going to wait.

When it started to rain, Jessica felt as if heaven was offering to cry the tears she couldn't. She moved from the curb to beneath a nearby awning, wishing that Brenda would hurry back with her clean clothes. At least they would be dry. Her heart was heavy, her spirit low. The only thing that was keeping her sane was the intermittent updates Stryker kept giving her.

The negotiations came to a standstill just before dark. At that point, Jessie's hopes dropped and fear took over her thoughts. How badly had Stone been injured? Had Erik Chang been able to stop the bleeding? Even now, was Stone unconscious and dying? Was she going to spend the rest of her life alone, grieving for a life they'd never had?

The town clock began to chime. Jessica wrapped her arms around herself, trying to get farther beneath the awning and out of the blowing rain, when out of nowhere, Stryker appeared, wearing a yellow police slicker and carrying another.

"You are without doubt, the most irritating woman it has been my pleasure to meet," he growled, and thrust the slicker in her face. "Put the damned thing on before you catch pneumonia. Stone will have my hide if I let you get sick."

It was the underlying sympathy that did her in. She

started to cry huge, quiet tears that ran down her face like the rain running into the streets. She kept missing one arm-hole, thrusting her hand over and over toward the sleeve without luck.

"Here, let me," Jack said, dressing her as if she were a child.

When she was covered from head to toe in the bright yellow slicker, he took her by the hand and led her toward an ambulance, knocking abruptly on the back door.

A paramedic opened the door and looked out. "Keep her inside with you," Jack said. "She's probably already sick as it is."

Jessica found herself bundled inside, and when Jack slammed the door shut behind her, she crouched down on the floor, thankful to be out of the wind and the weather.

One of the medics pointed to a gurney that was readied for action. "Here, miss, you're welcome to lie down."

Jessica looked at her slicker, dripping with rain, and then she thought of the patient who would be needing their help, as well as a clean, dry bed.

"Thank you," she said. "But I'm fine down here." And she lay down on her side, pillowing her head with her hands and listening to the rain as it hammered against the walls of the unit.

The last chime of the clock was drowned out by the sound of the rain, but it was eight o'clock, just the same. Twelve hours had gone by since Stone had been shot. The warmth inside the ambulance worked like a drug. Within moments, she'd fallen asleep.

Stone came toward her, moving silently on bare feet as he walked toward the bed. Jessie took a deep breath and then held it, mesmerized by the hard, flat plane of his belly, of his long, muscular legs, of the glitter in his eyes as he paused at the side of the bed and stared down.

"I want to make love to you," he whispered.

Jessie exhaled on a sigh. "I know."

"I won't make any promises," he warned her.

There was a terrible sadness in her voice, but there was also an acceptance on her face. *"I know that, too,"* she said, and closed her eyes, unwilling for him to see the tears.

The weight of his body pressed her deep into the mattress, and then all thoughts of tomorrow flew out of her head. She wanted to spend the rest of her life with Stone, but she would take whatever she could get. Even if they never married, she would find a way to accept it…if only he didn't stop loving her.

Jessie continued to dream, unaware of the tears running down her face and mingling with the raindrops that had yet to dry.

Stone sat slumped in an upright position, pretending to drift in and out of consciousness. Erik Chang was nearby, still playing his part as the conscientious medic. The teller, David Clark, was a broken man. He sat with his hands over his face, muttering to himself and crying nonstop. Ruth still guarded over her husband's body, while Bill Jackson, the bank's vice president, slept. Some of the other hostages were dozing, as well. But there were those who seemed aware that something was going on. They didn't know what, but more than one had recognized Erik Chang as another one of Grand Spring's finest, and their hopes were now pinned on the two cops—one wounded, both unarmed.

Stone and Erik watched and prayed as Cody Garrett was the first to lose consciousness. To their relief, he was on top of the president's desk, flat on his back and snoring loudly. Scanlan was standing guard, but more than once, Stone had seen him stagger. Garrett was pacing from one end of the hostages to the other, downing coffee in huge gulps in order to fight what he thought was fatigue. But it was Trigger who'd given Stone pause. Chang hadn't known ahead of time, and Stone hadn't thought to tell him, that Trigger was a junkie, although he'd probably figured it out by now. The junkie wasn't out. He was high.

Stone shifted position and winced. His shoulder was stiff and sore as hell, and he was shaky, which he knew was from the blood loss. But whatever the painkiller was that he'd been shot up with, it was working. Except for a slight buzz in his ears, he would do.

He kept watching the men for a sign of trouble. Every muscle in Stone's body was on alert. There was no telling what Garrett might do, or how he'd react, but whatever came, they had to be ready. This would be their only chance.

Suddenly, the cup in Scanlan's hands was on the floor. He seemed to look down in disbelief at the brown brew splattered on his feet, and then he crumpled, facedown, his body limp, his arms outflung, possibly in an unconscious effort to stop his descent.

At the sound, Garrett spun and then staggered, using the rifle to steady himself like a drunk with a crutch. When he saw Scanlan down on the floor, he jerked the rifle up toward an unseen assassin.

All of a sudden, Garrett saw the situation for what it was. His brother, Cody, was snoring. Scanlan was on the floor, while Garrett, himself, felt like hell. Everything and everyone kept wavering in and out of focus. What he had thought was fatigue now became something else. He looked around for Trigger, and when he saw him kicked back on a desk with his gun across his knees and staring and scratching at a spot on his arm, he started to curse. Trigger was high.

Garrett was coming undone and Stone could see it happening. When he started toward the row of hostages with his rifle aimed head high, Stone shoved himself up with a grunt. His whisper was low, but it was enough that Chang heard him say, "Garrett is mine."

Chang nodded and looked toward Trigger. While it seemed that Trigger's mind was in left field, that damned rifle across his lap made Chang nervous. Following Stone's lead, he moved from sitting on his backside to a squatting position, getting ready to leap.

Garrett's mind was slipping. He kept trying to remember why he was here, and kept wanting to lie down on the floor. And in that split second between unconsciousness and reason, he knew they must have been drugged. Rage filtered through the fog in his mind as he looked toward the hostages, whitewashing what little patience he'd been maintaining with a red, angry haze. And then he caught movement out of the corner of his eye and spun just as the cop hit him knee-high in a flying tackle.

They went down in a tumble of arms and legs, and Garrett's finger, still locked on the assault rifle's trigger, suddenly tightened. The spray of bullets that erupted from the gun sent hostages scrambling for cover, riddling the walls and ceiling and showering plaster and glass down upon them.

Trigger saw Chang coming and jumped to his feet with a curse, but when his rifle clattered to the floor, he looked down in surprise. As he scrambled to get it, the toe of Chang's shoe caught him squarely on the chin. He went down without a sound.

As Trigger lost consciousness, Garrett was still fighting to retain his. And it was the rage in his heart that made it happen. His rifle now lay off to one side, lost in his scuffle with the wounded cop. But he never saw Stone's fist coming, or felt his head bouncing on the marble floor as Stone rolled out from under him.

Stone was on his knees when the police came through the door. Afraid he would be mistaken for one of the gunmen, he held up his hands. His breath was short and pain-filled, and all he wanted was to lie down and sleep.

"I'm a cop," he said softly. And they were running and shouting and calling out to everyone in sight. "I'm a cop," he said louder. "Don't shoot."

* * *

The hostages' screams, along with the eruption of gun-fire, sent the police into action, moving on orders set in place long ago.

Jessica came awake and moved, all in the same moment, and was out of the ambulance just as the SWAT team went in the front door of the bank. She stood, frozen to the spot, with the rain falling on her face, praying as she'd never prayed before.

And then the shots stopped, and it seemed that the world was holding its breath. All she could hear was the rain falling on her slicker and the thunder of her heartbeat in her ears. It seemed like she was waiting forever, and then through the rain and confusion, she saw two men coming out of the bank. She took a step forward, and her heart soared. It was Chang and Stryker, and they were support-ing a third man between them. She started forward, un-snapping her slicker as she went. The rain was coming down now, faster and heavier than before, but she kept on walking.

Stone looked up through the downpour and saw her. He glanced at Jack in surprise.

"Don't look at me," Stryker said. "She wouldn't do a damned thing I told her. She's your little headache, not mine."

A quiet joy pushed past Stone's pain. *Mine.* He watched her, his entire focus on the woman coming to him through the rain.

And then she was standing in front of them, her hair plastered to her head, her clothes slicked to her body. She handed Stryker the slicker.

"Put it on him," she said. "He needs it more."

Jack took it out of her hands and draped it around Stone's shoulders as Jessica's gaze focused on the damage that had been done to her man. She had meant for the raincoat to shelter him, but when she saw his face, she walked into his arms, sheltering him, instead, with her love.

Stone leaned down and rested his face against her cheek and gave thanks for the fact that he'd been given another chance.

"Jessie."

She looked up. His eyes were dark and pain-filled, and her heart went out to him.

"Help me get him to the ambulance," she said, urging the two other officers to move.

"Not yet," Stone said, and cupped her face. "I have something to say to you and something to ask."

"But, Stone, you need—"

Ignoring Stryker's and Chang's presence, Stone focused on Jessie, instead. "What I need is you," he said.

"I'm here," Jessie said, trying hard not to cry.

"I love you, Jessie."

It was no use. Tears started anew. "Oh, Stone, I love you, too. I was so afraid. I didn't know if—"

"I know. Neither did I," Stone muttered, and pushed her rain-soaked hair away from her eyes. "But I made myself a promise while I was in there."

"You did?"

He nodded. "Jessie, I'm sorry."

"For what?"

Her face was so dear. Her voice so familiar. Her touch so compelling. He closed his eyes and swallowed, trying to still the quaver in his voice. When he looked, she was still there, waiting, just as he'd known she would be.

"For not believing you and for not believing in us."

"It's all right," she said.

"No, it's not, but the only way I know how to apologize is to beg your forgiveness and—" He took a deep breath, suddenly overwhelmed by the enormity of what he'd gone through as well as having been given back his life.

"And what, Stone?"

"And to tell you that I don't want to spend another day on this earth without saying these words. Marry me, Jessie. Live with me. Love with me. Please be my wife."

She lifted her chin, and the rain peppered her face and soaked her clothes to her body, but she didn't feel a thing except a spiraling joy.

"Oh, Stone."

He almost grinned. "Can I take that as a yes?"

Her heart was too full to speak. All she could do was nod.

He opened his raincoat, offering her the only shelter he had to give, and she accepted it without reservation. All she could see—all she could feel—was Stone's love, wrapping itself around her, warming her...forever.

Epilogue

Jessica came out of the room where she'd been dressing for her wedding, then stopped before a full-length mirror in the outer parlor to fidget with her hair. Even though the new growth around the scar on her head was almost as long as the rest, it didn't quite fit in with her hairstyle.

Giving it up as a lost cause, her gaze shifted from her hair to her dress. She'd spent nine and a half hours shopping in Denver's finest bridal shops for something that would make a statement. This was the end result. She turned, looking one way, then another, judging herself from all angles and smoothing her hands over the narrow, fitted bodice with satisfaction.

Brenda walked up behind her, leaned over Jessie's shoulder and stared in the mirror at their reflections.

"Oh, Jessie, you look like you stepped out of the past century, and not the back room of Squaw Creek Lodge."

Jessica's eyes were wide and slightly tear-filled as she gazed back at her sister through the mirror. Her voice was quiet, and for Jessica, unusually subdued.

"Brenda."

She looked up. "What, honey?"

"Thank you for being my sister."

Brenda's eyes filled. "It's my pleasure," she said quickly, and then pretended to fuss with Jessie's veil while Jessica gave herself a final study.

The Victorian style of her wedding dress suited her in a way she wouldn't have imagined—from the high-necked collar to the vee-shaped lace insert that almost revealed her bosom...almost, but not quite. The waist was narrow and fitted, with the waistline dropping to a vee, echoing the neckline. The sleeves were long and lace-tipped. The skirt fell in soft, voluminous folds around her hips to brush the carpet on which she stood. No cumbersome hoops, no boned-in stays for Jessie. She was a "what you see is what you get" kind of girl.

"There was a time when I thought this might never happen," Jessica said.

Brenda paused, her thoughts flying back to the thirty-six hours of hell they'd gone through while waiting to see if Stone would survive. She brushed at a speck on Jessie's shoulder.

"I know, honey. But that's all behind you now. You have to focus on the future, right?"

But Jessica's thoughts were still locked in the past and on the days of Stone's healing. When he'd told her to set the date for their wedding, she'd stunned him by announcing she didn't want to wait for a time when they could plan a honeymoon. She knew that the murder of Olivia Stuart was still a strong and ongoing case, and that Stone wouldn't be satisfied until it was solved. And that was all right with her. They had the rest of their lives to go play. But she wanted a ring on his finger and their names to be one and the same. Then she might be able to rest.

Jessica turned away from the mirror. There was a sarcastic grin on her face. "Well, there's something to be thankful for. At least I can't *see* into the future anymore."

Brenda rolled her eyes. "Perish the thought." And then she glanced at the clock. "Oh, look! It's almost time. Come on, sweetie. I'll bet there's a nervous cop waiting for you somewhere outside."

Jessica's grin widened. "And he deserves to be," she said. "Heaven knows he kept me waiting too long."

Brenda laughed. "Who would have known when Stone and I were dating that one day he would marry my little sister instead?"

Jessica brushed a speck off her bosom and pulled at her veil. "Well, I did, for one."

Brenda snorted softly. "Oh, pooh. You certainly did not."

"How do you know?" Jessica taunted. "Maybe even then I was *seeing* things no one else could."

Brenda started to laugh, and then stopped at the odd expression on her little sister's face. "Oh, enough about that. Come on, Jessie. It's time."

The ballroom of the lodge was beautiful. Baskets of flowers and greenery decked every nook and cranny of the room, compliments of Jessica's employers. But Stone was unaware of anything except the aisle between the chairs that had been set up to seat their guests.

The room was full. A low buzz of voices and the occasional chuckle from those assembled did little to soothe Stone's nerves. And then Stryker came up behind him and took him by the arm.

"Okay, partner. It's time."

Stone moved out in front of the guests, his gaze locked on the empty aisle and the doorway beyond. Jack said something, but nothing registered except the distracted tone of his voice. A flutter of white beyond the doorway caught Stone's attention, and he shifted, straining for a glimpse of Jessie.

Behind him, he heard the pastor take his place. And then music suddenly soared throughout the room and Stone saw a rose-colored dress as Brenda started down the aisle, and he thought, *wrong sister*.

As she came near, she gave him one last pointed stare and then took her place at the altar. It was a warning look he couldn't miss. Stone almost grinned. The audacity of the Hanson sisters never failed to surprise him. This one was daring him to make a mistake. What look, he wondered, would his Jessie be wearing?

And then the familiar strains of the wedding march suddenly filled the air. He tensed, and for a fleeting moment remembered hearing the same music at his wedding to Naomi.

Oh, God, please let me get it right this time.

Jessie stepped into the doorway, and Stone's breath hung in the back of his throat. When she started down the aisle, he inhaled slowly, remembering a time when he didn't think he would live to see this day. When Jessie reached his side, he was looking at her through tears.

After that, everything became a blur of sensations. The touch of Jessie's hand in his. The scent of her perfume. The quick intake of breath that she took before she responded to her vows. Stone was, in the true sense of the words, lost within the moment. And then, without warning, everything went dark.

Jessica gasped, echoing the emotions of the people who were gathered. Her first thought was *Oh, no! Not again!*

Stone's reaction was entirely different, but in keeping with the cop that he was. The last time the lights had gone out at this lodge, Jessie had fallen and hit her head. Remembering what had happened as a result of that fall, he grabbed her arm as he shouted aloud, making sure everyone in the room heard what he had to say.

"This is the police! Don't anybody move!"

A slight titter of laughter came from somewhere behind him, and he heard the rustling of clothing and the shifting of chairs as everyone settled.

"Is everyone okay?" he asked.

Murmurs drifted to him in the dark, and he moved his grip from Jessie's arm to her hand, threading her fingers through his in a comforting squeeze.

"Jessie, are you with me?" he asked.

"Hen scratch," she muttered. "I don't believe this."

He grinned, picturing the look on her face as she said that. Then he asked, "Pastor, you were saying..."

The pastor cleared his throat. "Let's see, where was I?"

he mumbled. "I believe Jessica had just finished her vows and Stone...Stone was—"

Jessica's voice was unmistakable. "Stone was promising to love me forever."

A soft wave of laughter filled the darkness, and Stone abandoned the formality of the ceremony to take Jessie in his arms. No one knew they were now standing face-to-face, or that he had lifted her veil and was cupping her cheek. Only Jessie experienced the intimacy with which he finished his vows.

His voice softened, and even though it was cheating, he leaned forward and brushed a kiss across her lips before he spoke.

"Jessie Leigh, I swear that I will love you forever, in sickness and in health, with love and laughter. That I will honor you, and keep you forever in my heart, and that I will remain faithful to you and you only until the day that I die." Then a tinge of laughter colored his voice as he added, "If I've missed anything, I'm pretty sure you'll remind me."

Another titter of laughter moved across the room like wind coming through the trees. Out of habit, the pastor looked down and then realized he couldn't see the words before him. But he'd said them before, so many times and in so many places that he knew them by heart.

"Having said this, do you, Jessica, take this man, Stone, to be your lawful wedded husband? Do you promise to cherish him and love him above all others, until death do you part?"

"I do."

Because of the silence within the room, and the darkness in which they were shrouded, her vow seemed more intense, as if the sound of her voice was the only thing left to hear.

The words rang in Stone's heart, and he pulled her head to his chest, holding her safe against the dark.

"And do you, Stone, take this woman, Jessica, to be

your lawful wedded wife? Do you promise to cherish her and love her above all others, until death do you part?"

"I do."

"With the powers vested in me, I now pronounce you husband and wife. Mr. Richardson, you may kiss your bride."

And then, like a miracle, light illuminated the room in a sudden and blinding burst of electricity. Sighs filled the air, but not for the return of power. It was from the sight that met the guests' eyes.

They saw a big man humbled by the weight of love as he held the woman of his heart. The traditional kiss had obviously come and gone, as Jessie already stood within the shelter of Stone Richardson's arms. Her cheek was on his chest, her arms wrapped around his waist. He held her close, one hand splayed low at her back, the other at the base of her neck.

The pastor's face was one big smile. "Well now, as the Master once said *'Let there be light.'* Ladies and gentlemen—I give you Mr. and Mrs. Stone Richardson."

Jessica was on her back and staring up through the trees, her head pillowed on the strength of Stone's uninjured arm. Still wearing the heat of the day, the ground kept them warm, although the mountain air was brisk and cool.

Stone felt her intensity as she lay without moving, staring up at the sky, seemingly suspended by the beauty above. Enveloped by the darkness in which they lay and the anonymity of night, he felt a peace unlike any he'd ever known. He turned his head, watching her profile and her unblinking stare, and then he saw her squint and remembered what he'd told her—about the stars through the pines, and how, if you looked at them just right and suspended disbelief, that they looked like ornaments on a Christmas tree.

Suddenly, she stiffened, and then impulsively reached

out and grabbed for his hand. A mixture of amazement and joy colored her voice.

"Stone, you were right! They're hanging right on the branches like bright Christmas lights."

Mesmerized by the beauty, she stared until her eyes began to burn from the strain. Reluctantly, she finally had to blink, and when she did, the image was gone. She sighed and turned in Stone's arms, looking up at him and the dear, familiar lines of his face, instead.

"Oh, Stone, did you ever see anything so beautiful in your entire life?"

He shifted and looked down at his wife in the dark. Only the barest of an outline was visible in the near-moonless night, but he knew the shape of her face by heart.

"No, Jessie Leigh, I can't say that I have."

Jessie didn't need light to hear the want in his voice. She smiled to herself, holding the thought of his love in her heart.

"Stone Richardson, are you trying to make a pass at me?"

He grinned, testing the theory by sliding his hand across the flat of her belly to the curve of her hip, pulling her almost beneath him in one move.

"And what if I was?"

The magic of the stars was forgotten as she fell into the magic of her husband's touch.

"Then I'd say...for an officer of the law, you're awfully slow on the draw."

Laughter.

It had been the first bond they'd shared. It would forever be the best.

* * * * *

continues with

CINDERELLA STORY

by Elizabeth August
available in November

Here's an exciting preview....

One

Nina Lindstrom breathed a sigh of relief as she hung up the phone. Her children were safe and happily pretending they were camped out in their grandmother's living room. When she'd learned that the electricity was out all over town, they had been her number one concern.

It seemed to be one of those days when plans went askew, Nina thought as she unfastened the frilly white apron she wore, then left the kitchen. She'd been counting on the money from this moonlighting job to buy a few extras for her children. But life had taught her never to count on anything happening the way she hoped it would.

Officially, the wedding reception was canceled. However, Melissa Howell had invited the guests and the wait staff to stay and help themselves to what was available. Wearing her best black cocktail dress, combined with her one set of good jewelry and her hair pulled up on top of her head, Nina looked as sophisticated as any of the other guests. *So why not go mingle with the blue noses?* she asked herself. It had been a long time since she'd been to a party and never one so high-class as this.

Alex Bennett stood leaning against a wall, watching the rest of the wedding guests. In spite of warnings about the roads, he was contemplating leaving. Weddings usually brought out the husband-hunting instincts in women, and he was in no mood to fend off a female with a ring on her mind. But then, there hadn't *been* a wedding. Women, he mused wryly, were unpredictable creatures with hidden agendas. Trying to figure out their motives for any action was a waste of time.

They could, however, turn an otherwise dull evening into something memorable, he added, noticing the slender, dark-haired female who had just entered and was making her way to the buffet table. His gaze went to her hands. No ring.

Thoughts of leaving faded. Alex crossed the room, picking up two glasses of champagne along the way. "I thought you might like a beverage," he said as he reached her.

Nina looked up at the tall, dark-haired man in front of her. She recognized him from other parties she'd worked. She didn't know his name, but she'd heard a couple of women refer to him as "the oil tycoon who'd built the summer place on the mountain."

"If I had a third hand, I'd thank you for your consideration," she replied, indicating the plate in her hands.

"It's a good ploy, don't you think?" He grinned. "Unless you want to go thirsty, you have to put up with my company. I'm Alex Bennett."

"I'm Nina." She chose not to add her last name. She was allowing herself a momentary fantasy and there was no need to reveal she was not one of the guests.

"Interesting nonwedding. Rather Gothic atmosphere, don't you think? The bride flees the wedding in the midst of a raging storm and the mother of the groom doesn't even show up. Now the groom is missing and we, the guests, are left to fend for ourselves by candlelight."

"A night fraught with intrigue," Nina quipped.

"And music," Alex noted as the strains of a popular song filled the air. "Would you care to dance?" Without giving her an opportunity to say no, he put down the glasses, took her plate from her, and drew her into a loose embrace. Nina was acutely aware of his strength. *It's just a dance,* she admonished herself.

Alex didn't think any woman had ever felt so good in his arms...her soft perfume, the curve of her hips, the velvet look of her lips. *It's this strange night,* he told himself, *causing my perceptions to be heightened.*

Nina felt herself wanting to move closer. Alex's breath played on the sensitized skin of her neck and her blood began to heat. Her senses reeling, she looked up, uncertain of what to say. Her gaze locked with his, and she felt herself being drawn into the lush depths.

"You have the most kissable-looking lips I've ever seen," Alex said, his face moving closer to hers.

Suddenly panic flowed through her. She was letting her fantasy get out of hand! When he discovered she was a poor widow with three children, he was bound to bolt.

"I just remembered something I have to do." She squirmed out of his arms and rushed from the room.

Alex followed her into the hall, but in the dimly lit passages, he lost her.

June 29th

"The end is near," the white-haired old man announced with conviction. "I can feel death breathing down my neck. I'd hoped to bounce a great-grandchild on my knee before I went to those oil fields in the sky, but that doesn't seem likely now. However, I'd die a happy man if I knew you'd at least found yourself a wife."

Alex studied his grandfather's lined, weatherworn features with concern. William Bennett was the only real family he had. He loved the old man and hated to feel he'd let him down in any way. A small lie couldn't hurt, he reasoned. "I have found someone. She's got raven hair...so black it shines in candlelight. Her eyes are hazel with tiny gold flecks." Startled, Alex realized he was describing the woman he'd encountered at Randi Howell's nonwedding.

"I probably won't live to see the wedding." The old man sighed heavily and grasped Alex's hand. "Bring her here. I want to meet her before I meet my Maker...."

As Alex drove back to Grand Springs later, the scowl on his face deepened with each mile. He didn't like lying to his grandfather. But on the other hand, seeking Nina out and enlisting her aid wasn't a bad idea. She had disturbed his peace of mind. Once he found her, she would no longer be a mystery woman and he'd no longer be haunted by her.

He'd just offer to pay her to play his fiancée for a couple of days. A sudden worry that she wouldn't cooperate crossed his mind. Then a cynical smirk distorted his features. Any woman could be bought for the right price....

But Alex never expected to have to pay with his heart....

Take 4 bestselling love stories FREE

Plus get a FREE surprise gift!

Welcome to the Towers!

In January
New York Times bestselling author

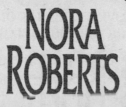

takes us to the fabulous Maine coast mansion
haunted by a generations-old secret and introduces
us to the fascinating family that lives there.

Mechanic Catherine "C.C." Calhoun and hotel magnate
Trenton St. James mix like axle grease and mineral
water—until they kiss. Efficient Amanda Calhoun finds
easygoing Sloan O'Riley insufferable—and irresistible.
And they all must race to solve the mystery
surrounding a priceless hidden emerald necklace.

Catherine and Amanda

THE Calhoun Women

**A special 2-in-1 edition containing
COURTING CATHERINE and A MAN FOR AMANDA.**

Look for the next installment of
THE CALHOUN WOMEN with Lilah and Suzanna's
stories, coming in March 1998.

Available at your favorite retail outlet.

Silhouette®

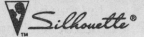
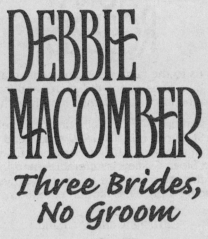

Indiscreet

Camilla Ferrand wants everyone, especially her dying grandfather, to stop worrying about her. So she tells them that she is engaged to be married. But with no future husband in sight, it's going to be difficult to keep up the pretense. Then she meets the very handsome and mysterious Benedict Ellsworth who generously offers to accompany Camilla to her family's estate—as her most devoted fiancé.

But at what cost does this *generosity* come?

From the bestselling author of *Impulse*

CANDACE CAMP

Available in November 1997
at your favorite retail outlet.

Candace Camp also writes for Silhouette as Kristen James

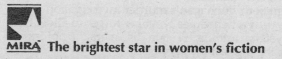

MIRA **The brightest star in women's fiction**

The Stars of Mithra

Three gems,
three beauties,
three passions...
the adventure of a lifetime

SILHOUETTE·INTIMATE·MOMENTS®
brings you a thrilling new series by
New York Times bestselling author

Nora Roberts

Three mystical blue diamonds place three close
friends in jeopardy...and lead them to romance.

In October
HIDDEN STAR (IM#811)
Bailey James can't remember a thing, but she knows
she's in big trouble. And she desperately needs private
investigator Cade Parris to help her live long enough to
find out just what kind.

In December
CAPTIVE STAR (IM#823)
Cynical bounty hunter Jack Dakota and spitfire
M. J. O'Leary are handcuffed together and on the run
from a pair of hired killers. And Jack wants to know
why—but M.J.'s not talking.

In February
SECRET STAR (IM#835)
Lieutenant Seth Buchanan's murder investigation takes
a strange turn when Grace Fontaine turns up alive. But
as the mystery unfolds, he soon discovers the notorious
heiress is the biggest mystery of all.

Available at your favorite retail outlet.

Daniel MacGregor is at it again...

New York Times bestselling author

NORA ROBERTS

introduces us to a new generation of MacGregors
as the lovable patriarch of the illustrious MacGregor
clan plays matchmaker again, this time to his three
gorgeous granddaughters in

THE MACGREGOR BRIDES

From Silhouette Books

Don't miss this brand-new continuation of Nora Roberts's
enormously popular *MacGregor* miniseries.

Available November 1997 at your favorite retail outlet.